I0714786

WHEN WREN CAME OUT

BLAIR BRYAN

Copyright 2022 by Blair Bryan

All rights reserved.

This is a work of fiction. Names, characters, businesses, places, events and incidents are either the products of the author's imagination or used in a fictitious manner. Any resemblance to actual persons, living or dead, or actual events is purely coincidental.

The best place to buy books by Blair Bryan and Ninya is https://tealbutterflypress.com/

There you will support the author and find the best pricing as well as exclusive options like autographed paperbacks and hardcovers.

The best way to buy my books is direct at tealbutterflypress.com There you can save 20-25% and find autographed paperbacks. They are available at most booksellers too.

I write under two pen names, Ninya for Non-Fiction and Blair Bryan for Contemporary Fiction.

Non-Fiction

Scotland with a Stranger: A Memoir

Treehouses with a Teenager: A Memoir

First You Then Him

Fiction By Blair Bryan

Back to Before

Better than Before

The Sweetest Day

The Funologist

When Wren Came Out

AnaStasia Lived Two Lives

Steamy Sexy Series Velvet Guild

Velvet Guild Collection 1

Velvet Guild Collection 2

Velvet Guild Collection 3

For J, who gave me a proper education in tolerance and understanding during our car rides to and from school.

It takes courage to be authentic, and you have it in spades. You make me proud. I love you.

SPECIAL THANKS TO THESE ALLIES

My editor said, "This book needs to land in big hands." I took that statement to heart and launched a Kickstarter to find those big hands. As part of the reward tiers, these allies backed this project in a substantial way and deserve my humble recognition. Thank you for joining me in this mission.

Platinum Level Sponsors

Gina Finical

Anna Osborne

Stephanie Hale

Brooke Zeno

Angela Mason

Gold Level Sponsor Jenni Williams

ONE

It only takes the snag of one thread to unravel the tapestry of a seemingly perfect life. You never know what event will cause that snag to happen, when the illusion of the public façade you've carefully built crumbles, and you are forced to see your world stripped bare and with fresh eyes.

The unraveling of our lives began with a phone call from the event coordinator, Marcy, desperate to fill a last-minute volunteer opportunity at my daughter's Catholic high school. St. Augustine's always hosted the Annual Show Choir Showcase for eight schools in the Minneapolis suburbs we'd lived in for the last four years. When the first email call for volunteers landed in my inbox, I was expressly forbidden by my daughter to sign up.

"It's so embarrassing when you come running up to school to volunteer every chance you get," Wren grumbled. "Why can't you get a real job like Sammie's mom?"

"I *have* a job," I'd remind her, "taking care of my family," while I folded John's white t-shirts into perfect squares. "But it would be nice if my coworkers would try to make it a little easier on me," I teased her, and she rolled her eyes and stormed away. Discounting traditional roles of womanhood was as easy as casting off dirty socks in the corner for her. I knew I was a dinosaur, about as far away from a card-carrying feminist as possible, and in Wren's judgmental teenage eyes, this fact was offensive. It diminished my value. Until she was hungry, and then my love for cooking, baking, and homemaking became more palatable qualities.

Now that she was sixteen, Wren was painfully aware of my presence and had started loathing my penchant for volunteering at her school functions. Not wanting to rock the boat, I gave in. Sure, it stung when she was so vocal about blocking my participation, but I chalked it up to the inevitable growth cycle of all teenage girls united in their shared mortification of their mothers. I remember mocking my own mother for her fashion choices and inferior make-up application techniques, and now Wren was doing the exact same thing to me. It was the circle of life.

During the first twelve years of our marriage, we moved seven times. We were an Army family, and her father was frequently deployed for long stretches of time, climbing the ranks to Master Sergeant. While he was away, I was Wren's constant companion. I was the chef and the taxi and the playmate. I was the confidant and the giver of hugs and the trusted advisor.

Then, around thirteen, our relationship shifted when Wren's coltish first steps toward adulthood carried her further away from me. She delegated me to the sidelines, where I gazed at her with my eyes brimming with hope and longing for an engraved invitation to slip back into her life. I probably should have insisted and interjected myself into her life more, but it wasn't my way.

It was a challenge, but I tried not to hover, instead branching out in the community and volunteering at our church. Making friends as an introverted adult is brutal. I'd rather be at home infusing bone broth and figuring out ways to sneak it into Wren's diet. Or gardening or reading, anything that didn't require wearing lipstick or pants with an actual zipper. When John retired and we first moved to Eden Prairie, for Wren's sake, I decided to put myself out there more. After the initial awkwardness and my social anxiety lessened, I had to admit it was starting to feel like home. A *real* home for the first time in our marriage.

Home was a weighty, elusive concept while we lived the nomadic life imposed upon us by the military. I was enmeshed in the duty of motherhood so fully I didn't realize what was missing until we moved to Eden Prairie, and I felt peace envelop me for the first time. There is a stillness in your heart where tranquility grows in the fertile soil of stability. It was a resounding steadiness and baseline contentment that let me breathe deeper and relax more fully, and in record time, Eden Prairie became our own little Garden of Eden.

With the thrill of fresh purpose unfurling in my belly, I ran up the stairs humming a jaunty *"When the Saints Go Marching In"* and threw on some bedazzled Converse sneakers I'd found at a garage sale. From a hanger, I pulled on the maroon St. Auggie's Show Choir t-shirt I had purchased at the beginning of the season over high-waisted mom jeans that covered a multitude of sins. A little soft in all the wrong places, I made peace with my body that enjoyed chocolate caramels a little too much and a little too often.

God bless the first designer who introduced spandex to denim. You, sir, are a saint.

With dainty features, a smattering of freckles across my nose and cheeks, and big brown eyes, I was labeled cute as a child, a descriptor that I never shook. I didn't think it was terrible company to be in. After all, puppies and babies are cute. I raked my fingers through my shoulder-length, brown hair, noticing a few glittery white strands catching the light from the fixture above the bathroom mirror. Trying to smooth them down with water a couple of times, I gave up after they stubbornly popped right back up.

I tugged the gold St. Christopher's medal I always wore to free it from catching on my sports bra—I was convinced underwire was a torture instrument of the devil—and centered it on the chain around my neck. I liked to keep my jewelry simple and utilitarian.

Who has the time to swap out earrings to match their outfits? God knows I don't.

I always wore the simple gold band John presented to me a month before he got called for active duty in Iraq, and on my ears, the conservative diamond studs he splurged on when he returned. They were a complete surprise gift to soften the rock-hard edges he developed from living in a war-torn country without us for nearly two years. I wasn't fussy, or someone who spent money or time on handbags or shoes. I was practical and prided myself on my frugalities. Where it was hard to buy myself a new pair of jeans unless the ones I was wearing developed significant holes, I doted on Wren, whose closet was bursting at the seams with jeans and sundresses. Many of them still with tags on.

Why is it so easy to spend money on your children, but infinitely harder to spend it on yourself?

Guilt colored most of my decisions my entire life. I was steeped in it. I know I shouldn't speak ill of my own religion, but even as a little girl wearing a plaid skirt at my own Catholic elementary school, I remember its source of origin. Guilt and Catholicism go hand in hand and travel together. I'm pretty sure it was the first official pairing to cross the gangplank on Noah's Ark.

Glancing at the stainless-steel watch that ringed my wrist, I had to hustle. My shift was starting in twenty-five minutes. I hesitated briefly, thinking I should probably send Wren an obligatory text to fill her in on the change of plans, but my desire to be punctual, and by punctual I mean ten minutes early, outweighed the need to inform her of the change.

Ten minutes later, I was guiding my sedan into a lucky open parking spot next to the wall of yellow school buses emblazoned with local school names. With a grin, I pulled the gold medal to my lips and kissed it, acknowledging my good fortune. The lot was packed, but I'd scored a spot only a few feet from the door.

St. Christopher for the win again.

St Auggie's was a typical school built in the eighties, olive green and drab with a bricked façade. A blanket of fresh snow covered the old roof that our parish priest disclosed we were going to have to replace next year at the last elder's meeting. Inside, ancient painted radiators tucked between the rows of lockers clanged and burned the dust, leaving a charred earthy smell behind. St. Auggie's

Catholic School was an old girl—a clean building, showing her age, but lovingly cared for by the shoestring staff. We didn't have the influx of property tax income the public schools did to pay for shiny upgrades and the latest technology. The school and church were supported by the tithes collected every Sunday in the gold church plate that was passed from aisle to aisle by our balding ushers.

Not even stopping to glance at my reflection in the rearview mirror, I hoisted my enormous black leather purse to a shoulder and hurried to the entrance. Peaceful snow floated to the ground as I navigated thick tracks of slushy trails in front of the entrance in an attempt to keep my feet dry. Once inside, I unbuttoned my coat, shook off the flakes like a dog coming in from the rain, and hurried toward the source of the sound, the rubber soles of my shoes squeaking on the speckled epoxy floors. Pop music pumped through the PA, and the roar of cheering and singing intensified with each step I took. At the entrance, the metal doors of the gym were a mouth gaping open wide as I merged into the controlled chaos, waving at acquaintances every few steps. The gym was packed wall to wall with people—parents relegated to the stands and teenagers sprawled across chairs and standing in rows closest to the makeshift stage. I picked my way through the crowd and up the wiggling bleachers to find a seat hidden in the mass of humanity that filled the maroon vinyl seats. Scanning the room, I searched for Wren's thin frame and long, dark blonde hair.

Sweet Caroline cued up on the PA system, and the crowd began to sing in unison. The notes bounced off the wooden floors with such intensity my heart thrummed and the bleachers I was sitting on began to vibrate. It was a song I knew by heart and had sung to Wren to calm her down when she was a colicky baby. I'd dip and dance around the pale green nursery, crooning into her ear with the perfect pitch singing voice I was blessed with and had passed down to Wren.

My heart ached to return to those sweet, heady, exhausting days where nothing mattered except keeping a tiny human alive. When you are in it, deep in the trenches of motherhood, sleep-deprived, and with hours passing without accomplishing anything tangible, people will tell you to hang on, it will get better. I never understood why they said that. Sure, I'd have sold my soul for four hours of sleep in one stretch, but I savored every moment. Wren even had the dreaded colic, unable to get comfortable in the evenings, her tiny belly distended and red. The inconsolable screaming didn't even phase me; it actually gave me purpose. I'd buckle her in the car seat and drive until she'd finally give in and sleep would overcome her. Her long, curled eyelashes and fat baby cheeks finally still, her mouth slack and then sucking a phantom nipple, then slacking again as she finally relaxed, as I drove down dark streets, warm and snug in the car with my sleeping babe.

John and I decided together when Wren was on the way that I would be a stay-at-home mom. It was a title I adored. I didn't shrink from it or feel unfulfilled like the talk shows always told me I should feel. I took my job of shaping this tiny life seriously. The days converged and melded from one into the next, her babyhood a mashup of library story hours and lazy afternoons at the park where I'd push her for hours in the baby swing. The wind rushing into her face would make her giggle and her eyelashes flutter from the breeze. Kicking her chubby legs in unison as she got closer, I'd sing out, "Wheeeeeee!" and grab her baby toes to tickle them while laughter bubbled up over us both. She'd ricochet back up into the air, looking like she was an angel baby floating in the clouds, only to return to me. I cherished the time spent holding her in my arms in the spring when the lilacs were in bloom. The sweet scent of them filled my lungs as she reached a chubby arm out to grab onto a stalk, her eyes crossed in concentration.

"Pretty," I said, talking to her like an adult, naming her world and taking great pride when her squeaky little voice repeated back a discernible, "T-t." Those days passed in a blink and seemed so far away now as I sat in the gymnasium.

"Bah, Bah, Bahhhh," I sang out from my perch on the bleachers in the throng of parents I was cocooned in. Rocking from side to side to the music, my singing voice was strong and steady, using my diaphragm to project it cleanly out into the chorus. Singing was an activity I enjoyed and a gift I felt compelled to share as one of the musical worship leaders at St. Auggie's. I occasionally made a little extra pocket money singing for weddings and funerals. It was squirreled away into the college fund I created for Wren before she was born, and I took pride in seeing that number grow a little each month and knowing it would give Wren options. I never went to college, but gosh darn it, my daughter would.

Singing the words loud and proud, I stood on my tiptoes and scanned the crowd, my eyes searching for the face it always craved—the beautiful face of my daughter. The one I lived and breathed for. The truth was I knew there were only two years left. She would go on to do great things, taking the world by storm, while I was left behind wondering how the heck the time went so fast. I'd then wait for her to grace us with her presence, accompanied by the expected loads of dirty laundry hauled from her dorm.

I loved being a mom. You could say I was made for it, begging for dolls for Christmas since I could speak. I always dreamed of being surrounded by a large, rambunctious family. Being raised Catholic, it is a fate almost expected of you, that and the result of relying on the rhythm method as the standard of birth control.

Motherhood is an exquisite study in contrast. While pregnant, you are biologically fused together with your child, but every single day outside the warm cocoon of your womb, there is a subtle tearing away. Even though the pull to separate is natural and part of the journey, it still hurts like all get out, this bittersweet symphony of life.

Every stage of childhood had something great to love about it, but then, before you could settle in or get used to the way things were, they would shift and change again. Leaving you forever grappling with figuring out where you fit in. Scrambling to establish your value repeatedly to this new version of your child. Parenthood is a million tiny endings to grieve. The day the crib and baby swing leave your house after sitting idle for a few months while you denied that you didn't need them anymore. Every day in tiny, almost immeasurable increments, your child is leaving you and embracing their autonomy. They are becoming their own independent being.

My eyes finally landed on the recognizable long, thick shock of curly blonde hair. Show Choir demanded the female performers' hair be styled identically in order to participate. Part of the uniform, it was required to be pulled back from your face and curled into long ringlets that cascaded down your back. It paired perfectly with the sparkly, floor-length, flared dresses each girl was asked to wear with heels. The overall look was cohesive, embracing the feminine, and every time I saw Wren in costume on stage in full hair and make-up, my heart swelled with delight. She was growing into her beauty, the awkwardness of the pre-teen years fading away to uncover the beautiful woman she would soon become.

Curling her hair for competitions was one of my favorite rituals. Spending the hour before the event with Wren held captive, perched on the edge of one of our sturdy dining room chairs while I got to work sectioning her satiny hair into even chunks. She had such thick hair it always took over an hour to curl it. I was proud she took after her father in the hair department and had successfully avoided the genetic weakness of my own limp, darker locks. Wren's delicate features and upturned nose paired with the layers of beautifully curled hair made her look angelic.

Today, my eyes landed on her with a smile that rapidly morphed into embarrassed confusion. A prickle of irritation needled up my ribs, watching her carousing with my best friend's daughter, Sammie, without a care in the world, oblivious to everyone around her.

She knows better than to sit on someone's lap at a school function. It is completely inappropriate. What will people think?

I glanced quickly around the crowd, feeling exposed as the first sliver of parental shame walked up my spine. I felt a flush of warmth rush up my cheeks and rubbed them with the palms of my hands. This latest stage of development had a willful Wren pushing boundaries and buttons harder and faster the closer she got to adulthood.

I made a mental note to discuss it with her on the way home, but I couldn't tear my eyes away from the interaction. Just a few feet from the stage, Wren was singing and swaying in the throng of teenagers. Her skinny arm, all elbow, was slung around Sammie's thicker shoulders. I saw Sammie's arms wrap around her waist, pulling her in tighter as a faint alarm sounded. In complete denial yet unable to look away, time slowed as I continued to study them from afar.

Wren's thick, curly hair fell forward as she leaned in closer to whisper something to Sammie that made them both laugh. It was a brazen act that my intuition understood and cataloged instantly. The exchange was *intimate*, unveiling a shocking affection that formed a lump in my throat and made my mouth an instant desert. My breath quickened and I felt myself flush again with shameful warmth. I looked down, giving myself an internal pep talk.

You're crazy. Wren would die if she knew you were thinking like this.

I forced my eyes back up, and they landed on Megan Stonewell. Her eyes narrowed and her head tipped and tilted toward Wren in such a tiny, nearly imperceptible movement I initially thought my mind was playing tricks on me. When her lips settled into a scowl, I couldn't deny her disgust. I pried my eyes from hers and wrenched them back to Wren, examining the interaction with Sammie, not wanting to rush to judgment. Wren was laughing and carrying on in a massive assembly of her friends and peers, completely unaware that I was watching from my perch on the bleachers. Lately, she had been hostile and sullen, hiding in her room under the pretense of studying for her upcoming SATs. Here, she was lighter and carefree, smiling widely and energetically engaged. The song ended, and Wren jumped to her feet with the rest of the audience, clapping and cheering along with the entire gymnasium.

The crowd rose around me as I sat stunned for a long second, unable to move. Panic and fear surged through me as I grappled to accept what my eyes had seen. Going through the motions, I finally found my feet and applauded, knowing it was what was expected of me, but internally, my mind churned. Reliving the last five minutes over and over in slow excruciating detail, I shook it off. As the crowd dispersed, I walked to my post at the coat check and busied myself with the task at hand, glad to have something else to focus on. There was a tingle of truth I refused to acknowledge. I stuffed it down along with the anxieties and worries that come with raising a child in this day and age.

She's just cutting loose, just having fun. You are losing your mind.

TWO

I've always loved birds. That's how you end up with a daughter named Wren. When six months pregnant, and I initially offered it up as a name suggestion, John vetoed it immediately. "It's too liberal, and we are *not* raising one of those."

He said it like being a liberal was an incurable disease like herpes, a flawed affliction to be avoided at all costs. A way of thinking that was detrimental to his way of life, the *Army* way of life. I didn't blame him for his beliefs; it was actually one of the things that drew me to him in the first place. Surrounded by tepid namby-pambies in my early twenties, immature *boys*, it was refreshing to finally find a *man* with real convictions—the kind you live or die by. The Army had left its mark on John. Loyalty, duty, respect, selfless service, honor, integrity, and personal courage— these seven core qualities were chiseled into him during basic training and became values he lived by every day after.

I'd always wanted to have four children, a nice even

number to successfully avoid the dreaded middle child dynamic. After a year of unsuccessfully trying, distilling our sex life down to the sole act of conception and using calendars and thermometers to monitor fertility, we finally conceived. We were both over-the-moon excited to be welcoming our first child into our family. The pregnancy was textbook, and I felt accomplished for growing this tiny human inside me. Each day, rubbing my belly where she rested, I prayed for her health. Knowing deep within, cells were doubling and dividing. Growing at an astonishing rate, creating fingernails and toes—it was a full-fledged miracle. I was in awe of the magic of being pregnant. Even the morning sickness was tolerable, knowing that as I spent mornings on my knees retching up the crackers, oatmeal, and fruit, she was becoming stronger. It gave my life purpose.

I didn't take so much as an aspirin for a headache the entire pregnancy. I ate salmon I hated and drank fresh carrot and ginger juice, even though it took half an hour to clean the stupid machine after using it. Becoming pregnant had been so difficult that I had one singular focus: giving this child the healthiest start my body could provide. John rubbed my feet, and at night would rest his head in my lap and read stories to Wren. The pregnancy brought out a side of him that I'd never seen before. Nurturing and sweet. Secretly, I congratulated myself on picking the perfect father for my child.

As my due date drew closer, John was promoted again and stationed in North Carolina, and his unit wasn't going to be deployed until after the baby was born. I'd written a birth plan, and we packed a bag and waited for the labor pains to begin. He whisked me to the hospital when the contractions were five minutes apart and coached me through sixteen hours of the most unmedicated pain I'd ever endured. Exhausted, I cried when the doctor confirmed that labor had stalled.

"Let's schedule a c-section."

I shook my head violently as another round of contractions gripped my belly. Pressing my lips together and blowing through them, I made a hissing sound.

"That is not part of our birth plan," John answered for me. His voice was direct and calm and filled with authority.

"But Corporal, your wife is exhausted and labor has stalled."

"In this scenario, our birth plan dictates the use of Pitocin to get things moving. Right, T?"

I nodded up and down as the last wave of pain left my body, and then I leaned back on the pillow drenched in sweat. Proud of my husband, who was a stickler for carrying out orders, whether from me or the United States Army. John stayed the course for four more hours until Wren's heartbeat plummeted and I was rushed into surgery for an emergency c-section. The last thing I remember before the anesthesia kicked in was John squeezing my hand. He smoothed my hair away from my sweaty brow and said, "It's okay, sweetheart. I got this." The fog swallowed me, and I peacefully surrendered to it, knowing all was well and in John's fully capable hands.

When I woke up from the anesthesia, it took a full minute to get my bearings. John was keyed up and jittery, hovering over the bassinet where, under a heat lamp, the nurse was checking the baby's vitals.

"It's a girl," the nurse sang out as she washed her

hands and then stepped closer to me. She gently pressed on my belly, and I gasped. Then she expertly peeled back the blanket and checked my incision.

A few minutes later, the doctor strode in, and in less than ten words, destroyed my world. Still groggy, he broke the silence in a brisk, matter-of-fact tone. "We had to give you an emergency hysterectomy."

"What?" Stunned, I struggled to sit up in the bed. The agony of movement tugging at my freshly stitched abdomen made me pant.

"I'm sorry, Mrs. Churchill. We had to take drastic measures to save your life."

I was confused and bewildered.

Why was he lying?

There's no way John would have let them cut my womb out of me. There wasn't. Panic set in, and my heart rate began to spike as the truth settled in deeper.

There will be no more babies for us? It can't be true.

"No!" I cried, shaking my head to keep the words from entering my ears and lodging into my brain. My eyes slid over to John, who raced over to my side of the bed.

"No," I mumbled, in complete denial. "There must be some kind of mistake. You're wrong... John?" My voice cracked as he moved closer. I tugged at John's shirt, balling my hands into fists as I felt wetness cascade down my cheeks. "No! No! No! No! This wasn't on our birth plan. He's wrong, right, honey?" The words tumbled from my dry mouth as my wild eyes were glued to John, looking for confirmation as the doctor continued to explain.

In shock, I struggled to understand his torrent of medical terminology. I closed my eyes, shutting out the offensive incomprehensible terms, feeling more tears leak out of the corner of my eyes. John stood by clutching my hand, and when the assault of words finally ended, I opened my eyes again and saw his pain. Defeat reflected in his eyes; it was an emotion he was completely unfamiliar with. Failure was devastating to the man who could always be counted on to make the right call under pressure.

I was inconsolable, a quality that rattled my *Army Strong* husband. A man who wasn't afraid of anything except overwhelming female emotions. Looking like a fish out of water, and eager to distract me, he awkwardly walked over to the warmer and was handed our bundled babe. Directed by the nurse, he brought her to me. "T... honey, don't cry," he pleaded, always direct with his words and giving orders, a way of navigating his life I was accustomed to by now. I swiped at my tears, brushing them away along with the dream that our house would be filled with children.

John maneuvered carefully toward the bed, his eyes glued to her tiny heart-shaped face, his shoulders tight and tense, protecting this little bundled creature wearing a tiny pink hat. In his desperation to stop the torrent of tears that still coursed down my face, my proud Army man caved the first and only time in our lives when he placed our sweet, swaddled daughter in my arms.

"Theresa, sweetheart, look... she's so delicate and perfect." He redirected my grief as he marveled at the tiny fingers that reached out to curl around his. And just like that, she wrapped her father around her finger without him even putting up a fight, without him even knowing. "She looks like a Wren," he cooed softly in an effort to comfort me as he looked down at her. His breath was warm on my cheek as he wrapped his strong arms around us. His perfectly timed concession stopped the flow of tears instantly, and I hiccuped and looked down into her sweet little face.

"Really?" I asked, my voice strained and hoarse from the torrent of tears, and he gave a tight little nod.

A flash of a gassy smile shifted her features to play-fully joyful when he said her name out loud.

"Wren. My little Wren," I crooned, my face inches from hers, the milky scent of my colostrum filling tiny pockets of air between us. "You like that, don't you?"

John kissed my cheek, and time stood still the way it does during the first magical hours of a new baby's life on earth.

"Wren *Elizabeth* Churchill." I looked into John's eyes with a concession of my own, and a small smile flashed across his face, acknowledging and appreciating my addi-tion of his mother's name.

"Wren Elizabeth Churchill," John repeated as his arms pulled me closer and I leaned into him, ignoring the twinge of pain that shot out from my incision. He wasn't an overly affectionate man, so when he offered it, I lapped it up like a kitten with cream no matter what state I was currently in.

Lying together in the hospital bed, we marveled at what our love had made. A living, breathing being who would have my eyes and her father's hair. Just twenty-four hours earlier, we arrived at the hospital as a couple but would leave there as a family. A threesome now filled with purpose, each of us getting a fresh start, a new beginning, a new title marked by the momentous occasion of birth. Mother. Father. Daughter. Even when I am old and gray in the nursing home, I will remember the warmth of that joy, wonder, and ecstasy seeping into every hidden space in my broken heart. Healing me from the inside out. The rest of the world fell away. There was only our new family huddled together against the brutal cold world. We became the Three Musketeers.

Wren latched on and nursed with such a ferocity it stunned me. Her first taste of the outside world held the clues to how she would approach everything in her life, with wild abandon and delight, unafraid to partake in the pleasures it offered. I was thrilled to see she took after her father in that respect and a little afraid at the same time that their sameness would bond them in a way that would perpetually leave me an outsider.

Since this was going to be my only babe, I was going to savor every moment we had together. As I stared into her wide-open eyes glued on mine as she gained nourishment from my body, I fell in love. A deeper love than I ever knew existed. Deeper than the love I had with John even on our best days. I would devote every moment of my existence to making her feel cherished and supported. She would have dreams and goals, and she would reach them with the determination and military precision of her father and the practical steadfastness of her mother.

Wren was now the sun in the center of our new universe, and we were reduced to planets revolving around her.

THREE

Time passed the way it does when you are a mother, speeding up, yet slowing down. The years truly are short, yet the days are long. Four years and two bases later, we were settled at Fort Bragg for only a month when John got his next deployment order. Instead of the usual thirty days' notice we'd gotten in the past, it was cut short by two weeks, leaving me panicking and frustrated. I knew my role and was ready to carry out my own orders; I was just beginning to resent being forced to bend to the Army's will. It was a frustration I bit back and chewed down, never sharing it with John.

We snuggled together on the bed after making love. I forced my brain to focus on the curve of his strong shoulders and the smattering of hair on his chest that tickled my face when he pulled me onto his chest afterward.

"Are you ever scared?' I asked.

"Can't afford to be," he answered. "My mind is busy keeping my platoon safe and making sure I can get back to you and Wren in one piece."

This was his third deployment, but he was instructed in advance it had the potential to be his longest. Wren was almost four, and for the first time able to comprehend her daddy was going somewhere for a long time.

I knew the next few precious minutes before she woke up would be the last we'd have alone together for over a year. When he came back, we'd have to fight our way back to this tender place we were now. There would be anxiety and sleepless nights, and oh so much awkwardness. That's the one thing people don't understand about being a military wife. It's not like a friendship that picks right up where it left off when you are reunited. When John was deployed, our marriage wasn't simply put on pause. No, instead, life continued. We were being tested every day by forces outside of our marriage that were fundamentally changing us both.

Overseas, John would be living in deplorable conditions, under absolute stress, and witnessing and enduring the atrocities of war. Those were the types of harrowing memories that left their mark on a man. Heart-wrenching moments buried deep in their psyches that only resurfaced when they returned home. If your soldier didn't come home in a casket, your husband still wasn't safe. The trauma of war lurked, waiting for the opportunity to be expressed in addiction, PTSD, or suicide. Each deployment changed him. John would become hardened and quieter, keeping to himself longer, and in that state, the only person who could reach him there and bring him back was Wren.

During his deployments, Wren and I were engrossed in our day-to-day life. School for her and piecing together odd jobs to make extra money for me. I learned early on it was never a good idea to allow yourself too much time alone to think during deployments. That was the key.

When he called, I always gave him the highlight reel of our lives. His calls were so sporadic I slept with the phone perched on the nightstand, anxious to hear his voice, day or night. The family intel I shared with him focused exclusively on the good stuff, the milestones Wren was hitting, and the funny words she'd say. The way she called fingers "skinders" and when she sang the Alphabet song, instead of L M N O P, it morphed into ARM-A-DILL-O PEE! The first time it happened, she'd burst into song with such utter glee, belting it out so proudly *I'd* almost peed. It was so cute I didn't have the heart to correct her. On our calls, I worked to translate bits of our lives through the phone line he could carry in his heart wherever his boots took him.

And finally, after waiting for months, forgetting what it was like to be a wife and have a partner, the day you'd waited for would arrive. Homecoming. Instead of pure joy and excitement to reunite, you'd lie awake at night the days before the ceremony, wondering if this version of your husband would fall in love with you again. Even though I was never one to spend much time preening in the mirror, on the morning of a homecoming ceremony, I'd find myself changing outfits six or seven times, trying to find the right dress paired with the right lipstick to make the transition back to wife easier. It never was. What worked for us were systems. A consistent way of doing things, a religious schedule to adhere to, and a clear division of duties with Wren.

"T., Look at me." We rolled toward each other, our heads resting on mismatched pillowcases. Tears were already welling in my eyes. "I know this is hard, sweetheart, but it's the life we chose."

I nodded through my tears. "I know."

"Remember the plan."

I began to rattle it off. "Stay busy, take lots of pictures and videos, and reach out to the other wives on base."

"And I'll stay focused and call as often as I can and look forward to the day when we are reunited."

I sighed. I understood the plan. I'd been through it many times before, but it didn't make him leaving any easier. There was the initial grief to process when he left, then there was the daily battle in my head against the worries of him getting wounded or killed in action. He didn't share any of the details of his deployments, and although I was sometimes grateful to be in the dark, other times, the not knowing was worse. I was getting good at creating fatal situations in my mind.

Through the wall between us, we heard Wren babbling to herself.

"Looks like Miss Thang is up," John said with a smile. "I'll make you some pancakes before we go to the send-off." He gave me a kiss and we scrambled to pull our discarded pajamas on. Four-year-old kids had a way of making surprise visits to your bedroom and not leaving until they asked a litany of embarrassing questions.

What were you doing to Mommy?

Why are you naked?

I'd just pulled my nightgown on when her shadow darkened the doorway. Wearing green footie pajamas and dragging her blanket and threadbare elephant behind, seeing her Daddy, she ran to him with glee.

"Daddy!" He scooped her up into his strong arms,

kissing her cheeks and then her neck with his scratchy stubble that made her giggle.

"Nom, nom, nom." He nuzzled, playfully nipping at her neck with his lips and scratchy chin, and laughter bubbled out of her throat, bouncing across the room from one wall to the other. I closed my eyes, mentally recording it. The deep teasing timber of his voice. His usual authoritative tone was tucked away while he frolicked with Wren. Her absolute joy at being the center of his attention. They were besotted with each other. Two peas in a pod, cut from the same cloth, each other's favorite person. I savored it, knowing the tears would come soon. Wren would be inconsolable at the base when we assembled for the deployment ceremony and he got onto the bus without her.

"Pancakes?" he asked when the giggles subsided.

Wren nodded up and down enthusiastically and followed him into the kitchen. I heard pots and pans clanging around, joined by the sounds of John's voice patiently explaining every detail of what he was doing and asking her for help. He'd talked to her like an adult since she was born. Filling her world with the sound of his voice, his patient instructions, and guidance. It was almost like he was banking them, creating a surplus and a store she could rely on to get her through the long months he knew would follow.

"Coffee?" I asked, ruffling Wren's hair and sneaking a quick peck on her soft, round cheek. She was standing on the plastic stool John brought home for her, next to him in front of the stove. He handed her a spatula and took her tiny hand in his, attempting to flip the first pancake. It flew out of the pan, and then the other half caved in on itself.

Wren burst into tears. She knew today was the day her

daddy was leaving, a fact she struggled to understand, and it keyed up her emotions. John pushed the pan to the back of the stove and swept her up into his arms. Her legs wrapped around his torso, and she gripped his neck tight as she sobbed.

"What's all this about?" he asked softly. "Everyone knows you have to throw away the first pancake anyway."

She pulled her head back. "Why?"

"Because it doesn't get as golden brown as it should."

She seemed to accept his answer and relaxed her hold on him slightly. I poured a cup of hot coffee and set it on the counter for him.

John dipped to set her down on the ground. "Go sit by your mama and I'll finish up here."

Two minutes later, he brought the hot pan to the table with a smirk. Using the spatula, he deposited a cast-off drip that had cooked into the world's tiniest pancake at only half an inch wide. He solemnly placed it on her plate and then placed the real pancake on mine.

Wren looked from plate to plate, her tiny brow furrowed, before shouting, "Hey! That's mine."

"No. That's your mama's. You have a pancake." He pointed at the little brown dot in a sea of white Corelle, then reached over and poured a river of syrup for her.

She plucked it up, swiped it through the sticky syrup, and gobbled it with an open-mouth smile. "More!"

"More?" He feigned shock. "But you already ate a whole pancake! I can't believe you're not full!"

Wren giggled in response. "I'm not full yet. More, please!"

"Okay, fine. Little miss is such a slave driver." He set back to work cooking up the rest of the flapjacks as I recorded the moment. A simple breakfast before a terrible day.

———

After washing the dishes, I was glued to the clock, watching the last precious moments tick away. My anxiety rose with each one that passed. On the drive over, Wren slept in her car seat in the back. I braced for the crankiness that would result from the double whammy of being rudely awakened from her nap too early and the departure of her favorite person in the world.

During the hour-long ceremony where the uniformed men and the occasional woman filed into the building, each taking a seat on one of the tan metal folding chairs set out in straight rows, an ugly reality reared up. The chances of all of these chairs being filled at the homecoming ceremony a year from now were nearly zero. The bitter truth set off a flood of fear in my heart as I focused on the chair of our soldier with Wren sitting on my lap so she could see.

Wren waved at John from our perch in the bleachers, and he found a way to sneak his one-finger wave at us when his superiors weren't watching. The Army band cued up a rousing exit song that was supposed to pump us up but felt forced. We poured out of the building, making our way to the three coaches that lined up at the curb, waiting for our final goodbye. In a few moments, he would load up B Company and they'd disappear. The tears that hovered at the surface all morning now coursed down my face. My reaction elicited the same in Wren. We clung to each other, scanning the crowd for John, desperate for one more hug.

In two minutes, my handsome soldier in his green beret swept us into his arms.

"I love you guys. Take care of each other while I'm gone and remember all the stories so you can tell me when I get back."

"We will, right, Wren?"

She nodded, still looking forlorn. He took a step back, standing her next to me, and saluted her. She smiled and attempted a salute back with her pudgy little hand, and then she burst into fresh tears and clung to my leg. She knew this was the end; it was always the last act.

He leaned in to hug us one more time and breathed into my ear, "I love you, T. Take care of our baby."

"Hey, I'm not a baby anymore!" Wren demanded.

"My mistake," he said, and I was sure I saw his eyes glisten. "Take care of this sweet young lady." He kissed her forehead one more time and pressed his lips together before crawling up the steps of the motor coach, disappearing from sight. We waved at the bus until it disappeared from view almost a mile away. It was the third time and still hadn't gotten any easier. What I eventually learned was that it never would.

FOUR

When Wren was six, we were living in a home off-base when John was deployed again. Being enrolled in school now, Wren quickly learned that the other daddies didn't have to leave all the time. She was starting to ask hard questions, and I struggled to choose the right words to explain why he had to do it.

Wren's first-grade class adopted his platoon, and they had been writing letters and sending care packages with handwritten cards, beef jerky, and socks. It helped the time pass more quickly and made Wren feel more connected to John. Once a month, the class spent part of their day doling out shelf-stable candy and snacks into boxes that reminded the soldiers of home. The children's care packages were always acknowledged with hand-written letters and postcards from the men in John's platoon.

When their homecoming was a week away, it was actually her teacher, Miss Spellman, a rail-thin twenty-something with a huge empathic heart, that suggested the platoon come to school and surprise Wren and the rest of the class.

That morning I was buzzing, anxious to see John again, helping Miss Spellman gather the supplies needed to have our own homecoming celebration. Chocolate cupcakes I'd iced to look like camouflage sat in a carrier along with a gallon of cherry-flavored juice and a plastic crate filled with milk cartons. I glanced at the watch on my wrist and smoothed my hair, excited. I was minutes away from seeing John. A flash of Army-green movement out of the corner of my eye sent a flutter to my chest and made me nervously tuck a stray hair behind my ear.

Wren's classroom was constructed of concrete blocks painted a bright white with enormous colorful motivational posters covering every wall. Numbers in bright primary colors and a huge handwritten set of classroom rules flanked the sides of the whiteboard. Ancient linoleum flooring was speckled pea green, and there was a stack of carpet squares in the front.

"Okay, class. Grab a listening square and gather 'round. We have a new letter from our Army friends to read to you." Wren's blonde head popped up at the news, and she scrambled over to the line by the carpet squares, then settled in the front row. "Criss-cross applesauce," Miss Spellman reminded as she waited for the other kids to gather next to Wren.

"This letter is from Sergeant John Churchill, someone who is really special to our class. Do you remember who that is?" she asked in her teacher voice.

"My daddy!" Wren blurted out, and my heart twinged.

"That's right." Miss Spellman smiled sweetly. "Wren's dad! He always has such incredible adventures to share with our class. Are you ready to hear what he's been doing?'

"Yes!" Wren was just one of many in the chorus of happy, childish voices.

I slipped out into the hallway where John was waiting, while Miss Spellman began to read the letter to the class. Finding him immediately, my heart burst as he swept me up into his strong arms, looking handsome in his combat uniform and hat. Behind him, the rest of his platoon stood quietly in fatigues and combat boots.

"She has no idea," I gushed as I pulled back and looked into his eyes, seeing a weariness there that always took root when he was away. I brushed my hand across his freshly shaven cheek.

"Perfect," he said.

"Remember to keep quiet as we enter the room, boys." He whispered the command to the men behind him, and they nodded.

"Let's go in."

Their boots were silent as they opened the door and began to slowly file into the room. At the front, Miss Spellman continued reading the letter. "Thank you for the snack boxes you sent last month. We've been living on cottage cheese and hamburgers, so to get some of our favorite candy is a real treat. Did you know Afghan children love to fly kites? Sometimes they have kite competitions, and some of the contestants will attach metal or glass to their kites to cut the strings of their competitors' kites so they can win. That's not fair, is it?"

"No." It was another loud chorus of tiny voices, outraged at the injustice.

Miss Spellman looked up at John with a smile on her

face, nodded, and turned the reading over to John, who continued where she left off. "We can't wait to come home…"

Hearing her father's booming voice for the first time in almost a year, Wren gasped, jumped up, and whipped her tiny body around to see her father drop down onto one knee with his arms open wide. The rest of the class chattered, confused about the influx of soldiers in their classroom wearing camouflage.

"Daddy?" Wren rushed to him, uttered a cracked sob, flung her body into his arms, and clung to him for dear life. She wailed in relief, her little body quaking. John closed his eyes, clinging to his daughter just as tightly. When you are a child, the passage of time is warped. Even after filling pages on our calendar with red crosses and counting the remaining days, she'd still ask, "When is Daddy coming home? I want him to come home." She'd cry herself to sleep some nights, having a harder time accepting it on those days than others.

"Class, this is United States Army Sergeant, John Churchill, Wren's father, and the rest of his platoon we've been writing to." She crossed to the whiteboard and in red lettering wrote a number. "Did you know our letters traveled 6,750 miles to get to their destination? That's a long way! If you got in a car and drove all the way across the entire United States, you would have to do it twice to go that far." She let the fact settle in for a moment before continuing. "Let's get ready to go to the bathroom and wash our hands. Our soldier friends have agreed to eat lunch with us."

"You're so lucky! We're having Walking Tacos today," one little boy chimed up. "It's my favorite."

"Mine too," John said, finally standing back up to his full six feet. Wren wouldn't let go of him. Her little hand clutched two of his fingers in a death grip, a huge smile on her face. I watched them walk down the hall. The uniformed men dwarfed the smaller children, who looked up at them in awe, chattering in excitement as they made their way closer to the lunchroom. Her daddy was home. Everything was right in Wren's world again.

FIVE

After the final performance of the day, Show Choir parents and teens slowly filtered past my post at the coat check. There was a lull in the action, and I waited inside the closet that was packed with parkas and leather jackets on hangers with numbers. The Dutch door's top half was sprawled open wide, and I stood behind it with a smile, waving at kids and parents I knew from various activities. Show Choir was like a family. Tight-knit, we came together to fundraise and host events. This was Wren's third year performing, and I often took new Show Choir moms under my wing to show them the ropes.

"Hey there, Theresa. I'm lucky number 13," Stan, one of the Show Choir directors said with a smile. "You make sure and tell Wren congratulations on being awarded a solo during the next showcase."

"Solo?" My voice cracked.

"She knocked it out of the park during the audition. Wren's got a voice like an angel just like her mom."

"Thank you," I said with a smile to hide the sting of hurt. Wren never mentioned auditioning for a solo.

Turning around, I heard Wren's voice. "What are *you* doing here?" Her words were harsh and came out as an accusation. I shrugged my shoulders and forced a smile and an explanation.

"Marcy called. She needed a last-minute volunteer."

Wren sighed, and her expression hardened to the bored teenager look I was used to seeing plastered on her face. "Can we give Sammie a ride home?" she asked.

My first instinct was to refuse. I wanted to talk to her privately, I needed to, but as I usually did, I gave in.

"Okay, but we won't be leaving for another twenty minutes." A significant number of coats still remained on the metal hangers. "Mr. Olson just told me you are going to be the soloist in the next showcase."

Her eyes flashed to mine, and her lips turned up with a sneaky grin. "Yeah."

"How come you didn't say anything? I'm so proud of you! That's amazing!" I gushed.

"Because I knew you'd act like this." She laughed at my excitement, but I knew part of her was secretly pleased.

"Can't I be proud of my daughter who has a voice like an angel?" I repeated the compliment, taking joy in it all over again. "I can't wait to see you perform."

"Settle down, *Theresa*," Wren mumbled, but the corners of her lips twitched up in a secret smirk of obvious pride. "Can I have some money for the concession stand?"

I pulled a ten from my purse, quickly handed it off, and watched her merge into the crowd of people pouring out of the gymnasium, knowing a line would begin to form in front of me in seconds.

"You're *welcome*," I chimed in her wake.

The next twenty minutes passed quickly as I returned coats to their owners while practicing my lines of the conversation I wanted to have on the ride home. I weighed the idea of including Sammie in it, then tossed it out. It wasn't my job to discipline someone else's child. I didn't want to step out of bounds, so I decided to wait until after we dropped Sammie off.

Pulling on my coat, I waved a hand toward the exit, and Wren and Sammie began to head toward the door. Once at the car, they both got in the back seat, reducing me to chauffeur status. I analyzed them in the rearview mirror. My heart quickened as they leaned closer, whispering, and my eyes locked on them.

"Mom! Car!" Wren screamed, and I slammed on the brakes, sliding on the icy road. The car careened precariously close to the bumper in front of me before coming to a stop. "Jesus!" she grumbled.

"Wren, don't take the Lord's name in vain," I said automatically as the pounding of my heart intensified in my ears. I exhaled loud with relief, thanking God we hadn't caused an accident, and decided to pay more attention on the drive to Sammie's house. In ten minutes, I pulled into their freshly shoveled drive and waved at her dad, Mike, who was leaning on the shovel while puffs of white exhaled air hung in clouds around him. He waved me onto the cleared part of the drive, and I saw his wife, Jennifer, walking down the steps while she yanked her coat on.

"Thanks for bringing her home." Jennifer was the type

of woman to write a thank you note when she received a thank you note. When we first landed in Eden Prairie, I discovered finding female friendships as an adult was infinitely harder. With our other posts, I kept to myself and focused on Wren. I consciously made the decision not to put myself through the painful process of working to find and maintain friendships for only a year or two before we would be shipped to the next post, never to see them again. Now that John was retired and an upper-level manager in the private sector, I was tasked to hold dinner parties and card clubs. Mike was on the security team John led. The first night we met, Jennifer showed up on my doorstep with an impeccable peach pie and a nervous smile, and we bonded as we worked through the massive pile of dishes after dinner. We had so much in common, the friendship was easy, and we often carpooled the girls together.

"Any time. You know we love having Sammie around."

"How was it?" she asked as snowflakes drifted down and disappeared into the camouflage of her salt and pepper hair. She brushed it out of her eyes. Her thick fingers were freshly manicured a tasteful blush of pink and swollen, her simple wedding ring nearly cutting off the circulation on her ring finger. She was encased in puffy down, rendering her shape to a lumpy square.

Eye-opening. Terrifying. Shocking.

The words were on the tip of my tongue, and I pushed them away. "You know how these things go. A gymnasium bursting at the seams with frenetic energy, but St. Auggie's got the trophy. We got a one."

A one was the highest score a Show Choir could hope to receive. Jennifer turned to Sammie, lifting the garment bag that looked weightless. "Where's your gown?" She asked as she shook the empty bag in the air. Sammie reached into her backpack and pulled out the obnoxiously sequined number and tossed it over to her mother.

"Sammie! You know it's supposed to live in this garment bag when it's not on your body!" she shouted out to her daughter, who ambled away. Jennifer turned back to me. "Seriously, they have no idea how hard we had to work to fundraise to buy these costumes."

I laughed and nodded in agreement. "I still have half a dozen butter braids crystallizing in the bottom of my garage freezer!"

"I must have made six dozen cupcakes for the bake sale. Tell me they are going to appreciate all this hard work someday."

I laughed. "I hope so, but the jury is still out."

"Congrats on Wren's solo," Jennifer said, a proud smile spreading over her features. "Sammie said she killed it, whatever that means."

"Thank you." I basked in the glow of her compliment. As a mother, there is no greater joy than when your offspring displays a natural talent and is publicly acknowledged for it. I felt myself flush with pride.

"Thanks again for dropping her off, Theresa." She reached over and squeezed my forearm. "Coffee, juice, and donuts after mass tomorrow?"

"We wouldn't miss it," I answered then rolled up the window as Jennifer walked away with the garment bag. I glanced over my shoulder. "Come sit in the front," I asked Wren. "I want to talk to you."

She replied with a huff but acquiesced as she opened the door and slid in next to me. "Did I do something wrong?" She sounded suspicious of my intentions, as any teenager would when a parent asks to 'talk.'

"Well, kind of," I began, scrambling to find the words I'd rehearsed in the coat check and coming up blank.

"What do you mean?"

"Honey, it's not appropriate to sit on someone's lap at an assembly," I finally explained and darted a sideways glance over at Wren. Her cheeks pinked up.

"You were *spying* on me?" She waxed dramatically.

"Hardly, you were carrying on in a *public* place." It was irritating how fast Wren took offense.

"See, Mom, this is why I don't want you volunteering at my school anymore." She crossed her arms around her flat stomach in a huff and leaned forward so her hair would curtain her face, hiding from me. "You always take every-thing the wrong way."

"That's not fair, Wren. When you are away from us, there is a standard. A way you need to conduct yourself that shows respect for yourself and your surroundings. Lollygagging on the laps of your friends doesn't show respect for your school, for yourself, and definitely not for Sammie. When did you two get so chummy, anyway?" I asked, walking the fine line between prying into her life and satisfying my thirst for knowledge. Questioning your teenager was like disarming a bomb; clip the wrong wire and everything explodes.

"You've been forcing her down my throat for years. I thought you wanted us to be friends?"

I grimaced as my intentions were revealed. I didn't realize I was so transparent. "I guess I'd hoped."

"Well, wish granted," she answered with a smug smile, crossing her arms and settling back onto the seat, continuing to stare out of the windshield ahead. "We're friends, that's all."

"Okay," I said, but as she sat still next to me, I pondered her response. I wondered if there were signs and signals, evidence of something more I missed. "Your dad would have been livid if he saw you carrying on like that."

"I know." She turned away to look out the window as we drove the rest of the way in silence.

They're friends. That's all.

It should have been the end of the conversation, but why did those four little words seem like the world's biggest lie?

SIX

Mass on Sundays was non-negotiable in our household. Always the early riser, John was showered and shaved and in the kitchen, sipping a cup of coffee and reading the newspaper. His reading glasses dipped down low on his nose. He wore the same haircut our entire marriage, high and tight, a close-cropped military style that fell firmly into the creed he lived his entire life by. "If it ain't broke, don't fix it."

He glanced up at me. "You were talking in your sleep last night."

"Really?" I asked with a yawn. It was hard to settle in last night. Doubts and worries I couldn't fully articulate chewed on the edges of my brain. "Did I say anything interesting?"

"Lots of passionate mumbles," he answered as he flipped the page to the Metro section. "Something on your mind?"

I leaned over to kiss his freshly shaven cheek. "Not really," I lied. It wasn't anything *yet*. Over the almost two decades of our marriage, I learned not to involve John in the worries of child-rearing and homemaking. He tuned me out anyway. I was trained to take care of most things myself, and if necessary, he could be consulted in an emergency. It's the way it works when you're an Army wife during long deployments. You develop an independent streak out of necessity, and you don't burden your husband with the day-to-day minutiae of life. John was a good leader and believed in delegation. He trusted me to take care of Wren and make decisions when he was away, but when he returned, I'd hand the reins over to him without skipping a beat.

I sipped on a cup of coffee and scrambled a couple of eggs, adding some cheese.

"Wren!" I shouted upstairs, "Come have some breakfast."

She eventually stumbled down the stairs and over to John. "Hey, Daddy." She smiled.

"Hey, sweetness." He shut the paper with a smile and handed the comics to Wren. She pulled out the seat and sat down next to her dad, and I studied them. She was a carbo copy of John. They both sat identically on the stools at the island—leaning forward on their forearms, fists made into tight balls as they read the paper. It was comical.

"Since I didn't get to see you come out of me with my own eyes, I should have demanded a DNA test," I remarked, taking another sip of coffee.

"Gross, Mom," Wren chastised.

"Yeah, gross, Mom," John teased. He secretly loved that Wren favored him. I handed them each a plate of scrambled eggs sprinkled with chives and freshly grated cheddar, then watched them dig in, both left-handed, both scooping forkfuls of sunny yellow eggs into their mouths in unison.

"It's like watching synchronized swimming," I said to myself, earning a hefty eye roll from Wren.

"What's this I heard about you getting the solo in the next showcase?" I prodded Wren purposefully in front of John, eager to share her newest accomplishment.

John looked up from his paper and glanced over at Wren, interested with warm eyes. "Did you?"

"I got it." She smiled, happy with herself.

"That's my girl!" John declared, pulling her in for a side hug. I swear I saw the briefest hesitation before she melted into his arms. "I'm so proud to see you working up to your ability." To John, rising to meet the fullness of your God-given talents was the holy grail, the reason for living. "Always choose excellence, sweetheart."

"Why didn't you tell me you were auditioning?" I asked the question I'd been dying to ask since I initially heard Stan mention it. The words were laced with a wounded feeling I couldn't seem to shake.

"It's no big deal."

"It *is* a big deal," I said as I brushed away her reason. "I can't wait to hear you sing."

With a nod, she turned back to her eggs and the comics, and next to her, John made quick work of devouring his own, then folded his glasses and tucked them into his pocket. He rinsed and put his dirty dishes into the dishwasher before walking down the hallway, saying over his shoulder, "You two better shake a leg. The bus leaves in ten."

———

Church plugs you into a community quickly. It was the easiest way to feel connected in a new town on a new base. I was raised Catholic and graduated from a Catholic High School and so had John. It was one of the commonalities we shared. Going to church was always calming for me—a place to think and reflect, filled with other people thinking and reflecting.

As Catholics, we got a lot of flak and a couple of black eyes when sexual abuse allegations surfaced that went all the way up to the highest positions in the Vatican. It was embarrassing to be so hated in the news, but I never wavered. I loved the consistency of mass. No matter what town we lived in, I could find a Catholic church near the base and attend a service. It always had the same rituals and songs, a weekly routine that I could depend on, year after year, no matter where we were stationed. There was comfort in the familiarity.

St. Augustine's was flanked with two sides of colorful Tiffany-era stained-glass panels depicting elaborate pictorials of Jesus's short life. The morning sun penetrated them, sending rainbows of color cascading onto the carpet and across the plastered walls. It featured stunning hand-carved pillars that held up the aging roof. On the cracked domed ceiling, frescoes had been painted in gold and were showing their age now, needing a full restoration to the tune of over two million dollars. The ornate sacristy and altar areas were cloaked in shiny brass and ivory. The church was gothically beautiful, and I always felt a sense of peace wash over me whenever I spent time there. The silence is what I adored. It was the one sacred place I wasn't endlessly questioned or tasked with chores. I was able to close out the rest of the world and recharge my depleted batteries in the silence and comforting chanting of responses that were an innate part of me. Sewn into the fabric of my soul, I often didn't remember responding, but I always did.

The sanctuary became *my* sanctuary, a place where my anxieties and blood pressure dropped to a more peaceful place when I breathed in the faintest whiff of incense. A place where I felt connected to something bigger than myself. It made me feel lighter. Walking out of church after mass, I always felt more grateful, more thankful, and more tolerant of the frustrations of modern-day life. It was my place of solace and renewal.

Mass was always around an hour unless Father McDonnell got off on a tangent as he was sometimes prone to do. He wasn't my favorite priest we'd ever been assigned, but you get what you get and you don't throw a fit. He was nearing his seventies, but robust, and his sheer height and weight cut an intimidating figure. Dressed in the long, flowing gowns that were like a velvet and linen poncho, his voice boomed through the ancient, crackling audio system, sounding like he was an instrument of God himself. He leaned hard on the fire and brimstone aspects of the bible, clinging to the notion that fear and domination would get butts in the seats. Behind thick Coke-bottle glasses, his hawkish eyes always felt like they were assessing you. Cataloging and identifying your missteps and infractions in the name of the Lord.

Mass passed by uneventfully. We sat in the same pew we always did, the one in front of Jennifer, Mike, and Sammie. It was always funny to me that we gravitated to the exact same spot every week like we'd been assigned seats. Wren sat sandwiched between us, stealing coy glances over her shoulder at Sammie. When her body began to shake in a fit of repressed giggles, John reached behind her and flicked his middle finger toward her head. The sound made a sharp *thunk* when it connected to the base of her skull. The act made her freeze, her shoulder tight to mine, her cheeks pinking in humiliation. I closed my eyes and bit down my frustration with his manner of keeping her in line. I stole a glance over my shoulder to see if anyone was watching. Jennifer gave me a small nod in agreement with John's behavior correction tactics, and I turned away feeling conflicted.

Wren had been spanked since she was little. Corporal punishment was the path we chose for discipline, and when I say we, I mean John chose it, and I upheld it when he was around. Initially, I wanted to try a different tactic, but it was the way I was raised, too. I vividly remember days when Mom sent me to the basement to wait for my father to come home to dole out a punishment. Trembling at the sound of his feet on the stairs, wielding a wooden paddle with bottle caps attached to it, I always wondered if they were decorative or served a more painful purpose, but never got the courage to ask my dad such an absurd question.

I couldn't bring myself to spank Wren, so when he was deployed, we used the time-out discipline technique. When he was home, she was spanked. As a result, Wren had two ways of behaving. She toed the line for her father but often dared to cross it for me. It was a split personality punishment style I was starting to question, wondering if it undermined my authority all those years ago.

After the closing processional, we got in line and followed the congregation down the creaky steps of the church rectory. I grabbed a cup of weak coffee and a maple and bacon long john. John stuffed a five-dollar bill in the donation jar, and we found a seat at a low-profile Formica picnic table.

"Mind if we join you?" Jennifer asked, and Sammie slid in next to Wren, their shoulders touching. Contact I cataloged, unable to stop myself.

Is it something to be worried about?

I loathed that I was reduced to weighing and measuring innocent gestures like my daughter sitting next to a friend at a picnic table together.

At the other end of the table, John and Mike settled into their tech talk. They listened to the same podcasts and could talk about things I didn't understand for hours, but that had strange names like Kubernetes and Pi-Holes. Jennifer and I learned to tune them out. Wren's head dipped toward Sammie's, whispering a secret that made Sammie laugh, and I picked apart the interaction, looking for nefarious intentions.

"You seem a little preoccupied," Jennifer observed, innocently forcing my attention back to her.

I flashed a quick smile. "Not any more than usual."

We settled into chatting about mundane things, sharing an instant pot recipe, talking about the sale at the meat counter and how at almost nine dollars a pound, the bread-and-butter pot roast just wasn't worth it anymore. My attention was divided. I listened and made the appropriate confirmation sounds and engaged head nods, but my eyes flickered away to the girls over and over. Stuck in a loop, analyzing their body language and the way they interacted with each other, looking for signs of something improper or unusual.

The crowd began to clear out, when to my surprise, Wren got up and gathered the trash with Sammie at the table without being asked. They carried it away, conspiring together and giggling as they stuffed the napkins into the plastic receptacle.

"That was nice of you. Are you girls trying to butter us up for something?" Jennifer praised with a smile.

"Wellll," Sammie dragged out the word. "Since there is a teacher in-service on Friday, we were hoping we could have a sleepover."

Inside, I cringed at the idea, but I plastered a tight smile on my face. I became very still, frozen, and unable to speak.

"Of course, you can," Mike piped up. "We love hosting Wren. She's a great kid."

John visibly puffed up with pride as he always did when compliments were being doled out to his daughter.

"Can I, Mom?" Wren asked, leaning into me.

"Um," I hesitated, unable to make my lips form the word yes.

"Daddy?" She moved on quickly, steadfast in her desire to lock down permission as quickly as possible.

"I don't see why not," he declared.

Jennifer leaned in and squeezed my forearm. "It's settled then. You know, a teenager's friends are either the biggest blessing or the biggest curse. We're lucky you landed in Eden Prairie. I feel so at peace knowing Sammie's best friend is from another God-fearing family."

I nodded as the smile drained from my lips. Normally, I would agree and feel a rush of warm pride wash over me, but there was this little niggling of doubt now. It clouded my judgment and fed my fears. I prayed it was just my tendency to overthink and read into things rearing its ugly head again. I wasn't ready to walk down the other path. I wasn't ready to give voice to them because then it would become real. For now, the fear only lived in my subconscious, and even though it swirled and swirled, there wasn't enough evidence to make an admission.

This is all in my head. I am making more out of a few touches than is necessary. I have to stop. It's innocent.

SEVEN

The next morning, I made a cup of coffee and sat at the island sipping it. A year ago, we remodeled the kitchen. It was John's idea, and I poured over Pinterest boards, feverishly pinning backsplash tiles and color schemes, cabinet door options, and drawer pulls. I was conservative, looking for second-hand, refurbished appliances. Although my days of pinching pennies were over once John retired and transitioned into civilian life, the frugal habits I'd leaned on early in our marriage lingered. John wouldn't have it and declared he was in charge of the appliances. He researched them using *Consumer Reports* as a guide. When the appliances were finally delivered, the stunning Wolf gas range in shiny stainless steel took my breath away. I stood in shock in our freshly painted kitchen, unable to speak.

"What?" he asked, feigning innocence, gratified by my reaction, a smirk crinkling the corners of his eyes. I walked over and wrapped him in my arms for a hug, glancing up at him adoringly. The hair at his sideburns had started a slow march toward silver, and his face was rugged, etched with a map of lines I could trace by heart.

"It's so expensive," I protested.

"I knew you'd never buy it for yourself," he said as we watched the crew hook it up to the new gas line John had also insisted on, another bucket list item I'd wanted but talked myself out of due to the cost. "This thing will outlive us. I did the research, T. It's worth the investment."

The first night after it was installed, I placed a pan on the burner and turned the knob, listening to it crackle to life and then *whoosh* to light as the blue flames lapped up the side of the pan. I marveled at it. I'd never cooked on gas before. "It's so fast!" I exclaimed and glanced over at John, who was acting like he was reading the paper, but his eyes were focused on me. A flicker of a smile turned the corners of his mouth up in a grin. A pat of butter dissolved in the pan, and I picked it up to swirl it around. With Teflon-coated tongs, I picked up the well-seasoned chicken breasts and laid them onto the pool of browning butter, relishing the satisfying sizzle. "Hear that?" I asked with a huge grin on my face. "It's dreamy!" Fifteen minutes later, I placed a white plate in front of him, holding chicken with a perfect sear, finished with marsala wine, mushrooms, and more butter.

Wren filtered in, not as enthralled with the modern appliances as I was, sitting at the table for dinner, a nightly ritual I insisted on. It was the one time of day that we gathered together to share a meal and to wrangle more than shrugged shoulders out of our daughter. John was an avid bibliophile and would often present Wren with ethical dilemmas as fodder for dinner conversation. Oftentimes, he would take opposing views on purpose to debate with

Wren. I listened to them argue with each other and marveled at Wren's intellect and articulation. The sharp set of her thin shoulders and the steely tone of her voice when she felt injustices were occuring. With her skinny arms crossed across her chest, she spoke eloquently, and I was proud of her for standing her ground and not being intimidated.

At the end of an especially long duel, John would shake her hand and say, "You were a formidable opponent, but I'd like to declare a cease-fire and commence our peace talks at *Dairy Queen.*" She'd roll her eyes and follow him out into the garage, and I'd finish up the dishes and give him his one-on-one time with her. I always wondered what they discussed at their Dairy Queen Peace Conventions, but they never spoke about it.

Now, nearly a year later, I walked out to the living room, where the dollhouse had been relegated to live after Wren turned fourteen and declared she was done playing with dolls. Crouching down, I opened the little door and looked into the miniature structure where a mom, a dad, and a baby had lived for almost a decade. A thin layer of dust coated the roofline.

After a deployment that left John particularly morose and moody, his therapist recommended he find a hobby. He'd taken to drinking more whisky than usual and had punched a hole through the drywall late one night. After seeing it in the light of day, he admitted he needed help, and after a few sessions with the integration therapist, he came home with a new purpose. He loaded up Wren, and they went to the lumberyard then disappeared into the garage for hours. He cut out tiny scalloped siding that

Wren helped him glue on the exterior. Small windows were made with sheets of see-through plastic film.

For a solid week, they worked in the garage together, creating tiny balsam wood chairs and bedroom sets, and inside I sewed up curtains and clothing for Wren's dolls that were going to live there. Building the dollhouse as a family brought pieces of John back to us. After each deployment, he'd spend a week with Wren in the garage, cutting and staining and painting tiny fixtures and furniture to fill our miniature house. It made life at our real home easier for all of us. We'd spent so many hours together creating it, there was no way I could ever let it go. Even though it was a significant pain in the butt to move, every time we got new orders, I'd insisted on it. Someday, I'd give it to our grandchild, but for now, it was relegated to our living room.

I traced my thumb across the peak of the roofline, glancing into the kitchen, which was a replica of our favorite house on base. The tiny chandelier that hung over the dining room table was a combination of wire and Swarovski crystals.

I studied the family inside, playing house. A mom, a dad, and a baby. A complete set, a concept that had always seemed so simple.

"I can move that up to the attic," John offered, trying to be helpful.

"I like it here," I answered, and I did. It had become a sort of time capsule of our lives. "Someday, Wren's daughter will get to play with it."

"You're such a sap, Mom," Wren said, breezing into the living room with a piece of cinnamon toast clenched between her teeth. Dressed in her St. Auggie's uniform, she had her hair braided tight to her head.

"I prefer sweet and sentimental," I offered.

"Sure, we'll go with that," she answered with a smile as she came over to give me a quick hug.

"You ready, kid?' John asked, stopping to put his shoes on at the door.

"Good luck on your math test," I called out after them as I followed them to the garage.

"Luck?" John replied as he settled his laptop backpack into the back seat of the SUV. "She doesn't need luck, she's a Churchill."

I watched him pull away and then closed the door and put my coffee cup into the dishwasher, telling myself not to go looking for problems. Plenty of them find you on their own.

EIGHT

The week slipped by like they do when you are knee-deep in the throes of mothering a sixteen-year-old. The taxi service ran like clockwork, and I quickly found myself in the driver's seat on the way over to Sammie's house with Wren next to me, a sleeping bag and her back-pack wedged into the floor between us.

My mind was on overdrive, listening to Wren chattering about typical mundane things. All week long as I carted her and Sammie to school dressed in their uniforms of navy plaid, white button-down shirts, and thick wool cardigans, it was easy to write off what happened. They were just two sixteen-year-olds going to school. The knee socks aged them down, making them appear younger to me. But today, seeing Wren dressed in jeans and a fitted crop top that she had been forced to layer over a tank top, or her father wouldn't let her leave the house, I noticed a new rainbow bracelet on her wrist.

A little internet rabbit hole I found taught me the

rainbow was a symbol of LGBTQ+ pride since 1978, and each color on the flag had significance.

"What's that?" I asked, trying to infuse my tone with neutrality, not wanting to pick a fight before I dropped her off.

"It's just a bracelet, Mom," she answered, her voice thick with condescension.

Is that all it is?

"Like it or not, what you wear sends a message. It can be interpreted in ways you don't want it to and can put you at risk as a young lady."

She huffed a loud, annoyed sigh and rolled her eyes. "I like the colors. You and Daddy read too much into everything."

I was afraid to pick away at her answer, remembering her love affair with rainbows that began when she was four. The Roy G Biv lesson in pre-school captivated her instantly and compelled her to draw rainbows on every surface. She was obsessed, coating her space in waves of color punctuated with puffy clouds at either end. There was an especially rough night when she'd drawn one on the wall in her bedroom in our rented apartment on base as John was reacclimatizing to being home with a small child after a long deployment. I still remember her dramatic wailing from the spanking she earned from that stunt.

"I want to get my license," she blurted, pulling me from my memories in a panic. It was a topic I avoided. Every day, my role became more and more obsolete, so I clung to the things that still kept Wren close to me. "I need you to sign me up for driver's ed."

I cleared my throat and answered, "We can talk about it with your father tomorrow."

"What is there to talk about?" she prodded. "I'm growing up and you both need to accept it. All my friends are driving. Sammie's birthday isn't for another three months, and she's already done with driver's ed."

My heart sank. Wren had a point. I knew we couldn't clip her wings forever. "But then we won't have any more of these wonderful drives and all this quality time together to look forward to," I offered with a sweet smile. It was a joke, a bad one.

"It feels like all you and Daddy want to do is keep me in this box, and all *I* want to do is break free."

She was right. I did want to keep her in a box where I knew she would be safe. It stunned me that she was self-aware enough to see it. A bubble of panic welled up. "We can definitely talk about it."

"Agh!! Talk about it?" Wren huffed in frustration. "That's all we ever do. I want to take action."

"You *are* your father's daughter," I responded. "I'll find out when the next driver's ed class starts. How about that?"

"Okay," she agreed as I wondered how far out I could schedule it. How long I could delay enrolling her before she would get frustrated. We drove the rest of the way in silence. On autopilot, I pulled into Jennifer's drive.

"I love you. Have fun and make good choices," I lectured as usual. It had become a litany of sorts that I subjected her to, knowing full well she was tuning me out but unable to stop my need to do it.

"I know, I know. Love you, too." Wren answered and then disappeared into the darkness. Yellow light spilled onto her face, and a door soon opened. Jennifer waved to me through the storm door with a smile as she invited Wren inside.

I put the car in reverse and headed home, looking forward to the peace and quiet that waited for me there. With an entire evening to myself, I thought I might get crazy and start a new cross-stitch. It was an easy, mindless hobby that I picked up during John's first deployment years ago. My life was filled with waiting and to stay busy, I filled the waiting with crafts. It was easier to focus on the dotted matrix of fabric in front of me instead of obsessing about where John was, if he was leading men through hostile territory, or if that dreaded government sedan would show up in my driveway with its terrible truth. I needed an activity to calm my busy brain that was endlessly conjuring up worst-case scenarios. Left unattended, I was prone to work myself into a panic. Wren's bracelet popped into my thoughts again.

You're doing it again, silly. Making mountains out of molehills. Just stop.

After a quiet dinner, where John fell into the routine of doing the dishes, letting me take up residence on the reclining end of our sofa, my mind finally started to unwind. I pulled the rainbow of colors from the cross-stitch kit, marveling at the beauty of them all.

It is *pretty. I see why Wren loves rainbows so much.*

I separated the colors one by one into neat piles and threaded my needle, knotting the end so I could begin to stitch, and got lost in the maze of tiny squares. Under the warm light cast from a nearby lamp, each tiny X I created had a soothing Zen quality. The fabric was stretched tight in a hoop in my hand. One by one, they began to fill in the small area I was working in.

An hour later, John appeared with a cup of chamomile tea. He set it down on the coaster next to me.

"Thank you," I acknowledged his efforts. It was his love language, acts of service, and one I always appreciated. I stood and stretched my arms behind me, lacing my fingers to pull my shoulders back. I felt the warmth of his hands on my shoulder blades. I leaned into him; the moments he chose to connect were often few and far between. I knew he loved me, but there was a sense of duty coiled tightly into the fibers of our marriage tapestry.

He leaned forward and planted a kiss on my cheek. I melted into him and closed my eyes, savoring the moment with a soft smile. I knew what came next. I knew my husband by heart. He wasn't a passionate man, but I had long ago decided I didn't need that. I far preferred a dedicated one.

He tugged me to the bedroom, and I followed, enjoying the quiet and intimacy. He was always freer and more open when away from our daughter's teenage ears. Satiated, I dozed off in his warm arms, content and relaxed, letting my body float away into a deep sleep.

A few hours later, I was jarred awake by the phone trilling on the wooden stand next to our bed.

Dazed, I blinked several times before glancing at the clock. Ten past midnight. My heart lurched as I pulled the phone off the stand and pressed it to my ear.

Nothing good happens after midnight.

"Come get your daughter." Mike spat the words out at me, I heard Jennifer chastising Sammie in the background and the sound of Wren sobbing.

"What?" It was the only word my lips could form.

Disoriented from sleep, I struggled to piece together what he'd said. It didn't make any sense.

"She is not welcome in our home anymore," he warned.

"Dad, no!" I heard Sammie on the other end, then the dead silence and dial tone.

Panicked, I shook John to wake him up. "Honey," I whispered urgently. "Wake up. Something happened at Sammie's. We have to go get Wren." In the darkness, I shivered and continued to rouse John from sleep. Years of sleeping in hostile territory gave him the ability to fall into a deep sleep anywhere. "Honey!" I said more urgently as I shook his arm relieved when he finally opened his eyes.

He slowly pushed himself up into a sitting position on the edge of the bed. Rubbing a thick hand over his face, he asked, "What in the Sam hell is going on? It's after midnight."

"I don't know, but we need to go *now*." My voice quivered as fear cut through my center. I jumped up and flicked on the light that stunned us both. John groaned and covered his eyes until they could adjust.

"What the hell is happening?"

"I have no idea, but Mike said we need to come now and get her. It sounded urgent."

We dressed quickly, and my mind spun in the darkness. John was silent in the driver's seat, focused on the task in front of him, and within fifteen minutes we stood outside their door. Standing on the front stoop, I knocked a soft timid knock with the back of one hand. Two seconds later, John leaned in and knocked more forcefully.

Mike yanked the door open, his expression already pulled into a tight scowl. "Go collect your trash."

"What did you say?" John responded in shock and confusion.

"You heard me," Mike answered.

John rankled at the insult, and his shoulders stiffened as he took a step into their house. I followed silently behind, stunned.

The lights were blazing in their kitchen where Wren and Sammie sat on oak chairs as far apart as possible, and Jennifer rocked herself on the other, sobbing.

"Calm down," John said to Mike, thinking it would disarm the situation as it had so often at work. "Wren, you better start talking."

"Yes, Wren. Tell your parents what you were doing."

Panic surged in my belly. My eyes widened as I searched hers. Wren's arms were crossed against her chest, and she was shaking. I fought the urge to pull her into my arms. Seeing her quivering in fear, it was a natural instinct to protect her.

"Now," John urged her, his voice deepening and sounding more ominous. I sensed the storm clouds gathering. Electricity crackled in the air, and I felt a significant shift.

"Sammie and I are more than friends," she admitted quietly. "Jennifer saw us kissing in her bedroom."

I gasped, and a hand flew to cover my mouth. Time stood still. The truth was shrapnel to my soul. No longer deniable, one of my deepest fears had been confirmed, and shame flooded in. John blinked several times, and a blanket of silence filled the room followed by a lightning bolt of truth that sent him reeling.

"What?" John began to deflate like a balloon. He staggered to the sidewall, leaning against it before regaining his composure.

"It isn't right," Jennifer muttered on repeat in the corner, again and again, then began to whisper *Hail Mary* under her breath. She dissolved into fresh tears at the end of each verse and then began again. Mike paced the room, ratcheting up the tension, grumbling to himself using words I could only grab in snatches. *Abomination. Against God. Going to hell.* The faster he paced, the more my fear grew. I stumbled forward to Wren and pulled her out of the chair.

"Let's go," I said to John, who was still dazed. Turning toward Wren, I barked out orders. "Get your stuff and go sit in the car." I tugged the keys from John's hand, and as Wren left, Sammie cried harder.

"Go to your room," Mike ordered. "I'll deal with you later." She stomped up the stairs, and a few moments later, the door slammed so hard family photos on the wall rattled in their frames.

I searched for words, my mind blank, and glanced over at John, the one who was always in control. My *Army Strong* husband who never backed down from a challenge was gutted and unable to comprehend what was happening, unable to pull it together and be the voice of the family. I summoned my courage but was relieved when he finally spoke.

"There has to be some mistake," he finally uttered. "You misunderstood."

"How dare you come into my house and question what my wife saw," Mike spat out. "Tell him, Jennifer."

There was a keening now, a low, sad cry as she

lamented. "They were on her bed, without shirts… Oh my God…" She trailed off.

John had enough. "We're leaving." Finally springing back into action, he strode across the room to exit out the front door, and I followed close behind, hearing the click of the door as I pulled it shut behind me. Wanting to lock the secret in and keep it there, hide it away in the dark corners, never letting it see the light of day. We got into the car, and Wren sat sullenly in the back seat. I glanced once more at the house as John backed out and began to pull away when Sammie rushed to the front picture window and beat on it with her hand, desperately mouthing words to Wren I couldn't make out. Wren shifted to the window, pressing her palm against the foggy glass, never taking her eyes off Sammie until we made the turn at the end of the block. I heard her sniffling and shifted in my seat to glance back. Tears coursed down her face. Usually stoic, I had to admit to myself that something profound had happened tonight. I quickly made the sign of the cross and fingered my St Christopher's medal, yanking it anxiously from side to side on the chain on my neck.

John drove the rest of the way home in silence and pulled the car into the garage. He turned off the ignition but refused to move. Wren couldn't open her car door fast enough, craving distance from us, and she disappeared into the house. I sat next to John for a moment. His eyes were focused on something ahead of him, unable to meet mine. I reached over to squeeze his hand and he recoiled.

"Did you know?" he muttered.

"Know what?" I asked, even though I knew exactly what he meant.

"That our daughter is a lesbian."

"No," I lied.

"Come on, Theresa, you spend every day with her. You had to know something."

"She's sixteen. She doesn't know what she is," I reasoned. "Come inside," I begged. "Let's sort this out."

"There's nothing to sort, Theresa," he said. "It has to stop. Our daughter is morally bankrupt. Since she can't seem to make good decisions for herself, I am going to start making them for her. I am talking about a total re-boot. No more extra-curricular activities. Things are really going change around here."

When my husband gets like this, he is immovable. Resigned, I sighed and then left him there in the garage. My heart was heavy as I climbed the steps into our home, and in the wave of confusion that currently cloaked every-thing, there was this underlying thread of truth. He was right. Things really *were* going to change around here.

NINE

The next morning, I made pancakes. Trying to smooth the feelings of the night before with maple syrup and bacon, it was a pitiful tactic that didn't work.

We gathered at the table, stiff and in silence. I passed the platter of bacon and pancakes to John, who stabbed a pancake with a fork and a grunt then set it back down in from of him, refusing to pass it to Wren. I sighed. This was going to be harder than I thought. Trying to diffuse the tension, I picked the platter back up and passed it over to her.

We ate in silence, our forks clanging against the Corelle the only sound in the room. I searched my mind for neutral topics to talk about around the breakfast table but came up short. Every tick of the clock on the wall in the kitchen felt like an eternity, and I cursed the pancake stuck in my throat that required almost an entire glass of juice to wash it down. I soaked up their anger and shame. I was a toxic sham-wow, the oddly absorbent infomercial rag from the early 2000s that was famous for mopping up spills ten times its size.

"You're grounded," John finally spoke without raising his eyes from the sports section laid out in front of him. His arms were crossed on the table, and he was dressed for work in khakis and a navy polo even though it was Saturday.

"For how long?" she dared to ask, and I silenced her further questions with a glare and widened eyes.

"As long as it takes," he answered. Knowing defiance would get her nowhere with her dad, she concentrated on eating her food as fast as possible. Two minutes later, Wren stuffed the last huge chunk of pancake in her mouth, desperate to leave the table. "May I be excused?" she asked, her mouth full, keyed up with anger and tapping her fingers on the table impatiently.

John said nothing, ignoring us with a soft grunt as he flipped the newsprint to the next page, engrossed in the details of opening season for the Minnesota Twins.

"Mom?" she asked, never one to relent, demanding an answer to her question. She was more like John in that way, never backing down, always pushing the envelope. It was a quality that when I first noticed it in her, made me proud. Wren would never be the doormat. She would be the boots. I didn't realize until recently how that similarity to her father would add to the tension in our home.

"Yes," I agreed, and she walked to the dishwasher to put her plate inside, her feet pounding hard on the steps as she climbed back to her bedroom. I was well versed in my role as peacekeeper. Navigating the distance between my husband and my child was a role I intimately understood, but this was uncharted territory, and I didn't know how to bridge this new and terrifying gap. John's walls were up, and I could feel his anger seething. Just below the surface, it boiled, only evidenced in the sharp line of his lips and the tension in his jaw.

"We have to get her back to church," he finally said, folding his newspaper back together and stacking it neatly next to him. "This will all blow over in a couple of days. Things will go back to normal."

I had my doubts. "Of course." I didn't see more church being the magic bullet like he did. She already went two days a week. Adding one or two more visits wasn't going to move the needle in any measurable way. "I was thinking we need to take her to see a doctor."

"A doctor?" He was outraged. "She didn't break a bone."

"I was thinking a therapist." The word therapist brought out a frustrated eye roll from him.

"I'm not going to have some liberal quack tell me how to raise my child," John said. "I don't need a professional to tell me I need to validate her feelings or some other emotional bullshit." Using finger quotes to signal his obvious disgust at a therapist using the word professional to describe themselves. "No." He pounded his fist on the table for emphasis. "She is confused, so I am going to take it upon myself to straighten her out. As long as she lives under my roof, she will adhere to our values."

He was a stubborn man, and I knew enough not to push back against his decision. It was better to let the emotion fade. Like a pressure cooker, I needed to wait and let the steam escape or we would all be burned. He got up, rinsed his dish, placed it into the dishwasher with a clang, and then left for work.

I sipped the rest of my coffee at the table alone.

———

Later that evening, I donned an apron and slipped some pasta into the boiling water. Dinner was always served promptly at 5:45. John was a creature of habit. He religiously followed a daily schedule. In the early days of our marriage, I adapted to it to keep my creature of habit content. Over the years, I'd actually begun to appreciate his itineraries because I knew what was expected of me. There was never a question of where I should be or what I should be doing. It was an unspoken covenant between us. A role we both stepped up to play.

I heard his key turn in the lock at 5:35. He coasted into the kitchen on a burst of cool air, delivering a kiss on my cheek as I stirred the sauce. The earlier tension etched on his face from breakfast had thankfully disappeared, and he complimented, "That smells delicious." After working a full eight-hour day, he felt back in control and capable. The office had a way of restoring order to his life. Computers made sense; they were easy to troubleshoot and they were logical—unlike teenagers. Work was his greatest escape, and I felt myself daring to relax, my shoulders dropping. I was glad to see a calmer version of him walk to the pantry while humming to himself as he opened a bottle of red wine.

After getting a pasta facial from pouring the streaming noodles into a colander, I pulled the garlic bread from the oven and set the table. A sip of red wine loosened my own tension, and I began to agree with his assessment. This was all going to blow over in a few days. Of course, it was.

"Wren! Dinner!" I shouted up the stairs where I could hear music faintly playing. She had disappeared into her room after breakfast, and I hadn't heard a peep. I knew she needed her space, too, so I stayed away to let her settle.

I spooned sauce into the deep serving bowl resting on the countertop. Hearing Wren's footsteps on the staircase, I hoisted up the heavy ceramic serving dish filled to the brim with a meaty sauce and began walking to the table. She cleared the corner and burst into my field of view. Stunned, I gasped and lost my grip on the dish, and it clattered to the ground with a crack, sending thick red sauce shooting up the walls and splattering across the baseboards. The bulk of it pooled on the beige rug under the dining room table, making it look like a crime scene as I stood frozen in place, astonished at the sight of my daughter's freshly shorn bald head.

Eyes bugging out and my heart quickening, I turned to look at John, whose back was turned away as he gathered silverware for the table. In slow motion, I watched him swivel around, humming to himself, and then freeze in total silence as all the air drained from the room. I began to wring my hands, preparing for another battle when we had barely survived the one at breakfast. Two in one day was a new record for our family, and fresh panic surged up again in my belly.

Wren ignored us and walked to the table, nonchalantly tugging to free her chair whose legs were tangled into the base. Finally free, she sat down on it and looked up at us with wide eyes.

"What did you do?" I cried. Both hands flew to my mouth to stop the other words I was afraid would spill out, already mourning the defiant act that discarded her flowing locks without a second thought. Her hair was one of her most striking features. Halfway down her back, I had braided it and combed it almost nightly from the time she was six. She'd gather in the living room at my feet, handing me a comb and spray detangler, and I would carefully unknot each section and pull the comb through it in long Zen-like strokes. I never realized the personal sense of pride I felt knowing it was beautiful until the moment it no longer graced her head. All of her gorgeous hair was gone and replaced by a bald skull with her pink scalp now visible. I ran upstairs to her bathroom, where her blonde locks had been discarded like trash, shoved into a wastebasket with used tissues and Band-Aids. Sinking down onto the toilet, I sobbed, grieving something I couldn't place. There was a deep sense of loss. A hole that opened in my heart.

From the kitchen, I heard, "What in the hell have you done? No daughter of mine is going out in public looking like they escaped Auschwitz!"

"Then maybe I don't want to be your daughter!"

The concentration camp comparison made me cringe. Words were powerful, unable to be unheard once they were uttered. In anger, John was prone to make outlandish and damaging statements that I spent the better part of two decades softening, but Wren's brazen act had stunned me. I gathered up the long strands of her satiny hair and tied them together with a ribbon, then tucked them into the bottom drawer of my nightstand. Then slowly, I walked down the stairs and back into the kitchen, where the sauce still lay on the floor, cooling down into a pool of lumpy crimson.

John and Wren eyed each other from across the room,

arms identically crossed, the same look of determination set in stone on their faces. Sizing each other up and strategizing a plan of attack in their heads. The silence was stiff and enveloping. I pulled the trash can over to the spill and began to scoop handfuls of sauce into it, my eyes blurred by tears.

"Look how upset you are making your mother!" he lobbed at her as they circled each other, stalking like I'd seen feuding lions do in a nature documentary.

Wren fumed, "It's my hair. My body, my choice."

"That is where you are wrong, sweetheart." He spit the words at her. "As long as you are under my roof, you will hold yourself to a standard."

"Whose standard? Mine or yours?" she asked, her voice like iron, her hands balled up and shifted to her hips.

"Mine and *your mother's*," he responded, dragging me into their battle. It was a tactic of his to make a unilateral decision for the family and then pull me into it when he got blowback from Wren, and for the first time, I felt used. "I will not be disrespected in my own home."

"This has nothing to do with you," she stated.

"This has everything to do with me!" he shouted. "Your actions reflect on us, whether you like it or not."

I stood ignoring their interaction, focused on the stain on the rug I was afraid would never come out. The greasy orange ring would remain and remind me of this terrible moment forever.

"What the hell is wrong with you?" John asked the question, the worst question you could ask any teenager. He didn't understand their quest to internalize every slam. To glom onto every insult and weaponize it to prove their parents didn't understand or love them. John was careening into scary territory and alienating us from our only child.

"John," I finally said, and his head whipsawed to mine as if he just remembered I was in the room in the first place. "Please." I begged him with my eyes, and he recalibrated.

"I'm going for a drive," he blurted and quickly departed, yanking on his coat and slamming the door behind him. We remained motionless in the kitchen, stuck in silence. I was at a total loss for words, kneeling on the ground, scrubbing at the stubborn orange stain. After a few minutes, I sat back on my heels and looked at Wren standing at the sink, staring out the window, her thin shoulders set in a hard line.

"We can heat up some leftovers," I offered.

"I'm not hungry anymore." She turned to me, and I saw her swipe at a tear on her cheek and her stance relax.

"I guess that's one thing we can agree on," I answered, my voice barely a whisper in the quiet. I looked at my daughter. Her bald head made her appear older than her sixteen years, but her shoulders sagged, undermining the notion. When John left, he took the lion's share of the tension with him. All that was left now was sadness and fear. I wiped my eyes and exhaled fully, puffing up my cheeks and blowing the air out in a torrent between my lips. I decided to take a different approach. "What is going on with you, honey?"

"Nothing." She was still closed off, her walls high and unscalable.

"It's extreme," I began tentatively, "this new look. I mean, what are all the kids at school going to say?"

"Who cares?" she answered, exasperated. "Who gives

a shit what those cookie-cutter posers think anyway? I am not scared."

"But prom is in a few months," I said. "It is going to take an entire year of living through the awkward growing-out stage for you to even have anything for them to style. And what about Show Choir? Hair is part of the dress code."

She laughed bitterly. "That's what you care about? Prom and Show Choir?" She shrugged in disbelief. "News flash, Mom, none of that is going to matter in five years anyway."

She was right, it wouldn't, but I was still afraid and trying to convince her otherwise. "But being a teenager is hard enough. Trying to fit in and understand all the unspoken rules. Girls are so mean."

"It's my life, not yours, Maybe I wasn't born to fit in," she mused, her eyes leveling on mine boldly.

I exhaled. Maybe she wasn't. It was hard for me to grasp the concept. I spent my entire life trying to fit in, trying to take up less space. Trying to conform to the ideals forced upon me by my husband, by the PTA, and by society. I never thought to question it.

Why did I never think to question it?

My head cocked to the side as I studied my daughter. My fearless, uncompromising daughter was boldly claiming her freedom, and I had to admit, I was bowled over by her audacity. To buck societal norms and forge her own path through life. It was a quality that I admired in others, but as her mother, it scared me to death.

TEN

After school on Monday, Wren opened the passenger side door of the car and then slammed it behind her. Her exposed neck was long and graceful now that there wasn't a cascade of blonde hair to cover it. Brow furrowed and lips pursed, I knew my daughter and she was livid.

"Hey," I said. "Had a rough one, huh?"

"It's been a shit day," she fumed, dumping her heavy backpack down at her feet.

"Whoa," I warned. "How about you try that again without the vulgar language?"

She was consumed by silent rage, staring forward, so I pulled the car out of the carpool lane and onto the street. "Is this about your new look?"

Just seven hours earlier, I'd driven a wordless Wren to school. I'd received grunts and one-word answers from my daughter all morning who, thanks to the haircut, didn't look much like one anymore. I kept stealing glances at her, completely exposed now. Her head was shapely and round, housing a big brain inside that was developing more and more connections inside it every day. Her face was pale except for the smokey eyes and long lashes that defied gravity and must have brushed across her eyebrows with every blink. She was wearing too much make-up, but I decided to choose my battles. Since I wasn't totally sure the one I was fighting yet, I'd opted to keep my mouth shut.

In the drop-off line, I'd slowed down. "Have a great day, honey." The words broke the silence a little too cheerily with the distinct tang of falsehood.

She barely muttered a response as she shut the door. I watched her pick her way through the lines of children and adults milling just outside the entrance. It was like watching Moses part the Dead Sea; two waves of teenagers drifted to opposite sides to create a wide path that Wren boldly stomped down. My heart dropped and I had to physically push away the urge to run to her and scoop her into my arms to protect her from the mean girls. In her wake, gaggles of teenage girls pointed and snickered behind her back, and then the wave converged back together into a sea of pimples and flat-ironed hair. I sat by the phone waiting for a call to come from the principal or from Wren herself, distraught and desperate for a pick-up, but it never did.

Now back in the safety of my car, she let out an exasperated sigh. "No, Mom, it's much more serious than that."

I racked my brain, searching for what could be more serious to a teenager than being judged by their peers about their appearance, when Wren blurted, "Sammie is getting homeschooled."

"What?" I asked in shock, remembering how Jennifer loved St. Auggie's. She'd graduated there herself in the early nineties and took immense pride in their legacy family status.

"Her parents were concerned about the kind of evil influences she was being exposed to at St. Auggie's." Wren used finger quotes to mock the word evil. "Me, I'm the evil influence corrupting their innocent daughter." She flopped back into the seat dramatically. "They're the evil ones. You know what I hate the most?" she asked, and when I didn't immediately answer, she continued, "Hypocrites." She spat out the word, her obvious disgust making her lips curl into a sneer.

I knew teenagers loved to expose hypocrisy. Wren's sense of justice was elevated and her view of the world was black or white. Her life experience wasn't long enough yet to include the painful morality lessons it would force down her throat. Tough lessons that would introduce her to the infinite shades of gray that made up the adult world. Her thin frame was stretched tight and taut in the seat next to me. I didn't want to poke the bear, but I also wondered what she meant. "What do you mean?"

"Isn't pornography considered a sin?" she started in. "Because Mike might have to go to confession for the stacks of *Penthouse* and *Hustler* we found jammed in his toolbox in the garage. Maybe *that's* what turned his daughter. Seeing *his* lewd and lascivious photos of barely legal girls."

"Well, that's a three-dollar word," I joked, trying to diffuse the tension. "I didn't even think you knew what it meant."

Her eye roll was barely contained inside the car.

"Wren," I cautioned. "Let's take a step back." I didn't want the visual of my daughter and Sammie pouring over smut mags, leering at centerfolds of naked women stuck in my head. There were already too many other images in there I could barely handle.

"Looking at magazines and reading books doesn't turn you gay," Wren explained. "You don't *turn* gay, Mom. There isn't one event that flips a switch. Attraction is a factory setting, direct from the big man himself."

I pondered that statement. "Then maybe he gets the wires mixed up sometimes?"

She huffed in frustration. "Ugh! You're almost as bad as they are. Great, so, you think I'm defective?"

"No, no, no." I tried to backtrack. "Stop putting words in my mouth."

She crossed her arms across her chest and stared straight out of the window for a long moment. When she was in a mood, it was a storm you had to let pass, just like her father.

"And, I decided I'm quitting Show Choir," she stated.

"What?" I screeched, slamming on the brake suddenly and jolting us both forward in our seats. "But, you love Show Choir."

"Not anymore. Mr. Olson took my solo away."

"Why?" I asked. "I don't understand. Why would he do that?"

"He's afraid we will get docked points because my hair is not to dress code, so he gave it to Maddie Stonewell."

"But you're the better singer," I stated. It was true, Wren's voice was a soprano powerhouse with a sparkling timber that was difficult to find in a person so young. Especially in a high school talent ecosystem as small as St. Auggie's. "That's not fair. I'll go talk to him."

"Don't waste your breath," she said. "I wouldn't do it now if he got on his knees and begged me to sing."

The rest of the drive was silent. When we got home, she flung the offensive Show Choir dress bag onto the floor and then stepped on it with her slushy boots. I wanted to tell her to pick it up, but I didn't. I wondered if she felt as dirty and discarded as the dress bag. I knew I did.

———

Later that night, John came to the bedroom whistling with a pamphlet in his hand. I put a bookmark in the book I was reading and set it next to me while I looked down at the thick cardstock of the pamphlet he thrust into my hand.

A bible verse screamed, "The truth of homosexuality is clear. Leviticus 20:13 (NLT)

"If a man practices homosexuality, having sex with another man as with a woman, both men have committed a detestable act. They must both be put to death, for they are guilty of a capital offense."

"At Hearts Restored, we help guide your child back into the loving arms of our Lord and Savior, Jesus Christ. They can unlearn this perverse behavior and be restored fresh and new, cleansed in the blood of the lamb."

"You can't be serious," I said in shock, looking down at the card that felt hot in my hand as a wave of nausea rolled in my belly.

"As a heart attack," he answered as he sat down on the edge of the bed, untying his shoes and pulling off his socks.

"Conversion therapy?"

"You *said* you wanted Wren to see a therapist," he answered like he had done something to please me.

"This is not what I meant at all." I stared down at the forced smiling faces of alternative teenagers that graced the front of the pamphlet, already knowing my daughter would never go easily. She would fight this kicking and screaming.

"I thought conversion therapy was illegal in Minnesota."

"It's not technically therapy, per se, but more of a youth group that reinforces our family values."

"That doesn't make me feel better about it at all," I admitted. "Besides, we don't even know if she's gay," I mumbled, leaning hard on denial. "She's never come out."

His chin jerked back as if he'd been slapped, and he palmed his face in frustration. "It seems pretty clear cut to me. She was kissing a girl."

"That might not mean what you think it means. Maybe she's just confused." I said the words more to try to convince myself than for his benefit, still trying to shove the genie back into the bottle.

"You need to read these." He handed me a stack of books. "Healing Homosexuality" and "A Parent's Guide to Curing Homosexuality."

Stunned, I flipped through the books, musty and old. He must have picked them up from the used bookseller he loved. Clearly from the late seventies, the photos of the teenagers on the front were rocking the Farrah bangs and hip huggers. The pages were yellowed and the previous owner underlined passages that stuck out like sore thumbs. "Homosexuality is a break in the psyche of a child, usually the product of abuse or neglect." I flipped it over in shock, noticing a faint smell of smoke that wisped from the cracked spine into the air. "Filled with personal stories from parents and children and ex-homosexual sufferers, this guide offers compassion and hope for all parents who seek to guide their child away from sin and back to wholeness in Jesus Christ."

I was starting to doubt my own deeply entrenched beliefs, where a month ago this issue was black and white for me. I'd always believed the homosexual lifestyle was a sin, but now it was clouded with doubt and disillusionment. I was waffling between the two, walking the line between my faith and my child. It was a tightrope I was on, and every step left me terrified and shaking.

"You're taking her. It's already been decided."

"No," I mumbled. The word was barely a whisper and my hands shook. I threaded them together and hid them under the blanket; I couldn't show him my weakness. I was barely clinging to my deeply seeded convictions myself.

"Theresa, I am the head of this family. You've trusted me to make all the important decisions up to this point. This might be the biggest test of all. We are fighting for our daughter's soul. Don't you get that?"

"You're right," I said carefully, knowing these words were the words he wanted to hear. "I *have* let you make the big decisions in our family, but this one does not feel right and I will not put our daughter through it. I need more information before making a rash decision. Conversion therapy has been banned by every major medical and mental health organization in the world. How can you willingly want to submit our daughter to something so damaging?"

Frustrated, he stood and walked to the bedroom to get ready for bed. I listened to his before-bed rituals. Water running, then the electric whir of his toothbrush, then the gagging sound he made as he gargled. I turned the pamphlet over in my hand, reading the success statistics of the center. Testimonials from mothers who gave them credit for controlling their daughters' urges and restoring them to spiritual health.

I tucked the pamphlet and the books away into the nightstand next to the bed and shut off the little lamp, pulling the covers up to my chin and covering my body with the thick down comforter. I couldn't look at him. A few minutes later, I saw his shadow on the wall as he crossed the room and then felt his weight sink into the mattress. He sighed once and then fell into a deep sleep, snoring loudly next to me. I tossed and turned for hours. All I could focus on was those books and pamphlets of paper buried in my nightstand and what havoc it was going to unleash on our family.

ELEVEN

For the next two days, John was a ghost in the house. He slept next to me, but he went through all the motions of our life in a trance, quiet and withdrawn. I laid next to him consumed with deepening fears, unable to rest. On Monday morning, he got up and went into the office earlier than five a.m., and I found myself at the coffee pot brewing some liquid energy. Tension was building in our home, and it touched everything in it. My stomach was tight and sour as I sat at the dining room table.

The sense of impending doom was hard to shake, so after I dropped Wren at school, I busied myself with washing sheets, pulling them off the bed in our bedroom, and setting the pillows on end. I climbed the stairs to Wren's room with the laundry basket at my hip. Tugging at the corner of Wren's mattress, I yanked at her sheet to pull it off. Seeing something sticking out under the mattress, I lifted it and found a stashed issue of GQ magazine, a notebook stuffed between the mattress and the box spring, and three pairs of men's boxer briefs. Out of place, the underwear unnerved me, forcing me to draw conclusions I didn't want to draw. It was another bone of contention, another truth I wasn't ready to see that ratcheted up my anxiety even more.

In her closet, buried under the mountain of dirty clothing that was giving the room a rancid smell, I found more pairs of men's boxers. Stuffed in a corner were non-stick tabs discarded from feminine pads, and pairs of bloodied underwear stuffed into plastic shopping bags and tied, shoved into a deep corner of the wall like she wanted to pretend they didn't exist.

"What in the world?" I said out loud to myself, resisting the urge to picture text Wren immediately. There was a flutter in my chest that intensified as I pulled out more masculine clothing, hats, and underwear. Working up a sweat, I pulled everything out of her closet and stacked the dirty laundry into two piles, the ball of doom in my belly growing with each revelation. Stacking the darks in one pile and the lights in another, I noted the absence of the pastel undies and pretty bras I'd purchased for her in the fall.

I dropped in exhaustion and defeat onto her mattress. Part of me wished they belonged to a boyfriend. That wouldn't have made it okay, but at least I would have known what to do. This realization left me scrambling and confused, unable to put the pieces together. I flipped through the GQ magazine, noting the folded corners on pages of men dressed in suits with impeccably groomed facial hair.

I opened the notebook. Doodles of rainbows and flowers, seeing Sammie's name in Wren's penmanship with a purple heart dotting the "I" made my heart accelerate. On the next page, at the top, the words "Bucket List" were scrawled in her familiar lettering. Afraid of what I would find there, I shut it quickly and stuffed it back under the mattress. Invading her privacy made me feel dirty. I'd always prided myself on giving her space. It didn't make me feel better peeking into her life without her permission. I was just so desperate for information, and it sickened me to see the new lows I was willing to sink to obtain it.

Something real is happening here. Is Wren having some sort of identity crisis?

I glanced around the rest of her room, scanning for clues, looking for items that were out of place, wishing the walls could talk. Wren had been spending so much time in her room lately, and I was certain there was something obvious I was missing. Posters of Matt Bomer were tacked to the walls. In the bathroom, tubes of mascara and liquid eyeliner were tucked away. Seeing all her cosmetics lined up neatly, I was able to push away the bulk of the fear. So what if she preferred men's underwear? No one could see it. Heck, if given the chance, I'd probably love to switch to boxers myself. Women's underwear was an instrument of torture designed by a mostly male-driven fashion world. I held up a pair of small grey boxers and noted how soft the cotton was. That had to be it, I reasoned, desperate to find a logical explanation.

Two hours of laundry later, the briefs were folded and put into her drawers, tucked away from prying eyes. I tucked them away in my brain, too, hiding them from sight, because if I couldn't see them then they didn't exist.

I hid the knowledge from my husband, knowing if he caught a glimpse, he would lose it. Confused, I was afraid to rock the boat, still lying to myself.

It's just a phase. So what if she's experimenting? Who will it hurt? No one.

TWELVE

The rest of the week passed, and as the champion compartmentalizers and chronic avoiders we were, we soldiered on. Falling back into our standard routines, the pit in my stomach began to loosen as the next few days unfurled without additional incidents.

"It was a nice surprise when you called," I praised John as we settled into his car, eager to get the night off to a good start. I hadn't expected his phone call from work that afternoon when he told me we were going out on a date. I was relieved to see John make the first step to reconnect, and I decided to tuck away the tension that had hovered over us and simply enjoy his company. "Where are you taking me?" With a smile, I patted my belly which was soft under the long burgundy dress I wore. "I'm starving."

"I thought my wife deserved a night out. Good food, good wine. We both could use a break."

"I don't think I've ever needed it more," I admitted, and he reached over to squeeze my hand. It was the first physical contact he'd initiated in days, and my stomach tingled.

"This is nice." I relaxed back into the heated leather seat of the car. My stomach growled, and I asked, "So, where *are* we going?"

I turned my attention to the windshield where the last fat heavy snowflakes of early spring splattered, instantly melted, and then drizzled down to the windshield wipers. "You'll see," he answered with a secret smile.

I squeezed his warm hand in mine, searching my mind for topics of conversation that wouldn't be inflammatory or send us down the path of ruminating over Wren. I needed one night off where I wasn't consumed with doubts and worries. Where I wasn't relegated to the diplomat, keeping the peace between them. I dropped his hand and reached out to scratch the back of his head. He turned toward me with a winning smile. His blue eyes crinkled and my heart tugged. Our recent distance made the contact feel foreign. He nuzzled into my hand, weaving his head back and forth and twisting into my palm as my fingernails gently scratched the back of his scalp. I felt his shoulders loosen, and I smiled and dared to relax.

Things have been bumpy, but we'll get there. God, I love this man. Even after all these years, he's still my best friend.

Flirting with my desire to connect with my husband again, but still harboring hurt feelings, I let the normality of the gesture woo me as the pressure valve opened slightly. Darkness fell, and he pulled into the parking lot of a building I didn't recognize. Looking around for restaurant signs, I was puzzled.

"Where are we?"

"One little pit stop before dinner," he said. "And then I booked us a table at La Fromage."

I squealed in delight. Cheese was my favorite food group—my husband knew me well. "Can we get the fondue?"

"Whatever you want, darling," he answered, and I clapped my hands together. My tummy let out another loud rumble at the idea of dipping deep-fried pretzel bites into thick horseradish gouda. My mouth watered.

I followed him into the building, where he waited at the door and held it open for me to walk through. "Thank you, sir," I said with a smile, feeling lighter and more carefree than I'd felt in weeks.

"My pleasure." He took my hand and led me down the hall. We entered a room where a group of men and women were gathered, their heads dipped in prayer, hands clasped in a circle. Confused, it looked like we'd stumbled into some sort of bible study. The group mumbled and chanted in low voices, raising their hands to the ceiling, a gesture that made goosebumps break out on my arms.

I glanced around the room to get my bearings. "God's love can heal the broken and the wicked."

Another poster taped to the wall prophesied, "Only when we repent and turn away from our evil ways can we fully know the kingdom of God."

"Only the Holy Spirit can transform a tarnished soul. At Hearts Restored, we help guide your child back into the loving arms of our Lord and Savior, Jesus Christ."

It was a phrase that gave me instant déjà vu. I rifled through my brain for its origin and came up empty. An overweight teddy bear of a man stood and lumbered toward us. His khakis were wrinkled and his shirt rumpled, bearing an orange stain on the front.

"John, it is great to see you again, and this must be the lovely Theresa you've been telling me about," he gushed as he offered a thick, sweaty hand that engulfed mine.

"I'm Jerry."

Larger than life, his persona was like another entity in the room, sucking up all the oxygen and overpowering the interaction. I pulled my hand back and tucked it into the pocket of my jacket, resisting the urge to wipe it on my hip. Instinctively, my radar went up.

"Please, have a seat," he offered. There were two empty chairs at the table where the rest of the group sat quietly.

His eyes were too small, too close together, and disappeared into his ruddy cheeks. His nose had the distinct red veins of a man who spent a lot of evenings deep in a bottle of scotch. "We are so glad you are here. John has filled us in on what's been happening at home, and we are here to assist in bringing your prodigal daughter back to you."

I felt the first stab of betrayal and yanked my glance over to my husband who blatantly ignored me, his full attention on Jerry.

"Our program has brought hundreds of children away from the wickedness of same-sex attraction and back into the loving arms of Jesus."

My mouth dried and I swallowed hard.

"Can I share my testimony with you, sister?"

I recoiled. His use of the word *sister* rankled me, but I nodded anyway, knowing the only way out of this meeting was to get through his 'testimony' as quickly as possible.

"I fell victim to the serpent when I was seventeen. A

man who befriended me came into my life at a time when I was floating, unsure of myself and who I was. His attention felt good, and I began to fantasize about him. My heart was filled with a devilish longing to lay with him that I indulged. It is not an action that I am proud of. But God forgives."

"Amen," the other people chorused together in a robotic way that was creepy.

"Yes, he does." Jerry pressed his thick lips together then licked them and began to continue. I focused on the beads of sweat that dotted his upper lip. "I fell deep into the belly of the beast. Prostituting myself with men, participating in lustful acts. It became an addiction. An addiction to depravity. I couldn't just stop. It took over my life, filling my heart with black soot. I hated who I was. Dirty and stained, a sinner."

John nodded his head in agreement, and I felt nauseous.

Jerry continued with a dry smile. "I remember during the deepest darkness of my trial, vividly listening to my namesake, the Reverend Jerry Falwell. I was surfing through the channels one night, desperate to settle down my brain that was obsessed with impure thoughts, and he spoke to me. 'Homosexuality is a moral perversion and is always wrong. Period. Every scriptural statement on the subject is a statement of condemnation.'" He waited again, and it was beginning to feel like performance art, a memorized monologue that had become his default setting during meetings like these. "God set me free and then revealed the true purpose of my life. He forced me through these trials so I could become the ultimate prophet and lead these broken souls back to him. It was truly my

Garden of Gethsemane." He paused for emphasis and nodded in a way he probably thought conveyed seriousness, but only left me craving a shower.

Broken? The word rattled me. I didn't feel like my daughter was broken.

"The Holy Spirit can transform your heart. It can give you new desires and wants." With a dry cough, he continued, "Homosexuality is not a person's normal or natural state. It is a cancer of the spirit that must be eradicated. One that we have sharpened our sabers and fought against for decades. We have to be diligent in the pursuit of the enemy."

I looked longingly at the pitcher of water sweating in the center of the table. As if on cue, he reached forward, poured two glasses, and offered one to me. I mumbled a thank you and fought the urge to put it to my lips. I couldn't bear to take anything from him.

After a long pause, he continued, "What's happened in her sixteen years that would lead Wren down this path of unholiness and depravity?" he asked then declared, "Theresa, the root of homosexuality is often childhood trauma."

His statement instantly offended me. I cleared my throat, the words I wanted to say sitting on the tip of my tongue. I detested hearing the sound of our names woven into his testimony and felt the walls closing in.

"The good news is we can save her. She will be washed clean with the blood of the lamb, transformed back into the child of God she was at birth."

Stunned, I was speechless. I glanced over at my husband, who was hanging on his every word. I struggled to return my focus back to Jerry, who was quickly becoming a caricature in my mind. His words burned, and I was offended. Rage bubbled up, and I struggled to contain it.

"We have raised our child in a godly home," I corrected, trying to set the record straight. "Wren had a very normal and happy childhood. John, tell him," I prodded, but John said nothing.

"Trauma can manifest in a myriad of ways, sister." Jerry leaned forward. The word 'sister' uttered again made me taste bile. Afraid he was going to touch me, I leaned back as far as I could in my chair and placed my hands in my lap, feeling my fingernails dig half-moons into my palms.

Childhood trauma? I focused on the phrase. Uncertainty filled me as he spoke. Wren was never traumatized. Was she? The doubt began to unspool, and I tried to come to grips with the claim. I wasn't with her every minute of every day, but we were exceptionally close. I would have known if she'd been traumatized.

He waxed on, his deep voice booming with the solution he thought we were ready to hear like he was our savior. "The good news is that we are going to heal your daughter before she gets trapped into the lifestyle. John explained during our first meeting that your daughter is just struggling with feelings. You are catching this in the nick of time. The longer this sinfulness plays out, the harder it is to return your child back to her natural state." He leaned forward again, and I could smell his rancid breath.

First meeting? Anger began to slowly simmer in my gut. I pressed my hands together to stop them from shaking.

"Here, she will have support. Be surrounded by a group of teenagers who understands her pain, who knows her brokenness. There is a comfort in that. I know when I went to my first meeting, the feeling of compassion within the group knocked the wind out of me. For so long, I was alone and afraid, thinking I was the only one who had these unnatural urges. I believed there was something fundamentally flawed with me. Stuck in darkness and unable to find the light."

"This is the trial God has tasked your Wren with in order to grow her spirit. There are many lessons God wants us to learn, and he often uses sin as a tool to lead us to a place of transformation."

I found my voice. "God is love. My God loves me unconditionally."

"Yes, he does. And while that is true, sister, it is often the sinner's heart that he calls into a relationship. He is using this development to draw Wren closer to him."

My eyes bugged. I struggled to accept the words that oozed like honey from his mouth. It felt like a performance, and the sentiment, though well-practiced, was hollow.

"The guilt, the shame, it led me to a place where I found myself late one Sunday night after spending a weekend indulging my desires, swallowing pills by the handful. Not wanting to face the destruction of my own soul and screaming for the pain to stop." He paused again, and John reached over to squeeze my leg. I pulled away and crossed them, shifting in the chair, fighting the urge to stand up and walk out. His voice intensified, "That night in a dirty hotel as dirty as my soul, I was once again on my knees begging for release. Shame obliterated me; the only way out seemed through my death. I drifted off toward the darkness as the pills and the booze numbed me out to the reality of the wicked life I was living. As I faded away, I saw an eternal fight break out over my soul. I saw the darkness and the shadows fighting against a shaft of light. The next day, I woke up in the hospital, and I drew a line in the sand. I said, 'Jerry, you are no longer going to participate in the destruction of your own soul.'"

I fought the urge to gag. Listening to him refer to himself in the third person was over the top, even for a character like Jerry.

"In that hospital bed, I pledged my future to Jesus."

I fidgeted in the chair and crossed my arms across my chest. I couldn't wait for this testimony to be over.

His voice deepened and proclaimed, "I was in bondage. But the Lord set me free!" Jerry raised his hands above his head and closed his eyes. "Yes, Jesus."

Another chorus of "Amen" filled the room, and I wondered if that was their only purpose. To cheer Jerry on with salutations of "Yes, Jesus," and "Come now, Holy Spirit." The way they waved their arms into the air like a toddler eager to be picked up was uncomfortable and leagues away from the controlled Catholic responses I was used to.

I'd had enough. "I'm sorry, but I need to leave." I stood on my shaky legs and walked proudly to the door and out into the cold night air. Sucking in huge gulps of it, I was desperate to get the stale and mildewy basement air out of my lungs.

Five minutes later, John burst through the door. "That was rude, T. At least we know where our daughter gets her flair for the dramatics from," John accused.

"You can't be serious." My chest tightened. "No way."

"An extreme response is warranted here," John answered. "The longer we let this carry on, the harder it will be to turn her around."

"Do you have any idea how much that destroys a child's mental health? Have you done any research on the long-lasting effects of this kind of pseudo therapy?" I spat out at him. "The practice is outlawed in most states. And the fact that Jerry is hiding this disgusting reprogramming under the cloak of religion!" I shouted. "It's outright criminal." I shook my head back and forth, pacing up and down the sidewalk and burning with rage.

"We need to *do* something," he begged, still unable to connect the dots as he paced next to me.

"We need to *love her*," I cried. "We need to show her that, no matter who she is or what she does, she is loved. That, at the end of the day, when the world does its best to destroy her, we have her back."

"I can't be asked to go against my personal values," he argued.

"She hasn't even officially come out!" I shouted at him, knowing the statement was weak the moment it left my lips.

"Come on, T. If it walks like a duck and talks like a duck…"

"Then it's a gay duck?' I shot at him sarcastically, but I couldn't resist. "We don't know *what* she is, and I doubt she does either."

"Fundamentally, I believe homosexuality is a sin. I cannot accept it. I cannot condone it in my household."

"Then you are participating in hate. God didn't make a mistake. He made her the way she is, and whoever that turns out to be is beautiful." I felt the gravity of the situation and began to plead. "She needs you to love her, and right now, she is testing us. She is floundering, trying to figure out who she is and how she fits into the world. Our only job is to love her, and I don't believe God would fault us for that."

"We have to guide her in the ways of the Lord," John argued. "The bible is clear."

"It is also the most misquoted and misconstrued book on the planet," I countered.

"It sounds like you are losing your faith," John judged me, and I was stunned.

"If keeping my faith requires me to find part of my child repugnant and unlovable, then maybe I am."

There were no more words on the way home. Where there was distance between us before, I now saw a clearly visible line. On one side was Wren, and on the other was John. I had been trying to straddle the line between them for far too long. I studied my husband as he drove us home, his shoulders tight and his stance unyielding. Though inches away, there was a deepening chasm between us. A bridge he couldn't bring himself to cross. For the first time in my marriage, I wondered if he ever would.

THIRTEEN

Internally, I was untethered and shaken. The events of the past few weeks were like a time bomb set off in our lives. Collateral damage was everywhere. Where once we were the Three Musketeers, we were now engaged in a triangular power struggle. I jockeyed between my husband and my daughter, feeling the pull and guilt when I was focused on one and disregarded the other.

Is she gay? What does that mean for her? For us?

She hadn't been in *any* romantic relationship *at all*, let alone a same-sex one. I'd been waiting and watching on the sidelines for evidence of her first crush. Part of me took pride in the fact her head wasn't turned by boys at sixteen. I hadn't been as level-headed, having had crushes on boys since I was in kindergarten and had my first pony-tail tugged on the playground. Wren didn't admit any of these feelings. She wasn't boy crazy or confiding in crushing on anyone.

I thought her lack of interest in dating gave me one less

thing to worry about. I didn't encourage her to date, so was that the reason we were here? If I had been more open-minded, would it have made a difference? It's amazing the questions your brain asks under assault and the way it struggles to assign blame.

Unable to concentrate, yet desperate to understand what was happening to my family, I opened Google and searched for confirmation. Typing ambivalent search questions like: When did you know you were gay? Why do girls wear boys' clothing? Clicking on articles titled: "Is your child a pre-homosexual?"

What does pre-homosexual even mean?

"What *not* to do when your child comes out."

"Parents who reject their gay children."

Wading through news stories of girls declaring themselves tom-boys with a willingness to battle boys on the playground rather than engage in playing with dolls. I filtered through my memories of her childhood, searching for clues. She didn't show an interest in dolls until the dollhouse was built, but that wasn't it. Was it? Wren wasn't outwardly masculine; she was probably just curious. A curious child who spent a fair amount of time in a make-believe world with friends of both sexes. There wasn't a single event to pinpoint or an ah-ha moment.

Did I miss it, the definitive moment in time where she crossed over? Was there anything I could have done to stop her from becoming...

Becoming what? The internal tug-of-war was wearing me down. I couldn't articulate what she was becoming. I didn't know, and I highly doubted Wren did either.

When did life become so convoluted?

Confusion swirled as I clicked through article after article, combing the dusty corners of the internet in search of information that would help me understand who my daughter was morphing into. Hours disappeared as I scrolled through blog posts and read articles. The assault of information did not bring clarity, just more turmoil.

"Is sexual orientation a nature or nurture event?"

"What to do when you suspect your child is gay."

"What is the official Catholic teaching on Homosexuality?"

Then I stumbled onto a Wikipedia page on the history of violence against the LGBTQ+ community. The words seared into my soul. I couldn't tear my eyes away.

Gabriel Fernandez. His mother and her boyfriend beat Gabriel, bit him, burned him with cigarettes, whipped him, shot him with a B.B. gun, starved him, fed him cat litter, and kept him gagged and bound in a cubby until he was found dead on May 22, 2013.

Eight years old. Tears made my vision blurry, swimming in the gory details of a life brutally taken. I clicked deeper and deeper. Reading more, sickened as a mother at the atrocities carried out on him. It made my heart sick.

A massacre at the Orlando gay nightclub *Pulse* left forty-nine dead and fifty-three wounded. It was the largest incident targeting the LGBTQ+ community in United States history.

Matthew Fenner. Twenty members of his church punched, beat, and knocked him down for two hours. Throttling him by the throat to shake him free from the homosexual demons that held him prisoner, all in the name of the Lord. I scrolled and scrolled through so much hatred cataloged in one place, line by devastating line.

Stabbed more than twenty times.

Set on fire while they were sleeping.

Broken jaw.

Stabbed and mutilated.

Raped and strangled.

Each brutal account destroyed me. I scrolled, sickened, and the page seemed endless as I scanned down it. If anything, incidents were *increasing* in frequency as each year passed. On and on, I scrolled down the page, finally coming to the end of it. With a sob, I buried my face in my hands, unable to take in any more atrocities, devastated by what I had learned. I was gasping for air to quell the surging panic. These victims were someone's *children*. The hate inventoried there was so intense, I had to look away. I did not want this for Wren. I didn't want this for *any* child. No human being should have to endure the brutalities cataloged here.

The door slammed. I wiped the tears on my face, quickly closed the Google windows that were open, and shut the screen to my laptop before forcing a smile on my face.

Wren ignored me and walked into the kitchen, searching for after-school snacks as usual. I trailed in behind her and impulsively pulled her into my arms for a hug. Her body tightened and then she relaxed. Closing my eyes, I breathed in the vanilla body wash I'd tucked into her stocking last Christmas. The scent grounded my hammering heart.

"You need to learn to let go, Theresa," Wren joked, pulling away from me.

I instantly burst into tears.

"What happened?" she asked, fear pooling in her eyes,

staring at me while I tried to regain my composure enough to get the words out.

I swiped away again at my cheeks and asked, "Can we talk for a minute?"

"Sure?" Her response came out like a question. Wary, she relented, and I crossed to the countertop and pulled out a stash of emergency cookies. Taking the time to pour us two glasses of milk, I was stalling to figure out an opening for a conversation I didn't want to have.

"You're scaring me," she admitted, sitting down at the kitchen table. Her backpack slid down her long legs to rest against the legs of the chair. Her eyes were wide.

"Things have been really difficult lately around here, and we haven't had a chance to talk."

"About what?" she asked innocently, and for a second, I considered dropping it completely. Shoving it under the rug and forgetting about it altogether.

Instead, I pressed forward. "Just the stuff with Sammie and the drastic change in your look. It feels like a cry for help. Is it?"

"I don't know," she answered quietly, her forehead scrunching up and eyes narrowing.

"I just read the most horrific page on Wikipedia," I continued. "A History of Violence against the LGBTQ+ community."

Wren swallowed and the blood drained from her face. I looked down at my hands shaking in my lap. "I'm scared for you," I started. "I feel like I don't know you anymore, and you are heading toward this reality that could hurt you, and I want to protect you from it."

"Maybe you can't," she tried to explain.

I clung to the one shred of hope I had. Denial. "Are you sure?"

"Of what?" Wren asked. "That I am attracted to women?"

"Are you? I mean, yes… but, no." I stammered and stumbled over the words, her bold revelation making me unravel.

"I don't know, Mom. I'm sixteen. I'm just trying to get through today."

"That lifestyle goes against everything we believe in as a family. All the values we hold dear. I don't know how to reconcile a reality like that in my heart."

"Whoa." She held up her hand, indicating I should stop. "You don't get to put that on me." Anger flashed across her beautiful features. She crossed her arms, closing off to me, and leaned back in her chair. "And using the words *that lifestyle* makes it sound like a choice. Being gay is not a choice, Mom. It's just another natural characteristic that makes up a person, like having blue eyes."

I wanted to understand, but the concept seemed so foreign. How could it not be a choice? Wasn't attraction a choice? Instead of compromising, I decided to hit her with a dose of tough love, thinking maybe I could shock her straight.

"We are the adults. Your father and I decided long before you were born how we were going to raise our children and what part our faith would play in the process. To see you outright reject it is a brutal truth that I don't know we can accept."

"Don't you think I know that?" she answered. "Do you hear yourself?" Her shoulders were stiff and approaching her ears. "I didn't realize your love had conditions."

"That's not what I meant." I back peddled, knowing I was on thin ice and needed to diffuse the situation that was quickly spiraling out of my control. "I don't know," I mumbled. "Why do you have to do this? Why do you have to make your life so hard?"

"It's harder not living authentically. Not feeling comfortable in my own skin."

"When did this happen?" I asked, scrambling to understand. "How long have you felt this way?"

"A while."

The confession hurt. I realized how much of my identity was wrapped up in thinking I had a daughter who could come to me for anything. She didn't feel that way anymore, and it stung. I gulped and tried to bring my thoughts back to center.

"It's not a sudden change, Mom. I've had these feelings since I was little. In kindergarten, I had my first crush on a little girl with curly blonde pigtails."

"You have?" My voice cracked, and I cleared my throat and took a sip of milk. It just felt thick and suffocating. I searched through those faded early childhood memories deep in my mind. "Madeline?" In shock, the name surfaced.

She laughed stunned, that I was able to pull the name out of thin air. "I'm surprised you remembered. Yes, Madeline. I just remember the yearning. She was so beautiful and I wanted to touch her hair. I got caught hugging her in the coat room, and Ms. Keeling told me to keep my hands to myself. I had to miss a recess."

I remembered the incident, too. At the time, I didn't even think twice about it. Wren was a loving child; she just needed to learn physical boundaries like any normal five-year-old. Was that the first inkling? Were there other hints I missed along the way?

I was starting to understand Wren's heart was an iceberg. I got to see the part that stuck out above the water line, the part she wanted me to see. But below the surface, there were countless chambers I didn't even comprehend. How could I be so clueless? All this time, I thought I was plugged in. How could I have missed something so huge? How could I have not seen the fundamental truth about my own child? The realization was deeply unsettling. It was like waking up one day and realizing that everything you knew was a lie.

"How do you know?" I asked, pushing for a reason. An event to pin this development on.

"You wouldn't understand."

"Try me."

Her eyes met mine, her gaze stony at first but began to soften. She sighed. "Don't you think, if there was a way to force myself to be straight, I would have done it? No kid wants to be different. Do you have any idea how many times I've cried myself to sleep, begging God to change my heart?"

"You did?" I was astonished.

She nodded.

"Why did you hide this?"

"I was hoping I was wrong. I was hoping it was just an infatuation that would go away. I tried to talk myself out of it so many times. I knew Daddy would never be able to accept it."

"Are you 100% sure? It seems more fashionable to be gay in this day and age, like it's the new thing. It was a slippery slope after Brittany Spears kissed Madonna at the Super Bowl a few years back."

Wren's eyes rolled. "Oh my God. You'll never understand. You will never get it. The God that you have spent your whole life worshipping and spouting about having a personal relationship with created me this way."

I shook my head, unable to accept what she was telling me.

"Who are you then?"

"I'm trying to figure that out."

"You're so far away, I feel like I don't know who you are anymore."

Wren laughed a bitter, little laugh. "That makes two of us."

The confusion held me hostage. "So, I guess this is the questioning part of it then, huh?"

She thought about it for a minute and nodded slowly while nibbling on a cookie. My stomach was in knots. "I have homework," she finally said, breaking the silence that engulfed us both.

"Okay." I stood and picked up her empty glass and busied myself with starting dinner. My thoughts circled and taunted me. I had clung to the hope her recent behavior was just a stunt for attention. After our talk, I had the distinct inkling I was wrong. Shamefully, I wanted to hide the truth, to ignore it, and bury it deep, but Wren had a different agenda. She wanted to shine a bright light on it and forge into the unknown to discover who she was. Fearlessly, she demanded that we see her as a whole person, autonomous of us. The woman she would become, not the child we struggled to raise with faith and values in our Catholic home.

It was getting harder to ignore the truth, to put a pretty bow on it and pretend all was peachy keen. It was impossible to write it off, to reason she was going through a phase and would eventually come around. Wren wouldn't allow it.

FOURTEEN

I walked into the basement of the hospital where a group of men and women were gathered in small clusters. My stomach fluttered in nervous response. I stood frozen in the doorway, unable to enter the room, hesitant and filled with anxiety. I'd driven to the other side of town to avoid running into anyone I knew.

"Admit it. You want to turn around and never come back." The voice startled me; it was deep for a woman.

"Is it that obvious?" I asked, turning toward the voice, trying to keep things light. Afraid if I started to cry I would self-destruct.

"Come on in. We don't bite." She walked toward me, and I saw her for the first time. Tall and elegant, she was dressed in a simple green dress and boots. Her hair was a thick shock of silver that cascaded down her shoulders. She extended her hand and I shook it. "I'm Sarah."

"Theresa," I answered.

She cupped her cheek with her hand and whispered,

"Between you and me, the coffee is terrible and weak, but luckily, the folks in here are wonderful and strong."

I nodded, crossing my arms protectively around my stomach, feeling exposed.

"Hey, guys," she said to the clusters of people standing near the coffee pot and a tray of cookies. "This is Theresa; she's new. Let's make her feel extra welcome."

Faces turned toward me with smiles, and a few gave me a wave. Sarah walked to the circle of chairs and sat down. "Let's have a seat and get started." I walked toward the chairs and grabbed the one closest to Sarah, taking a moment to unzip my coat and shrug it off onto the back of the chair.

"Welcome to Fearless Parenting, a support group for parents of at-risk LBGTQ+ youth."

Hearing the words *at-risk*, I cringed. It was an identity I didn't want to claim. One I had fought tooth and nail against my entire life.

"I'll kick off the sharing today." She stood. "I'm struggling to accept my child's self-hatred. I was called to a parent meeting at Rhyne's school. His teacher…" She stopped abruptly and then began again, "*Their* teacher," she emphasized. "God, I swear I'll never get it right."

"Their?" I asked, confused.

"Pronouns," Sarah answered without skipping a beat. "Rhyne's preferred pronouns are they/them."

I nodded and then clamped my lips down to avoid any other questions from slipping out.

"Their teacher and principal spread out the body of work Rhyne has been creating for their AP art class, and it was troubling."

I tipped my head closer, listening intently.

"I have to say, when I first saw the pieces, I was struck by their complexity and stunningly horrific dark beauty. All were self-portraits, and each struck a nerve in me." Her hands became more animated the longer she talked. "With burned edges and claw marks. Scars and darkness. I mean, on one hand, I want the administration to acknowledge the level of artistry and skill of the pieces. They were exceptional. But on the other hand, I could see why they were worried and understood why they insisted on the meeting. He… I mean, *they* have a real gift. Their art moves you and brings up a range of emotions you cannot ignore. The kid thrives in darkness, and I can't seem to get them to turn to the light." She smiled and then continued. "As the school meeting went on, I sat there wondering why Rhyne was being singled out."

I shifted on my chair, wondering if I would have the same reaction.

"Next, Rhyne was brought in to defend the work, and they were understandably angry and frustrated. No one doubted the skill, but it was the message. This artwork makes the school uncomfortable. It's too tormented and dark for a sixteen-year-old."

Sarah looked down for a moment, and I felt the distinct pang of mother's guilt overwhelm her. She recovered and continued. "They passionately voiced their opinion on how art is a healthy form of self-expression that should never be censored, no matter how hard it is for administration to accept." She smiled. "They are too damn smart for their own damn good." She shook her head, laughing. "Rhyne can be extremely articulate and convincing when they are passionate about something. Honestly, I don't think I was ever more proud of them. After an hour of back and forth, Rhyne promised to work on telling more of a story of hope and transformation. We'll see how that is portrayed in their new pieces. Rhyne can be hard-headed and stubborn like his momma." She was quiet for a long moment. "I wish raising a queer kid came with an instruction manual." There were murmurs of agreement from the group. Then she sat down and turned to me with a smile.

"Theresa, do you want to tell us who you are here to support?"

I cleared my throat and stood, folding my shaking hands together and began, "My daughter, Wren, is sixteen. Things kind of took a turn in the last few weeks, and I just feel lost. I don't know who she is anymore."

"Who can relate to that?" Sarah asked, and the whole circle nodded in agreement.

"She's acting out, shaved her head bald. My husband is an ultra-conservative retired Army man, and they are butting heads daily. It's a constant power struggle between them, and I feel like the referee. It's exhausting. He's talking about conversion counseling. Like he can force her to be normal against her will."

"Did she come out?" Sarah asked.

"I don't know how to answer that. I mean, technically, she was kind of forced out, if that makes any sense." My cheeks pinked up in embarrassment. "After a disastrous sleepover, a lot of disturbing behavior came to light." It was hard to say more than that. I felt like I was telling her secrets, and the shame crept in.

"Did she make it official?'

"Not really," I replied. "She admitted having her first crush on a girl in kindergarten."

A few heads nodded in agreement.

"I guess I am struggling with the morality of it," I answered. "I was raised Catholic, and it was drilled into our heads that homosexuality is a sin. I am having a hard time reconciling my faith with the love of my child in my heart."

"Our children are not an extension of us," Sarah answered. "As much as we want to believe they are, and as much as society lies to us and reinforces that belief." I crinkled my brow, trying to take in what she was saying. "They are here on their own mission, and their journey is *not* your journey. Part of the human experience is discovering who they are and what their purpose is, and we can't take that away from them, even if we try to cloak our actions in love. That is not what love is. Love allows."

It went against everything I thought I knew about motherhood, but there was a thread of truth buried in her words I couldn't deny.

"The truth is you cannot change who they are, and by rejecting a part of them, we send the message that they aren't lovable. That a part of them is flawed and dirty and wrong. Teenagers especially can internalize this message. It leads a lot of LGBTQ+ youth to dark places. Suicide, self-harm, drugs and other addictions."

"How can I accept something that is so wrong in the eyes of God?"

"Only you can answer that," Sarah said softly. "Personally, I believe God doesn't make mistakes. He created Wren exactly as she should be. There is nothing to be ashamed of."

That was a difficult one to swallow. I was being asked

to accept something I'd been taught since I was a child was a sin, punishable by eternal damnation.

"My God is a God of love," Sarah went on. "He is the ultimate father who loves his children no matter what. I'm sure you're familiar with The New Law? In the new testament, the ten commandments were distilled down to two basic laws. Love the Lord your God with all your heart and love your neighbor as yourself."

I chewed on that statement.

"There is no room for hate in love," Sarah added. "They can't co-exist in the same space."

I turned the phrase over and over in my mind. Absent-mindedly, I tugged at the St. Christopher medal around my neck, deep in thought and considering her words.

"Thank you for sharing," Sarah said, and I took my seat as another couple that looked vaguely familiar got to their feet.

"We are Mary and Craig, and our son, Tristan, was the victim of a hate crime. He passed away over a year ago." Mary's voice cracked and tears welled in my own eyes. In shock, I remembered the headlines from the newspaper about the event. It lit off a powder keg in our community, dividing the conservatives from the liberals, and after a short investigation, two men were arrested and charged with hate crimes and one count of first-degree murder and kidnapping. He'd been found naked in subzero tempera-tures, badly beaten, and they had carved the words God Hates Fags into his chest. It was all Wren talked about for weeks. There it was, another sign I missed. How did I miss so many?

I was riveted. This was my biggest fear, the terrible reality Mary and Craig endured.

"It's every parent's worst nightmare," Craig continued. "To see your child desecrated like that. Spit on, his face was so badly beaten we needed dental records to confirm his identity."

I closed my eyes. It was too much. I physically felt their pain. The agony of their loss cued up a fear response in my own.

"We're here because we're consumed by hate and anger, and we don't know how to deal with it," Craig answered.

"That's understandable," Sarah answered. "The sense of loss you feel comes with a whole host of emotions."

I opened my eyes, and Craig's glance landed on me. The lines around his weary eyes drew me in.

"Theresa, I know you don't know me from Adam, but I want you to hear this."

I sat up in the chair and listened intently.

"I wasn't the most accepting when he came out," Craig revealed. "I wish I had handled it differently. We wasted so much time locked into this battle of right and wrong. I wish I could have that time back. I wish I could have a do-over. This time, I would pull him into my arms and tell him I loved him, no matter who he chose to love. This time, I would push away my own selfish wants for his life and accept him fully. I would listen to every word he wanted to say, and I would reserve my judgment. I would have loved him. That's all he wanted. That's all any child wants, to know without a doubt their father loves them." He broke down, and Mary reached out to steady him.

"He knew you loved him, honey." She turned to the group. "They reconciled a few months before he died."

"I want that time back," Craig whimpered. "They took

away our boy, and now I want them to pay. An eye for an eye. I have fantasies about someone stabbing them with a shiv in prison. I have dreams where I watch them bleed out in the shower, watching them take their last breath and not doing a goddamn thing to help them."

In shock, I swallowed. His pain was palpable, like a twin in the room, taking up space, following him everywhere. Preceding every sentence he would say, carved into the lines on his face and the weariness in his eyes. This was a father pushed to the edge.

"You can't live in death, Craig. Tristan wouldn't have wanted that for you." Sarah finally broke the silence. "When you participate in this dynamic, it holds you prisoner. You have to break free. You can't let the last moments of his life define the rest of yours."

"I hear your words, Sarah, but I can't figure out how to do that," he admitted. His head hung in his hands. His shoulders slumped. "I don't know how to smile when he's not around to see it. Or how to enjoy a warm summer breeze when he's not here to feel it on his face."

"We went to a psychic," Mary admitted, and I leaned closer. If something happened to my child, I would probably be compelled to do the exact same thing. To find a way to communicate with her, even if it was all a farce.

"She knew things," Craig answered. "She mentioned the stone I carry in my pocket that has his name carved on it, and she told me that Tristan is around me always and that it is okay to move on and live my life. But I don't want to do that. I don't want to do anything without him."

"I bet that visit brought you peace," Sarah said. "But now, it is time to forgive yourself."

"I don't know how to do that." His voice cracked, on the verge tears.

"Sit in the quiet, and it will come to you. Recall the happiest moments you had being Tristan's dad. The moments when you were so full of pride you felt like you'd burst. Focus on those slivers of time, and you will feel a shift. You will find a way. Love always finds a way."

FIFTEEN

I tossed and turned all night long and got up before the alarm went off for church. It was my turn to be the worship leader, and I had to leave earlier than my family. Half an hour later, John and Wren were walking down the center aisle to claim their usual seat in the second pew. I watched as Wren slid in next to her father, yawning and distracted, irritated to have her dream of sleeping in on a Sunday crushed by the hand of God. She sat in the pew, sullen and bored. I pushed my desire to study her away, smoothed my hands down the front of my skirt, and adjusted the microphone in front of me.

"If you would please stand and join me for our opening hymn, on page two-hundred and-forty-nine, Praise God From Whom All Blessings Flow."

The organist began pecking at the keys high in the balcony on the massive pipe organ that filled the cavernous church.

At my perch, a small stage was tucked into the front corner where brown industrial carpet was frayed at the edges and a trip hazard on some of the stairs. Since the congregation was only getting older, it had been duct-taped down, which only contributed to the overarching theme of neglect.

It was always a challenge to get butts in the seats at church. The priest we'd been assigned was nearing seventy and a stodgy judgmental figure with a penchant for delivering sermons too frequently about the joy of tithing. Instead of breathing life into God and connecting him in a real way with the younger generation, he stuck to the classics. In his estimation, God was a punisher, and any moral infraction would send a person on the fast track directly to hell. Forgiveness was often absent from his lengthy sermons, bellowed out at the pulpit to echo in the practically empty church.

"Praise God from whom all blessings flow…" I sang out clear and strong as peace washed over me. Singing was one of my gifts. I was proud of the voice I'd been given, and leading the congregation was a task I enjoyed. It was a place where I felt capable and worthy. From the back of the church, Father McDonnell began his procession down the center aisle followed by the altar boys. When he got to the front, he bowed in front of the altar and then walked to his chair, an ornately carved throne, and waited until the song was over.

During the first part of mass, I was on autopilot. The first reading was read by Stan, his voice steady and strong. Then I led the congregation for the responsorial psalm, holding up my hand to indicate when the churchgoers should join in. The congregation sat down as Father McDonnell stepped forward to read the second reading. He adjusted the microphone, and his deep, booming voice rang out into the silence. "A reading from Romans Chapter 1 verses eighteen through thirty-two."

In the congregation, there was a flutter of paper-thin pages as bibles opened obediently to the correct place. "For the wrath of God is revealed from heaven against all ungodliness and wickedness of men who by their wickedness suppress the truth."

"Therefore, God gave them up in the lusts of their hearts to impurity, to the dishonoring of their bodies among themselves, because they exchanged the truth about God for a lie and worshiped and served the creature rather than the Creator, who is blessed forever! Amen."

"For this reason, God gave them up to dishonorable passions. Their women exchanged natural relations for unnatural, and the men likewise gave up natural relations with women and were consumed with passion for one another, men committing shameless acts with men and receiving in their own persons the due penalty for their error."

Out of the corner of my eye, I saw Wren straighten in the pew next to John. Typically tuned out during mass, I was shocked to see her lean forward and press her lips together in a frown. Her brow knit together as she avidly listened to the priest's disparaging words. Next to her, John's head nodded gently in agreement, and I saw Wren look at him with disgust and subtly slide a few inches away from him in the pew. I felt a flush of warm shame crawling up my chest.

Father McDonnell droned on in his deep, baritone voice, "And since they did not see fit to acknowledge God, God gave them up to a base mind and improper conduct. They were filled with all manner of wickedness, evil, covetousness, and malice. Full of envy, murder, strife, deceit, malignity, they are gossips, slanderers, haters of God, insolent, haughty, boastful, inventors of evil, disobedient to parents, foolish, faithless, heartless, ruthless."

During the reading of this laundry list, for emphasis, Father McDonnell pounded his fist after each one, punctuating every word.

"Though they know God's decree that those who do such things deserve to die, they not only do them but approve those who practice them."

"This is the word of the Lord."

"Praise to you, Lord Jesus Christ," I repeated and sat down for the homily with the rest of the congregation, the pews creaking in protest. After a long moment of silence, the priest began.

"This is an important message of guilt. God is commenting on the fall of mankind and the destruction of morality." He leaned forward, gripping the podium. "Doesn't it feel like a prophecy? Today, we glorify homosexuality, a deplorable act that is clearly defined as a sin in the word of God. The very definition of an abomination."

Tension knotted in my gut as I listened, riveted to Wren's reaction sitting in the pew.

"Make no mistake, Godly love is a sacrament between a man and woman. It doesn't matter whether modern society accepts homosexuality, glorifies it even, in books, television, and movies. It's a plague, a stain on our souls. We've gotten so far away from God, I have to believe that when he comes back to earth and has seen what we've done with the laws he gave us on judgment day, there will be a reckoning. We will be forced to stand before our God and explain why we have allowed men to lay with men and women to fornicate with women. Not only allowed it, but actively championed it. We've become a wicked society desperate for titillation at any cost. Following each other down into the rabbit holes of hell and pornography, deeper into a sin that I am not sure we can recover from."

Wren jumped to her feet, her hands balled at her hips, and glared at him. The priest paused and stared down at her from the podium. Her shoulders rankled, and she refused to budge. Then the whispering began, and far away, a baby began to wail. My face flushed hot and red, and I pulled the bulletin from my purse and began to fan my face with it. I was breaking out in a sweat at my hairline and down my backbone. I wanted to run to her, to pull her into my arms and hide her from the watchful eyes of the congregation. I wanted to yank her back down into the pew. Anything to cover up reality and this horrifying scene that was playing out publicly. I couldn't breathe.

Please, honey, sit down. Just stop.

In the pew next to her, John's face was stony and turning red with rage. A crimson pilgrimage clawed up his neck and across one of his cheekbones.

Wren promptly turned on one heel and walked ten feet away to the new pew Sammie's family had claimed since the disastrous sleepover. She held out her hand to Sammie, and my breath hitched in my chest. This was a public gesture that could never be explained away. There would never be a rational reason as to why my daughter reached to hold the hand of her girlfriend that didn't induce hushed, judgmental conversations. Sammie started to rise, but her shoulder was roughly shoved back down by Mike's hand. Sammie's eyes beseeched Wren's, tapping out a woeful apology in morse code. Jennifer spoke out of the side of her mouth, and Sammie rushed to cover her eyes with her hands.

Alone, my beautiful, fearless daughter turned again and strode down the center aisle of the church. A murmur swept through the congregation as they watched her depart. Heads swung back, mouths agape, and eyes widened in shock. I wanted the ground to open up and swallow me whole. Red slashes cut across my cheeks, and I tried to control my breathing. My heart hammered as their judgmental eyes swung to me. Seeing the disgust in them, their scrutiny made me feel dirty. From the podium, Father McDonnell started in again, undeterred.

"Homosexuality is a disease. A curable disease. The devil uses the weakness of youth to pull our children to him. With a maturing spirit, anyone can be cured of this affliction."

The rest of the sermon was a blur. We drove home in silence. I waited for John's rage to erupt and for Wren's fury to be unleashed. I was walking on eggshells with them both now, and I hated it.

SIXTEEN

S unday dinner was a silent, futile exercise. John sat at one end of the table, violently stabbing into roasted potatoes with his fork and grunting while passing the plates. Wren stuffed bites into her mouth, chewing twice and swallowing hard, eager to be released from the obligation. I sat at the other end of the table wondering how we had gotten here, so far from each other. Physically sharing the same space, but knowing our hearts couldn't be further apart.

All I ever wanted to be was a mother. When I was little, my most often played game was house, where I would stuff pillows under my shirt to create a bulging belly and then carry around my cabbage patch dolls that smelled like stale baby powder. It was my identity, and I wrapped my life around it, snuggled the desire deep in my heart while reading parenting magazines well before I was pregnant. With this growing divide in my family, I struggled to find answers. What would become of us if we couldn't navigate this challenge? Would we be three people, tolerating each other until our obligations to each other were over? Would my role as a mother be destroyed? These questions circled and circled my brain, consuming my thoughts as I picked at the food on my plate.

Families are tenuous things, often held together by a thin thread of commitment and flimsy promises. I didn't want my family to be labeled broken, and yet it felt like it was. Fundamentally, unequivocally broken.

After lunch, John rinsed his plate and stacked it in the dishwasher, then went out into the frigid garage where his tinkering projects awaited him. Currently, there was a broken space heater that he was sure he could rewire and restore to working order. I'm sure he wished he could apply that same step-by-step logic to our daughter.

After washing the dishes, listening to music to fill the void, I pulled on my jacket and walked out to the garage, where John sat at the bench with his reading glasses on. Pieces of a computer were strung out on his workbench. In the corner, the air compressor rumbled to life as he blew the dust out of the machine. The hammering sound was loud and then abruptly stopped. I waited for an opening as he tinkered with the pieces in front of him.

"That was quite a stunt she pulled today," John began. His voice was filled with authority, honed by barking out orders to soldiers for almost two decades.

"Yeah," I agreed. I didn't know what else to say.

"We need to do something, Theresa. We're losing her." That was when I saw the fear in his eyes. He *did* believe he was on a quest to save her soul.

"She's growing up," I offered. "Learning how to use her voice and stand up for what she believes in. Where do you think she learned how to do that?" I smiled, trying to diffuse the tension with a sincere compliment.

He blew hot air through his lips with a sigh. "That's just it, our daughter's beliefs are in stark contrast to our own. She can choose to live her life the way she wants when she's an adult and living in her own home."

"Will you approve of her choices then?" I asked and surprised myself with the directness of the question.

"No," John admitted, "but when she is out of the house, I can't control anything she does. If she wants to live in sin, that is her choice. God gave us all free will." He muttered as he palmed his weary face. "God help us." He sighed.

"I don't know if He can." I mumbled softly.

"Are *you* okay with her lifestyle choices?" he asked, his voice raising an octave at the end in shock.

"I don't know," I answered truthfully. "All I know is that she is our daughter. She is struggling to discover who she is, and we have to support her."

"No matter who that turns out to be?"

"Honestly, I think the right answer to that is yes," I said. "But I didn't say it would be easy."

"I don't know if I can do that." His honest declaration detonated a bomb in my heart.

SEVENTEEN

W e tiptoed around each other into the middle of the next week. I felt absolutely torn in two and afraid to interact with either of them. The house was a powder keg, and I worked to diffuse the tension.

"Let's get out of here, take Wren for some ice cream," I offered, trying to convince John. "Come on, a chocolate malt might just do the trick."

"And what trick is that, dear?" he asked directly again. "Is a chocolate malt going to magically make everything all better?"

"No, but it's a start," I offered. "We need to spend some time together as a family." He finally gave in, and I picked up my phone to get Wren on board.

"Daddy wants to take us for some ice cream," I fibbed, sending a tentative text, and was relieved to see the incoming text bubble. Then it disappeared. After a few minutes, I realized I wasn't going to get a response, so I walked to her closed bedroom door and knocked on it with the back of my hand.

"What?" a sharp voice I barely recognized as my daughter's asked from behind the door.

"Get your shoes on. We're going for ice cream."

The door opened and she glanced at me quickly, then retreated into the darkness of her room.

"What's that?" I asked when I noticed a pile of clothing almost four feet high in the corner of the room.

"Stuff we can donate to Saint Vinnie's."

I began to go through it, recognizing every dress and skirt I'd purchased. Every ruffled blouse and pink sweater. In defeat, I plunked the items back on top of the pile and sat on the chair at her desk.

"Trying a new look?" I asked, trying to maintain neutral.

"I don't feel comfortable in them. It doesn't feel like me."

"What do you mean? They are just sweaters and skirts."

"It's more than clothing, Mom. It's telling the world who I am." She stood with her legs apart. Defiant and challenging me. Exhausted from the battles, I changed the subject.

"Daddy's waiting. Let's go."

She begrudgingly put on her shoes and followed me downstairs, then got into the car without a word. We ran through the drive-thru, and twenty more silent minutes later, Wren and I were each holding enormous cones in our hands, and John got his malt. I was happy to have something to do. The sugar hit my bloodstream and Wren's at the same time. She leaned forward between the seats.

"There's something I wanted to talk to you both about." She licked a fat drip from her cone, and I silently prayed for small talk. Every conversation seemed too heavy lately. Every exchange was a battle in a war John was fighting, determined to win. We waited for her to speak.

"I've decided I want you to use they/them pronouns when you address me from now on." Proud of herself, she leaned back in the seat and began to nibble on the edge of the cone.

"Absolutely not," John spat out. "You're becoming one of them, buying into the brainwashing. This country is going to hell in a hand basket. It makes me sick that I sacrificed years of my life to defend Theybies."

"Wow." Wren was stunned. "When did you become so hateful and ignorant? I used to think you were the smartest person in the universe."

I thought about the group where Sarah made a real attempt to use her child's preferred pronouns, even when her son wasn't there to hear her. Was it really too much to ask? I couldn't figure out where I landed on the topic.

"How come total strangers can respect me enough to use my preferred pronouns, but my own father can't?"

"Respect is earned." John clamped down on the steering wheel as he drove us toward the house.

Wren sat in silence in the backseat, her building rage heating the back of my head. I tried to bridge the gap. "Isn't they reserved for more than one person? It feels weird to use it to refer to a singular subject." My words sounded hollow and desperate to fill the air. "I've been taught my whole life that they or them refers to a group of people." I stopped chattering, shifting in my seat to make eye contact with Wren.

"That's an invalid argument," Wren answered my question. "What do you say when you go to pick someone up at the airport?"

"I'm going to pick them up." I fell for it, then corrected, "Or I am going to go pick her up."

She rolled her eyes again. Educating us on her new pronouns was proving to be exhausting to her paper-thin teenage patience.

"Seems like there should be another word, so it's not so confusing. Does it really matter?"

"Yes, it matters," she said.

"I wish there was a totally different word."

"There is. You can use ze, zir, zem," she offered.

John laughed. "You have got to be kidding me," he shot back. "The theybies coined new pronouns to define themselves? That's ridiculous."

"And did you know there are over sixty recognized genders?"

"Recognized by who?" John demanded.

"By the world."

"Not in my world," he answered as he sucked hard again, and the straw made a screeching noise in protest.

"You're not even trying to understand," Wren accused.

"This is just a cry for attention. A cry for help," John explained. "Look at me. I am different." His voice twisted up in a high-pitched, mocking tone. "There is no way I am going to participate in this foolishness. It's selfish and over-indulgent."

Understanding that her father was immovable, Wren stopped talking. She stopped trying to connect and trying to explain. I looked down at the drops of melted ice cream on my leggings, then rolled down the window and threw the cone out for the birds. I couldn't stomach the sweetness any longer.

This wasn't a good idea. It wasn't a good idea at all.

EIGHTEEN

The house was quiet the next week, and I was glad to have a moment to myself. Pulling my hair back into a bun, I rolled up my sleeves and began to tackle the dishes from breakfast. I heard the *thunk* of the mail box shutting and opened the front door. The first burst of warmer spring air was welcome, and I breathed it in, letting it calm my nerves. The sun warmed my shoulders as I absentmindedly fished for the mail in my mailbox.

Back in the kitchen, I rifled through the contents. Junk mail circulars that never stopped coming due to placing one order at L.L. Bean eons ago. I set it aside for later as I still liked to flip through the catalog filled with old lady clothes according to Wren. Next, there were two bills, which I tucked behind my pinky and would deposit on John's desk in the study. The last item was a plain white envelope with blocky handwriting I didn't recognize that leaned hard to the right. I wiggled my index finger into the corner of the envelope to tear it open and yanked up.

A sharp cut made me yelp in pain and stick my finger

into my mouth. I pulled out a letter and shook it open. It was handwritten in the same block print as the envelope.

To Whom it May Concern:

Your daughter is going to burn in the eternal fires of hell. God hates fags.

It was filled with scripture verses and hateful rhetoric. The words swam together, and I couldn't bring myself to read it all.

I gasped, and the letter dropped to the ground, scissoring down and then sliding underneath the stove where it was completely hidden. For a moment, I considered leaving it there. If it remained invisible, I could pretend it never existed, but then I got down on my hands and knees and fished it out with a chopstick left over from our Chinese takeout last week.

I read it fully this time, on the floor leaning against the stove for support. The words still held their power, making adrenaline course through me. Seemingly carved into the pristine white of the paper, the author pressed so hard, fueled by hate, you could feel the impression on the back side.

Who does this? Who takes valuable time, effort, and energy out of their schedule to pen this kind of venom against a child? A coward, that is who. A troll living in hate sitting under his bridge on a judgmental mountain. I crumpled the letter into a ball and shoved it deep into my pocket, deciding to hide it from John. It would only add fuel to the fire that was burning between us.

I felt dirty and exposed, and the letter rattled me. I tried to brush it off and concentrated on making a chicken pot pie. It was a family favorite, and rolling out the flaky piecrust gave me time to think. It calmed the chaos in my brain. I sprinkled the flour onto the granite with a flick of my wrist, and then with the wooden pin, rolled it thin and draped it into the pie plate, crinkling the edges and covering them with tin foil so they wouldn't burn in the oven.

The phone rang; it was Marcy.

"Hello," I said calmly into the phone cradled between my head and shoulder as I wiped my wet hands on a dishtowel. "Are you looking for volunteers for the St. Auggie's Open House this weekend?" I tried to force cheerfulness into my voice and it fell flat.

"Actually, um…" Marcy started then stopped. After a short pause, she launched into, "This is difficult, and I truly hate to be the bearer of bad news, but Father McDonnell wanted me to reach out. He thinks it's a good idea if you take a break from being the worship leader so you can have more time to focus on what is going on at home." Her voice had a nasally, detached quality that I had never noticed before.

"What do you mean?" I asked, wanting to make this conversation as uncomfortable for her as it was for me. It was a means of payback that I couldn't explain, but that made me feel slightly vindicated.

"You have to admit something is going on with Wren," she said, then her voice dropped so low I could barely hear her next words. "And Jennifer filled us in on what happened at the sleepover with Sammie."

"Ah. Now I see." There was a sting of rejection again, another betrayal, proving my friendship with Jennifer had been destroyed. Another casualty of the war I was pulled into and had been forced to fight.

"We thought you might need some extra time to tend to Wren, and we didn't want you to feel obligated to volunteer. You're so giving of your time, and we know how hard it would be for you to step down."

"Who's we?" I prodded to a now silent Marcy.

"Well…" She paused and then stammered, "The… you know… your church family."

"Family?" I repeated, my voice gathering steam as the words began to flow out. "Family? That is laughable. If we're a family, it's the most dysfunctional family that ever existed." A bitter laugh bubbled up at her audacity. "It's not contagious, you know," I said, unable to stop myself from exposing what a judgmental shrew she was being. "Being gay, or questioning, or anything else. It's not like you can catch it from rubbing shoulders with me or my daughter."

"We have a duty to our congregation to hold our worship leaders to a moral standard," she went on. "We can't have a scandal like this. It makes it look like we condone your child's behavior. It's immoral." She paused. "I'm sorry."

"You should be," I spat out and then hung up the phone, my hands shaking. I'd saved her behind at least once a month for the last year, being flexible and filling in for her at the last minute for a myriad of church functions. We sat on many committees together. I knew all of her children by name. I thought we were friends. I was sick to learn just how fickle her friendship turned out to be. My world got even smaller, shrinking again. My family was being exiled, cut off from the life we'd constructed here, and that was when Eden Prairie stopped feeling like the Garden of Eden and more like the first ring of hell.

NINETEEN

It was easier walking into the building for the support group this time. I raised my hand to tentatively wave at Sarah as I walked into the room, recognizing a few of the people gathered there but not others. Sarah walked toward me with a bright smile.

"So, we didn't scare you away after all." She busied herself making a pot of coffee in the ancient percolator that sat in the center of a faded and worn card table. "I don't know why I go through the motions with this beast; no one drinks it anyway."

"You've just described my entire life in one sentence," I mused with a wry laugh.

Sarah reached over and squeezed my arm. "How are things?"

Things. It seemed like a loaded word. I considered it, mulling it over in my mind.

"Not great," I admitted with a small, sad smile. "My daughter walked out of a sermon on homosexuality, and I was asked to forfeit my cantor position at the church." It was the first time I'd said the words out loud, and they stung, my cheeks reddening in shame. I still hadn't been able to bring myself to tell John.

Sarah thoughtfully nodded. "Isn't it interesting how staunch churchgoers can be the most judgmental people of all? Do they think there isn't enough of God's love to go around or something?"

"Feels like it," I admitted. "I had a pretty small circle to begin with, but now that my family is a pariah at church, it's so lonely." I poured a glass of ice water into a Styrofoam cup. "Four years of relationships burned to the ground. It's hard to not be bitter about it."

"Then it's a good thing you're here," she said with a warm smile.

"Faith has always been important to me. It was the cornerstone of my life. The one thing I could count on. But if I'm honest, I find myself losing faith, and it feels like another loss. This whole revelation has been steeped in destruction. A collection of tiny deaths strung together, a fresh one surfacing nearly every day." I felt the burden shift on my chest slightly as Sarah listened.

"I understand why you would say that," Sarah agreed. "You have to grieve the life you dreamed about for your child. The expectations you had for them, the desires you had for their future. You trade dreams for judgment and shame, and if that isn't a bitter pill for anyone to swallow, then I don't know what is."

"It feels like a death, the dreams I had for her. I'd always hoped she'd eventually get married and raise a family."

"What makes you think she won't do any of those

things?" Sarah asked innocently, and I was stunned speechless for a moment. "Have you asked her?"

"No," I admitted. "I just assumed with this new development it would never happen."

"Oh, dearie." She grinned at me and wrapped a warm arm around me, pulling me in. "You're going to have to learn to stop the assumptions. That's the one constant. Sure, she might not get married in the Catholic church, but there are many other denominations that allow same-sex marriage if that is the path Wren chooses to go down."

I was stunned again. I had identified as Catholic for so long, it didn't even seem like an option for me to consider another religion. It felt like a betrayal.

"God is God, no matter what path you take to get access to him," Sarah said. "People forget that with all the man-made laws and rules we've shrouded religion in. The only thing that matters is your heart and your desire to be in connection with Him. He is everywhere, not only choosing to grace organized religion with his presence. They don't have a monopoly on God. He's here." She pointed to her heart. "He's in your home and in your heart."

Tears welled in my eyes, and I had to look away. The comfort her words ushered to me cracked my heart wide open.

"We need to start, but if you ever need a sounding board, call me." She dug into her purse and produced a business card that she placed in my hand. It felt like a lifeline.

"Thank you," I whispered. "You're so kind."

I took my seat in the circle as Sarah spoke up, "Let's get started. Who would like to share tonight?"

Mary waved her hand in the air and stood as Craig found his feet with a hesitant smile. I was stunned; the heaviness I noticed in the prior meeting was gone.

"We thought about what you said last time. 'Love always finds a way' and the missus and I made a decision." He turned to gaze at his wife for support and gave her a nod. Intrigued by the change in his demeanor, I leaned forward in anticipation.

A huge smile dawned on her face, transforming her grief into joy. "We're taking the money from Tristan's college fund and going to be awarding scholarships for LGBTQ+ youth who are going into social work and psychology programs." Her eyes radiated fresh purpose and newfound warmth that was missing during their last sharing session.

"That's incredible," Sarah offered. "What an amazing gift of hope you have found in such a hopeless situation!"

"It was supposed to help Tristan on his own journey to make his mark on the world," Craig began. "I'm hoping it can give us some purpose to all this pain."

"I know it won't bring your son back," I heard myself say. Normally, in groups, I hung back and lurked, afraid to share anything that would paint me in an unfavorable light or call attention to a failing of my family. "But that is such a generous act of love that will truly make a difference. It will take the hateful reality that you were forced to live and turn it into something beautiful and meaningful."

Mary smiled and reached out to squeeze Craig's hand. "See, sweetheart? You were right." She turned back toward the group. "I'm a little ashamed to admit, I didn't see this idea the same way Craig did initially. I took some convincing."

Craig hiked a thumb toward this wife with a knowing smile. "She's the stubborn one. Everyone thinks it's me, but this one can dig in like an Alabama tick."

Mary rolled her eyes at his reference. "It felt so final. It felt like if we liquidated the account, it was officially closing the most important chapter of our lives and leaving Tristan behind. We scrimped and saved for years in order to build a nest egg for him, and to know without a doubt he would never be able to use it…it crushed me. I was content to live in denial and wasn't ready to make a decision that momentous."

"We put our first dollar in the account when he was six months old. Our boy was going to take the world by storm," Craig chimed in. "I didn't want him to be forced to work in a factory for thirty years of his life like I did. Don't get me wrong, I don't regret it, but I didn't have a choice. We wanted our son to have a better future." His voice cracked. "They robbed him of his future the night he died, and ever since, I have been filled with rage. I'm furious with God, with Buddha, with whoever the hell you all pray to. How could a merciful God let this happen to our sweet boy?" Mary leaned closer to him and wiped at the tears in her eyes. "Since he died, I've been consumed with rage and hate. It's eaten away at me from the inside. After we started coming here, I started to wonder if the rage would last forever. If we would ever be happy again. He was our only child, and all our hopes and dreams were pinned on him and felt like they died with him, too."

I felt a twinge of pain. Wren was our only child. I leaned forward and felt tears spring to my own eyes. I'd never considered it before; if something would happen to

Wren, technically, I could no longer call myself a mother. The concept flushed me hot with panic.

"Tristan wouldn't want us to live like that. He was the most loving boy and had a huge group of friends who have still kept in contact with us even after all this time. Tristan was pure love. So, I guess what I am saying is—love wins. Even after all the destruction his killers unleashed on our lives, that will not be his legacy. His legacy will be love."

Two more women stood to speak, and I was lost in my own thoughts.

"Does anyone else want to share today?"

I got to my feet. "I never knew what hate truly was until earlier this week. An anonymous letter was delivered to our house filled with spiteful words and highlighted bible passages." I clasped my hands together, trying not to relive the moment. "I have always leaned on my faith in moments of pain, but seeing God's word blasphemed and weaponized like that was shocking. I feel a little lost and undone."

I stopped for a moment, trying to pull more thoughts together. "And the same day, I got a call from the volunteer liaison at St. Auggie's and was asked to take a break from my cantor position so I can better attend to my problems at home."

A quiet murmur filled the silence. "I'm starting to doubt everything I held dear. If they can wrap this kind of hatred and bigotry around the actions of a child, I don't know if I can continue to believe. It has shaken me to my core. I'm losing faith, and it's leaving me feeling exposed and rattled."

"It's a tough one," Sarah agreed, "when people hide under the guise of religion to spew their hate. This path gives you a chance to evaluate everything in your life in a much deeper way. You get to look at your profoundly entrenched beliefs and values and question them, much like your daughter is questioning her sexuality and identity right now. Youth is full of questions and blissful self-expression. It's only when we get older that we learn to hide our hearts, the sacred parts of ourselves that long for authentic connection."

"Why do they feel so threatened? Why can't people just live and let live?"

"Because they don't understand, they are afraid of it, and what people fear, they hate," Sarah offered in explanation. "And when they are so consumed with pointing out your shortcomings and failings, then they do not have time to assess their own lives. To see their own weaknesses."

I nodded and mumbled a thanks and sat down as Sarah stood up. "I want to share something with you that has been on my mind for a long time. I believe sexuality is not black and white, but a spectrum." She spread her hands as wide as she could. "On one end, there is total heterosexuality, and on the other is complete homosexuality, but in-between are most of us just trying to figure out where we land. It's hard enough for us adults to understand ourselves at this level. Can you imagine how much harder it is for our kids, who are bursting with hormones, stressed with school, and spending too much time on social media looking for acceptance and attention?" She paused, and I took her words to heart.

"The world is very different from the one we all grew up in. All you can do is love them, provide a safe space for your children to figure out who they are, and give them the freedom to choose. Unfortunately, that is really difficult for most parents to understand. We think we know better and can see around corners, and we want to prevent them from making mistakes. We think we can, that we are that powerful. Truthfully, any child is a singular soul first, sent here to gain understanding. If you look at it from this perspective, then the only worry you need to concern your-self with is if you are helping or hindering their progress. Thanks for coming. We'll see you next time."

"Mom?" One tearful word, three letters. Wren's voice cracked at the end of the phone line, making a prickle of fear walk up my spine and my breath quicken. Wren was supposed to be working on a group project at Austin's house. It was forty percent of her final grade and required a day-long marathon on Saturday to complete. John was in Atlanta for an IT conference, and his flight didn't get in until after midnight. I was supposed to have spent the time cleaning out the refrigerator, but instead, I escaped into a book—a good one that had me ordering takeout instead of cooking and enjoying a lazy Saturday. I had just run a hot bath, swirled in some Epsom salts, and added two quick dashes of lavender oil when the call came.

I sat still on the warming porcelain of the tub, looking down longingly at the bath I now knew I wasn't going to be able to indulge in.

On the other end of the line, Wren's voice trembled in fear and my heart ached, drawing me back in.

"Honey? Where are you? What's going on?"

"Don't be mad," she started to explain, and dread filled my belly with lead.

I squeezed my eyes tight and tried to calm the ten thousand terrifying scenarios being enacted in my brain.

"We're downtown. Can you come get us?"

"What?" In shock, I lost my ability to understand. "But you were supposed to be at Austin's."

"We finished early," she replied.

"Who's we?" I questioned, my fingers dipping into the hot water.

"Me and..." She hesitated, and my heart dropped. "Sammie."

"Oh, Wren…" Her revelation stunned me. I had no idea they were still in communication. Wren never uttered Sammie's name in my presence anymore, so I'd assumed they'd drifted apart. I'd thought Jennifer and Mike's efforts to isolate their daughter destroyed any chance they ever had at a real relationship.

"I know," she interrupted. "We screwed up. And I am ready to accept my punishment, but we really need you to come *now*."

"Of course." I hung up the phone in a panic and raced around trying to find my shoes. Shoving them on, I hopped out to the car in an effort to start the drive as fast as possible. Quickly, I backed out of the driveway, the tires screeching as I stomped on the gas pedal and followed the directions to the location pin Wren dropped. The deeper I drove into the city, the more anxious I became. Dirty sidewalks were littered with trash. Bail bondsmen, vape shops, and check cashing stores with bars on the windows began to pop up on every block. I pulled to a stop at the curb, seeing two thin figures huddled together in the dim light, not recognizing it was Wren and Sammie until they began to sprint to the car.

"Let's get out of here," Wren said after she slammed the door and jumped into the front seat and Sammie was settled in the back.

My eyes darted around the area, and I pressed the lock button on the door. Hearing the metallic *thunk* as the doors secured only made the tension worse.

I whipped the car into oncoming traffic, hearing a few irritated horn blasts and running two yellow lights, eager to get to the other side of town.

"What were you doing out here?' I asked.

"We heard about a drag show and wanted to go."

"A drag show?" I questioned, my voice taking on a shrill quality. "But you're sixteen. It's a bar. How'd you get in? How did you even get downtown in the first place?"

"We took a bus," she answered. "When it was over, we started to walk back to the bus stop, but two men dropped in behind us and were following too closely. I was holding Sammie's hand."

A wounded cry came from Sammie in the backseat.

"They got closer and started to make threats, trying to intimidate us. Said they wanted to 'teach these two dykes a lesson. We can turn them,' one of the guys sneered. 'All they need is to see a real cock.' They cornered us in one of the alleys and shoved us up against the walls." She kept turning to glance back at Sammie, her face pinched and tight. "They spit on us." Wren finally uttered, "Pigs."

Stunned, I turned toward Wren. Her head hung in shame, refusing to make eye contact.

"One of them held Sammie against the bricks," she admitted, her anger evident. "I got my phone out and slid the button to send an emergency SOS, and when the alarm sounded, they took off."

"That was quick thinking, but Wren, they could have…" My voice trailed off. I couldn't bring myself to finish the sentence.

"I can still smell the cigarettes on his breath," Sammie wailed from the back. "I can't get it out of my head."

"Sweetheart, we need to report this. It's assault. We have to go to the police."

"No!" Sammie's voice was panicked. "Just, please, take me home. I want to go home." She began to rock back and forth as I snuck glimpses of her in the rearview mirror.

Jennifer and Mike were going to be livid. Showing up on their doorstep with their distraught daughter, whom they expressly forbid from seeing mine, would only fan the flames of their rage. I was not looking forward to the face-to-face meeting.

"I will take you home, but first, I think we need to calm down and catch our breath for a minute."

I drove them to our house. Wren climbed back into the back seat and reached for Sammie's hand. Sammie leaned her head on Wren's shoulder as Wren made soft shushing noises and stroked her hand. Eventually, the sobbing stopped and Sammie relaxed. I even saw Wren crack a joke and illicit a little laugh from her. I couldn't tear my eyes off the rearview mirror. Witnessing my daughter be so sweet and affectionate with someone she cared about was a side of Wren I'd never experienced. I was fascinated, observing for the first time the bond they shared without judgment. The truth startled me. How was this act any different than the hundreds of times John comforted me? Why was it considered sick? Why did I swallow the indoctrination I'd been spoon-fed at church for decades? This was love, pure and simple, at its very basic level. How could it be wrong?

A wave of confusion engulfed me. I struggled to the surface for air and sputtered for the truth. At the house, I pulled the car into the garage and shut off the engine.

"Let's take a beat. Get something to eat and calm down, and then I can take you home," I offered. Wren jerked her chin, physically taken aback by my words. Her shoulders sank, and I could tell she'd been bracing for a different reaction.

"We'll deal with your consequences later," I informed her, and she nodded in understanding.

In the kitchen, I pulled out cookie dough I always keep frozen in balls, so I could make fresh baked cookies at a moment's notice. There was something about a warm cookie that was endlessly comforting, and even though I was angry, I wanted to bring them comfort.

Sammie sat on the sofa in the living room with Wren. With a spatula, I slid the cookies off the tray and onto a platter. Bringing them to the table with three glasses of ice-cold milk, I had to stop myself from calling out, "Gir... I mean, the cookies are ready." Wren walked to the table and pulled out a chair for Sammie and then transferred a couple of cookies off the tray and placed a small white plate in front of Sammie before serving herself. They were quiet and withdrawn, and we took the first few bites in silence. I noticed Sammie's hand shaking.

"Can we talk about what happened?" I asked.

Wren's shoulders shrugged, and I took it as a yes and

continued. "Whether you like it or not, we are living in a world full of hatred. I can see you care about each other, that much is obvious"

"I love her, Mom," Wren interjected, and my heart plunged, unprepared for her outburst.

"I love you, too," Sammie whispered, reaching out to grasp Wren's hand. Wren's face said it all. A huge smile I hadn't seen since God knows when broke out across her features. Her cheeks pinked up, and she brought Sammie's hand to her lips and kissed it. I found myself wondering if this exact scenario was playing out in front of me, would I have reacted differently if Sammie was a boy? The question was heavy on my heart as I considered it.

I would still hate that she lied to me, I would still ground her for breaking the rules, but would they have even needed to break the rules in the first place? That was the ugly truth I got hung up on.

I sighed with a smile. "Unfortunately, the world we live in is not always going to react favorably to your love. You don't have the luxury of holding hands in public or kissing each other. You need to always be aware of your surroundings, to be able to read the room. Public displays of affection can be dangerous for you both, as you learned tonight."

"But it's not fair," Wren complained.

"You're right," I agreed. "It's not fair, but that's just the way it is. This is the world we live in." I looked down at my empty glass of milk and nervously began to accordion fold my napkin, grateful John was out of town. This conversation would have gone very differently if he had been present. "You must always be aware of people around you. Be vigilant. You never know who is filled with hate and who can be triggered by one innocent act."

"By holding my girlfriend's hand?" Wren asked.

I nodded. "Yes. An act as simple as that can end in tragedy. There's a couple in my support group who lost their son. Did you guys hear about the Tristan Meyer case?"

"You're going to a support group?" Wren asked, stuck on the first few words, her forehead crinkled in confusion. "Why do you need to go to a support group?"

"I'm grieving the life I wanted for you," I said truthfully. "I'm doing my best to reconcile all the feelings I have, and I'm getting there, sweetheart."

"I hate that we live in a world where you have to do that in the first place," Wren muttered. "The alternative is to live a lie for the rest of my life, completely ignore who I am to keep you and Daddy happy."

"I would never ask you to do that," I told her quietly. "I want you to be free to express who you are, and I want you to love with all your heart." I stopped for a minute. "But you have to give me a chance to accept this shift in you. You have to give me time to put to bed all the dreams I had for you that will never come true."

"Like what?" she asked.

"The silly, traditional things like getting married, having grandchildren."

"What makes you think I don't want those things?" Wren asked.

Flabbergasted, I was silent and she continued.

"I don't know what I want or where my life will lead me, Mom, but someday, I *can* see myself getting married, and someday, I can even see myself having children. The only difference is I may choose to have them with a woman. I know that is probably not what you wanted to hear. I know it's not the life you wanted me to live. I get that, Mom, I do. But I can't be something I'm not just for you."

I burst into tears and pulled the paper towel to cover my face. I was ashamed. I blew my nose and reached my hand out to a confused Wren.

"I have to be true to myself."

"Wren, I love you. It's the only thing I know right now."

"Okay," she finally relented.

I looked over at Sammie. "Now we have to talk about getting you home."

Sammie stiffened. "My mom and dad aren't going to be as accepting as you are, Mrs. Churchill."

"They love you," I offered.

Sammie's eyes widened, and she shrugged off the possibility. "They love *their* version of me," she uttered. "The good little Catholic girl they raised, not this one I've become."

"Give them time. They'll come around." I tried to console her, but I had my doubts too. I was afraid to voice them. "It's time to face the music." I stood.

The drive over was uncomfortable and silent. I hadn't seen Jennifer since the sleepover disaster, and I was on edge. I pulled into the drive as Sammie and Wren clung to each other in the backseat. Giving them a few minutes to say goodbye, I stared straight ahead.

"Girls! The door just opened, and she's coming out," I warned, and they sprung apart as if electrified.

I rolled down the window and tried to smile, but the look of disgust on Jennifer's face made my hope fizzle.

"What are you doing here?" she demanded, her expression pinched.

I didn't know what to say so I stayed silent.

"Get out of the car," she spit at Sammie as she yanked open the door, Sammie slid out and Jennifer grabbed her arm. "Look at me, young lady."

Sammie's eyes darted to me then over to her mother, almost black and filled with fear. "Now, you listen to me. I forbid you to see these people ever again. Do we understand each other?" Sammie flinched as Jennifer tightened her grip. "Do we?"

"Yes, ma'am," she finally choked out, and Jennifer released her arm as she ran inside the house in a fresh burst of tears. My heart hammered as I watched their interaction. I was afraid for Sammie. Jennifer turned to me, shaking with rage, her cheeks slashed with red.

"You are not to have any contact with my child, Theresa. You pull a stunt like this again, and I will file a report with the police."

"For what?" Wren spoke up in the back seat, and I shot her a look in the rearview mirror that silenced her.

"Neither of you are allowed to have any contact with my daughter," Jennifer repeated.

"I understand," I said sadly. "But there is something you should know..."

Jennifer cut me off, "No more contact, or I will call the police."

I nodded, then rolled up the window and pulled out while she marched back inside and Wren fumed in the back seat.

"She can't do that!"

"She can do anything she wants," I said. "Sammie is her child, and there is nothing we can do about it."

"Homophobic bitch," Wren muttered under her breath as I drove us back home and pretended I didn't hear. We'd survived another emotional rollercoaster, and I just wanted to go home, lock the door behind me, get into bed, and forget any of this happened.

Wren stomped into the house and up to her room. There was a slam and then all was quiet.

TWENTY-ONE

T he next morning, it was work to pull my exhausted body out of bed. Sleep was elusive, and I tossed and turned next to my snoring husband, unable to find a place to settle. I'd pretended to be asleep when I heard him come in after midnight, grateful that he was out as soon as his head hit the pillow. I stared at the ceiling while thoughts circled in my brain, finally falling into a fitful sleep after three. Groggy, but hearing the stirrings of my family in the kitchen below, I finally sat up in bed and planted my feet on the floor. I glanced over at the clock that read seven a.m. and cursed the four hours of rest I'd gotten, knowing it would not be enough.

"What in the hell are you wearing?" I heard my husband's deep voice rumbling through the studs and drywall below. Panicked, my heart began to quicken. I threw on my robe and a pair of slippers and descended the staircase to see them engaged in yet another battle.

Wren stood across from him, wearing a crop top that exposed her midriff and was covered in a graphic rainbow with the words "born this way" scrawled across it. Rising above the men's skinny jeans was a thick waistband from boxers that sat just below her navel.

"You're a *girl*, Wren. Why can't you just be a girl? You look like a freak."

"I can't be your little girl anymore, Daddy, just to make you happy."

"The hell you can't!" he shouted.

She dug in, standing on her tiptoes, refusing to back down. "I'm gay, Dad. You have to accept it."

His eyes bugged and a vein in his throat surfaced and surged. He crossed the room in three steps and grabbed her arm just above her elbow, yanking hard. "Take it off. Now!" he directed, and I raced toward him.

"John, stop." Feeling torn in two, I struggled to get in between them. Wren stood her ground, refusing to back down from her father.

He continued to pull at the offensive shirt as I yanked at his elbow that refused to budge. "As long as you live in my house, you will obey my rules. I will not allow you to wear anything that goes against my values."

"No!" Wren shouted. "I will not pretend to be someone I am not. Not anymore." She stood her ground, and without thinking, he lunged forward and yanked the shirt up, ripping at it. I heard the fabric tear, then caught a glimpse of peach-colored hair peeking out of her armpits.

When had it gotten that long?

My brain flashed to a happier time. When she was thirteen, I'd gotten her a package of pink razors I tucked into a drawer in her bathroom, and to her complete dismay and humiliation, also gave her a leg shaving instructional lesson we barely survived.

Back in front of me, they jostled and struggled, and I heard her yelp and another tear as he continued to yank at the shirt.

Wren's eyes bugged in shock as she struggled in vain to escape his grip. "It's mine! I bought this shirt with my birthday money!"

"John, don't! You're hurting her," I begged as I pulled on his arm, but he shook me off. Obsessed with tearing the blasphemous shirt off her, he was singularly focused, and warning bells were screaming in my brain. One more tear and it was balled up in his hand, and she stood there exposed in her sports bra as nausea bloomed in my belly.

Finally freeing the repulsive fabric from his daughter, he crossed the room to where a basket of clean laundry sat in a chair from the day before. He plucked a t-shirt from the pile and flung it at her. "Put it on. We're going outside to the burn barrel."

The burn barrel.

In a daze, I followed behind them, tears coursing down my cheeks. The only thing I was certain of was that undeniable emotional damage was being inflicted right now, and every detail of this encounter would be seared into our psyches forever. Powerless to stop it, I begged.

"John, no! Stop!" Ignoring me, he strode to the burn barrel and flung the shirt on top, dousing it with lighter fluid while Wren and I watched in horror. Striking up a match, a whiff of sulfur from the matchstick wafted toward me, and a second later, I felt the *whoosh* of warm air hit my cheeks as the flames burst forth. Staring at the barrel, I watched the flames eating their way across the shirt, licking at the rainbow decal that was distorting and snaking further into the wall of orange fire. It was like gazing into the pit of hell. "This is where you're headed, young lady. You'll burn in hell if you continue down the path you are on."

Sobbing, her thin body shook. I tentatively took a step toward her, and her eyes flashed at me in rage. Her lips set in a hard line. She shook her head and stepped away from my grasp.

"John…" In shock, all I could seem to do was repeat his name. This was not how we acted. This was not how we treated each other. I stared into the flames, pulled back into the past, remembering a camping trip almost a decade ago.

A six-year-old Wren sat next to John on a rock near the fire pit at our campsite. They'd spent the last fifteen minutes scouring the woods for the perfect marshmallow roasting sticks while I cleaned up the picnic table and the remnants of the hotdogs and potatoes we'd roasted on the fire. My heart was swollen with joy, watching him walk her into the forest while instilling survival knowledge into her little brain that was starved for her father's attention.

Twenty minutes later, they emerged with smiles and wielding three long, green sticks. He pulled out his pocket knife and explained, "When you hold a knife, it needs to point away from your body. Like this."

He scraped off three sections of the stick, carving it into a fine point. Then testing it, he pulled her chubby hand toward it and pressed her thumb delicately against the point. "See? You can use this to catch fish or grill a hotdog."

"What about marshmallows?" she'd asked with a leading grin.

"Marshmallows, too," he answered with a smirk as he

grabbed the bag I pulled out of the camper to hand to him. He speared two marshmallows on the stick. "The key to a golden-brown marshmallow is to turn it evenly over the fire." Resting the stick on the outside fire ring, he rolled it in between his fingers as it began to turn golden brown. "If you get it too close, it will burst into flames. You have to be patient."

Next to him, dressed in a little sundress and pigtails, Wren nodded solemnly.

"See this?" He pulled the stick out of the fire, pleased with the toasted color he had achieved. He pulled it off and offered it to Wren. She popped the whole marshmallow into her mouth, her cheeks full as a little string of it coated her chin.

"Your turn," he instructed. "Fire can be dangerous, Wren. Come here." He patted his leg and she walked over to where he was, happy to be sheltered in the warmth of her father's flannel-covered arms. He relinquished the stick, and she held it with both hands while he speared two pristine white marshmallows onto it. He held the end of the stick and helped her turn it in two complete circles. "Ready to go solo?" She nodded enthusiastically and took over. The first turn was successful, but the second one was too vigorous and connected with an ashy log before erupting in flames. Wren burst into tears—inconsolable.

Just like tonight. Only five feet away from me, but it felt like a mile. I yearned for John to pull her into his arms like he had the night she'd burned the marshmallow, but he didn't. He sat stiff as stone watching the shirt burn. When it was completely dissolved into gray ashes that drifted up like reverse snowflakes in the sky, he turned on his heel and left us there.

"Honey…" I began, wanting to start damage control but unable to find any words to say.

Her eyes squinted in betrayal. "No." Wren said the word so calmly it was unnerving. "You don't get to do that. I am so sick of you making excuses for him." She broke my gaze and stomped back toward the house, leaving me alone near the fire that made me feel anything but warm.

I stared into it as fresh tears began their descent down my cheeks, and for the first time, I understood the only real fear I had in life was coming to fruition. My family was the one constant in my life I held dear, cherished and protected. But what if I couldn't protect them from each other? What if the biggest threat to my family was the internal destruction of it? What if the chasm that was growing between my child and my husband only grew bigger and eventually destroyed us all?

Defeated, I went to the kitchen to make some tea. I was chilled to the bone as I searched through the cabinets for the chamomile. The door slammed again, and I jumped. "Get out of my house!" John heaved a heavy basket of her clothing onto the dining room table, dumping them out as Wren reached out to collect her jeans and boxers.

"Mom!" Wren was panicked, black eyeliner running down her cheeks from the trail of her tears.

"John, what are you doing?" I asked softly.

"Did my money buy these?" He thrust a pair of Wren's boxer shorts into my face. His face was red and his eyes bloodshot. He was becoming someone I barely recognized. Basic instinct kicked in, and I took steps toward Wren, desperate to protect her.

"No," I answered. Wren was shaking, and I pulled her

into my arms. Sobbing, she clung to me as he stuffed the pairs of offensive men's underwear into a trash bag then yanked it out of the bin and strode to the door.

"What are you doing?" Wren's voice hit a fevered pitch as she pulled away from me. "Mom?" She followed behind him and pulled at his arms, but he shrugged her off effortlessly on a mission back to the burn barrel. I trailed behind them as panic surged in my belly.

"John, please," I begged. "You need to stop."

It only made him walk faster.

"Those are mine. I bought them with my own money."

He dumped them on the red coals, and they burst into flames instantly. Bright orange reflected in his eyes as he watched them burn, his jaw set into stone.

"If you want to act like this, get out. Get out of my house. You disgust me. As far as I 'm concerned, I don't have a daughter anymore."

Wren gasped and ran back into the house sobbing. Stunned, I held my ground. "That's enough!" I found my voice. "We're leaving."

"Where will you go, sweetheart?" he asked, the word sweetheart infused with so much sarcasm it made me flinch.

"I don't know, but we can't stay here." I scrambled. "You are alienating yourself from your only child. Do you know how much those words will scar her? She... I mean, *they* will never be able to un-hear them. They will be imprinted on *their* soul. Forever."

"They?" He mocked my decision to use Wren's preferred pronouns. "You've always been over-indulgent when it comes to Wren." He exhaled a hot breath. "She doesn't need a parent who waffles back and forth. She needs one strong enough to hold the line when morality comes into question."

"Maybe you're right," I lamented. "I don't know where I land on homosexuality, and obviously, I *am* conflicted. Any parent would be. It's not the life I wanted for Wren, but it is her journey. And if the choices in front of me are love or hate, I am always going to choose to love my child."

"At the end of my life, when I stand in front of God on judgment day, I want to be able to tell him that I did my best trying to raise my daughter," he argued.

"If that's true, then you need to rethink your actions because, from where I stand, it doesn't look like you are."

I turned on my heel and walked back to the house, pausing at our bedroom to pull two suitcases from the top shelf of the closet. John didn't follow me; we'd already used up all the words between us. I was emotionally exhausted. Spent. He went out to the garage to find solace in his projects. With one empty suitcase in hand, I walked to Wren's door and knocked on it with my knuckles. Inside, I heard sniffling.

"Yeah?" she answered weakly.

"Can I come in?" I asked with a sigh.

The door opened to her darkened bedroom. "Pack a bag. We're going to stay at a hotel for a while. Be thorough. I don't want to have to come back here. Your father needs some time alone to think."

She nodded and swiped at her cheeks with her hands.

"Come here," I whispered as I pulled her into my arms. "I'm sorry he acted that way. What your father has done is abusive, and we cannot tolerate that kind of treatment. Home is where you should always feel safe and loved."

She felt so thin and fragile in my arms. She shivered and let out a long breath.

"Sounds like you've been holding that in for a while," I said as I pulled back and cupped her face in my hands. "I love you. Do you know that? And there is nothing you could do that will change my mind. No matter what, you'll always have me. Now, get this suitcase packed, and let's get out of here. It's so toxic I can barely breathe."

A few minutes later, I shoved the suitcases into the gaping hole of the trunk in the garage where John was using a soldering iron to repair a wire on a circuit board. He ignored us, engrossed in his activity, and when I pulled out of the garage and backed into the street, the garage door began its descent without me even pushing the button on the remote. He closed himself off into the garage like he couldn't bear to see us for one minute longer.

TWENTY-TWO

I drove for an hour, consumed with fear, up and down streets while accompanied by the soundtrack of a wailing Wren. When she began to quiet, I settled on a location close to Wren's school and pulled into a Motel 6 close to the interstate.

"Wait here. I'll get us a room and then we can relax."

Wren nodded, her face pale and forlorn. I didn't have any more tears either. I felt hollow and empty. Drifting toward what, I didn't know.

I yanked open the door and headed toward the lobby, taking note of the crushed cigarette butts spread like confetti outside the entrance. I rubbed the St. Christopher's medal at my throat and was grateful when the lobby was immaculate. There were shabby carpets and cracked tiles, but hallelujah, at least it was clean. Behind the counter, a clerk smiled, her nose ring winking in the light. Her eyebrows were drawn on so garishly I almost couldn't take my eyes off them. Far from the thinned-out, sparse brows that were popular when I grew up in the nineties, these arches were dramatic and kept her face in a constant state of intrigue and wonder.

"How many nights?" she asked, breaking me out of my distracted trance that circled since we'd left. It was an inner dialogue of self-doubt and fear I wrestled to contain, and my shoulders were almost grazing the bottoms of my ear lobes. Noticing it for the first time, I forced myself to relax.

"Can we start with two and go night-to-night after that?"

"Of course, I'll just need a major credit card to get you registered."

I pulled my visa from its sheath in my purse and handed it to her, glancing around, noting the oak stand crammed full of brochures with local attractions that seemed to be a fixture in motels across the country. She swiped the card, and the expressive brows squeezed together. I crooked my head, wondering what made her eyebrows dance like that. Looking up at me with a nod, she swiped again, and once more before giving up, then offered me a sheepish smile.

"I'm sorry, but it's been declined. I have to keep it."

"Keep it?" I was stunned. "There has to be a mistake. I just used it at the gas station."

"I'm sorry, ma'am. It's throwing up a fraud alert." She lifted the machine and held it up for me to see. Across the cracked screen, the fraud warning was offensive and cold with blue robotic letters. "Do you have another one you'd like me to try?"

"Sure." I dug into my purse for the Discover card and handed it over. It was our emergency-only card. I sighed a hot, heavy breath as I drummed my fingers on the counter, the anxiety fueling a flood of energy my body was eager to dispel. She swiped again.

"I'm sorry, but this says declined, too."

Taken aback, I froze as she handed the card back to me. I looked at the traitorous card in disbelief, shoving it deep into my purse.

What in the world is happening?

"We can take cash." She offered, pity coating each syllable.

"But I don't have any." I never carried cash. I'd always put every purchase on my card to get the cashback points, then faithfully paid it off every month. It was how I paid for Wren's Christmas gifts every year. Frustrated, I dialed John, balling my hands into fists, preparing for battle. My forehead cooled against the glass of the door, out of earshot of the clerk, as embarrassment flushed up my cheeks.

"Yes?" He answered on the first ring like he had been waiting precisely for this call since we pulled out of the garage.

"Did you do something to my credit cards?"

"You mean, did I protect my interests when my wife deserted me and took our only child?" His words were venomous, and I felt the sting. Black and white. Everything was black and white with him.

"You can't cut me off," I blurted, devastated that I had to verbalize what I believed was blatantly obvious. "We've always had an agreement, you and I. My job was to keep the family unit running, and your job was to support us."

"Then I suggest you come home." His matter-of-fact tone jarred me. I never realized he was capable of acting so cold and detached, and a shiver rippled through me.

"You can't be serious," I murmured in hushed tones into the phone, my eyes darting to the counter where the clerk waited for her next guest, filing her talon-like fingernails. I took two more shameful steps away. "Come on, John, you have to admit how destructive your words were. It was spiraling out of control. I had to protect Wren."

"From her own father?"

"Unfortunately." I swallowed my pride and continued. "Don't you think we all need a break from each other? A little time out? Just a couple of nights. We have to calm down the situation, then we'll come home."

"That's out of the question."

My shoulders tensed and dread filled my belly. I'd never seen this side of John before, the ruthless cunning side that would strategically do anything to win. It worked for him in battle and in business, but I never thought in a million years he would apply the same cold, logical strategy to his family. I was shocked he didn't grasp the need to deescalate the situation.

"You're overreacting again, T. Just come home. We'll get Wren in some therapy and things will calm down."

"Your version of therapy is vastly different from mine. We need space from you right now, and I will not subject Wren to any more abuse." I shivered at the word; it was the one I knew would hit him the hardest.

"Abuse?" he repeated in a low growl. "I could say the same thing for the permissive and morally bankrupt ways you've been raising our daughter. I never agreed to that."

Getting nowhere fast, the anxiety transformed into rage. "I can't believe you would turn your wife and your daughter out onto the streets. I never thought you would stoop so low. It's making me want to rethink every aspect of our marriage. *I....*" my voice lingered on the single letter, strengthening and almost shouting the next six words into the phone, "WOULD HAVE NEVER AGREED TO THAT!" Then I punched the button to end the call, ignoring the vibrations from a string of explosive texts that came next from John. To keep my sanity, I put him on do not disturb, vowing to only check texts once a day.

I pressed my forehead against the cool glass of the windowpane as I sorted through my options. My hands trembled against the window with the feverish aftershocks of rage. My options were few. I banged my head against the wall, punishing myself for the reality I was living in. I had given up all my power. It never occurred to me that one day I would be sitting in a Motel 6 parking lot with my child being forced to consider sleeping in the car. I never saw this path as an option John would ever exercise. Seventeen years of trust crumbled into dust in front of my eyes. I was in freefall now without a net. My lips dry, I reached into my purse searching for a ChapStick, but instead, my hand grasped a thick card. *Sarah's card.*

I pulled it out and studied it for a full five minutes in the lobby. Subjecting only the hotel clerk to having to listen to me grovel and beg, I didn't want to add any further trauma to Wren's already overflowing plate.

Shaking, I dialed her number, and a wave of relief washed over me so powerfully when she picked up on the second ring, I burst into tears.

"Who is this?" she asked.

"Theresa… from group," I finally mumbled. "I need help."

"Why don't you take a breath first and then tell me

what you need?" she offered. I followed her directions, tugging at the St. Christopher medal at my neck, rubbing the surface of it with my thumb, begging for the right words to appear.

"Wren came out to her father, and then he yanked her clothing off her body, gathered up all of it, and dragged us out to the burn barrel."

"Oh my God, that is terrible," she commiserated. "Are you okay?"

A small, mirthless laugh escaped my lips. "We're about as far from okay as you can get. I'm at a Motel 6, and he cut off all my credit cards."

"Wow," she said.

"I never saw it coming." I felt the shame again that I was so clueless as to what he was capable of doing to win. "We can't go home. Not right now."

"That's obvious," Sarah agreed. "I don't have a ton of space, but we can manage. Come stay with me and Rhyne."

My voice trembled in relief. "Are you sure we wouldn't put you out?" I was backtracking in an attempt to smooth things over and talk her out of it, then I abruptly stopped myself. I didn't have any other options. Jennifer was out of the question, and I kept my circle small. This was my introverted personality's biggest shortcoming, and I didn't realize until now that it had the potential to destroy my life.

"Of course not. I'll text you my address. Come over as soon as you want." She paused. "And Theresa, you did the right thing for Wren."

"I know I did, but it feels so wrong."

"You'll see. Just give it some time. I'm proud of you

for getting her out of an abusive situation. You get in your car and you come over right now. You can stay as long as you need to."

A strangled cry escaped my lips. "Thank you." Her generosity overwhelmed me, and I was shocked at the ease with which she opened her home to us. A woman she'd met a couple of times and a daughter she'd only heard about.

The text notification jingled, and I tapped on her address and left the motel lobby, heading to the car.

"We're going to be staying with a friend instead," I said to Wren, who didn't move. She was strangely subdued, and I repeated myself, forcing my words to seem sunny.

"Okay," she said woodenly, and I was shocked. Normally, there would be a whole host of questions. She'd say something like, "I didn't think you *had* any friends." But today, she was deathly still and it concerned me. I drove the route as my phone guided us, still stuck on John's selfishness, ruminating in it. I hated I was so trusting and gullible, but this was an out-of-bounds knee-jerk reaction I would have never taken against him, and the betrayal was hard to stomach.

Twenty minutes later, I pulled up in front of a small clapboard house painted a vibrant purple with deep green shutters. Attached to the front post, a rainbow Pride flag danced in the breeze. It caught Wren's eye, too, and she remarked. "Whose house is this?"

"A new friend," I answered, ecstatic that she was speaking at all. Her silence on the way over was deep and suffocating.

Sarah opened her front door with a big smile and a

wave and navigated the steps. Behind her, a tall teenager with a mohawk and a full face of make-up pranced behind. I opened the doors and stepped out of the car and into Sarah's arms. She squeezed me so tight, the shattered pieces of my heart softened. She whispered into my ear, "You did the right thing. It's okay to relax; you're safe now."

She pulled away and faced Wren. "I'm Sarah, and this is my child, Rhyne. They prefer they/them pronouns," she informed us like she was telling us his hair color. Wren's surprised eyes shot over to Rhyne, and I felt her listlessness dissipate.

"Um, excuse me, your *favorite* child," Rhyne sang out, correcting her with a huge open smile that matched his mom's. Waving his arms around animatedly, limp wrists bobbed in tune with the Pride flag above his head. He was a tightly wound ball of infectious energy.

"You're the *only*, so I guess that's *technically* true." Sarah winked at Wren, pulling her in, who offered her the first authentic smile I'd seen grace her face in a long while. I felt my tension hiss in release.

"Well, when you hit perfection the first time out of the gate with *this Queen*," he waved a perfectly manicured black stiletto nail at himself, his head bobbing like a snake-charmed reptile, "you had no need to keep going." Rhyne's sculpted eyebrows waggled at me, and I couldn't resist laughing. The child was *charming*. His limbs were long and lean and had an androgynous look, with fingernails painted black and wrists ringed with colorful beaded bracelets. They spanned his delicate wrists and up his hairless forearms. He wore platform shoes that made him tower over all of us. Wren's eyes widened in awe, and she couldn't tear them away from him.

Sarah rolled her eyes. "See what I'm dealing with?" She turned to Wren, who was hugging her backpack to her chest, watching their interaction with interest. "You must be Wren?" She held out a hand. "What are your preferred pronouns, my dear?"

Wren was taken aback. I nudged her, and she stretched her hand out and shook Sarah's. "They/Them," she answered with a shy smile. "Thank you for asking."

"Rhyne, want to take Wren inside and get them settled?" Sarah asked. Rhyne took Wren's hand and led her up the stairs, babbling away about his favorite drag queen.

"That's quite a look," I said, watching him navigate the stairs with his seven-inch heels better than I ever could.

"It's an acquired taste," she offered. "I figure, in the grand scheme of things, what they wear has so little to do with the type of human I am trying to raise. Who cares if they express themselves the way they want? Rhyne's been screaming for the world's attention since they were a tiny baby. Now, they're just doing it with seven-inch heels and a fabulous eyebrow arch." She laughed and then continued, "I just want him… I mean, *them* to be good to people and feel comfortable to be who they are meant to be." She leaned in toward me again. "The pronouns, I really try, but I still struggle. Lucky for me, Rhyne gives me a lot of leeway. As long as I make the effort, it is good enough for them."

Standing there in her coat over a colorful printed dress, I marveled at all the color in her life. Vibrant and unadulterated, rich technicolor washed over her home, swept down her body, and adorned her child. This was a woman who was vital and alive, all her senses aligned, filled with strength and self-love. Not wallowing in shame and fear and hiding the truth of the authentic identity of her son. No, this was a woman who embraced it. I wondered if I would ever get to a place where I felt the same. In Sarah, I saw a reflection of the woman I wanted to be. Loving, accepting, authentic, and free.

"How did you reconcile all this? You're the most accepting person I've ever met."

"I wasn't always this way," she offered in explanation. "It was a process to let go of the son I thought I wanted them to be and accept the person their soul yearned to become."

Her easy admission of own her shortcomings put me at ease. "You are refreshing. Is that weird?" I tried to explain myself, "I've never met anyone so open-minded and kind."

"I've worked really hard to get that way." She smiled and continued, "And you can, too. That is what Wren needs more than anything. Open acceptance. Did you know that having one accepting adult decreases the risk of suicide by over forty percent for LGBTQ+ young people?"

"Really?" I *didn't* know that, but the revelation lodged deep into my brain and stuck there. Suddenly, it wasn't just a matter of letting Wren dress a certain way or indulge her interest in exploring her sexuality. It was a matter of life or death.

"Yes," she said and squeezed my arm. "That's all I needed to hear to persuade me. The rest of the world can look at my son and write them off and categorize them as a freak or an abomination. And trust me, they *will*. But when they walk through the doors at home, I want them to know, without a doubt, here, they are loved. Here, they are safe. Here, they are accepted."

I instantly teared up in the face of her absolute love.

"It didn't happen overnight, Theresa. I get the sense that you are beating yourself up right now. It's taken me a few years to reconcile this in my heart, too, and that is okay."

"I am afraid for her… them," I corrected, really trying for the first time to get the preferred pronoun right. The word still stuck on my tongue. For the first sixteen years, it was her, she, and my daughter, so to correct this was going to take work and focused attention, but now I saw the absolute reason it was necessary. "Life is hard enough when you fit into society's normal constraints, but when you go against what is socially acceptable, you open your-self up for battles. I wanted to protect Wren from that reality."

She nodded. "The truth is you can't."

"I am learning that the hard way." I laughed bitterly.

"Besides, who wants to conform to the boring require-ments of society? Who made those rules for all of us?" she asked with a smile. "Old, white men," she answered herself. "That's who."

Her answer made me laugh. Old, white men—like John.

"Wren is going to find their own way, and as much as you want to see around every corner and protect them from every threat, you have to accept that you can't. All you can do is love them and be their safe haven."

She took my keys from my hand and popped the trunk, pulling our suitcases out, then shut it before continuing. "You're still fighting to control the uncontrollable." She leaned back against the corner of the car. "It might be hard to swallow this next piece of advice I need to give you, but you need to look inside yourself and find the origin of the part of you that wants to control the actions of another human being. What is driving you to do that?"

At first, her comment stung and I was silent. I never saw myself as controlling. Trying to see myself from her point of view made me uncomfortable.

"You're not alone," Sarah said with a smile. "Any good mother is a bit of a control freak. We're wired to protect and lead our children at all costs. But if you think about it, the cost of control is ultimately weakening our children. We want them to succeed, and we have all this incredible life experience to draw from, and think we know better. But we need to step back and let these immature souls find their own path. We need to be cheerleaders instead of bus drivers. They need to drive their own bus."

"But what if where they are driving is dangerous? Then what?"

"The hardest thing you will be asked to do is watch your child drive into the ditch. But that is where all the learning and character development happens. That is where they learn the essential life skills of determination, self-awareness, and that their decisions always yield consequences." She assessed my current state. "It's been a long, emotional day for you. I can see you're exhausted, so let's go inside and have a glass of wine and relax."

I followed behind her like a little duckling, going over her words that rang of truth. Inside her home was filled with all the colors of the rainbow. An elaborate, abstract mural covered her dining room wall. I stood in front of it, entranced by its beauty. Mandalas in stunning combinations of yellow and blue, orange and purple were woven together with dots and swirling lines.

"It's beautiful," I complimented, astonished at how the brush strokes tugged at my heartstrings, the color washing over me and energizing my battered soul.

"I can't take credit for it. It's Rhyne's." She stood next to me, enjoying my reaction to something she was so used to seeing on a daily basis. After several long minutes, I glanced around the rest of the modest great room. A comfy sectional in grey microsuede was tucked into one corner. Fuzzy blankets in ochre and tangerine were folded into neat rectangles and placed on both ends. A collection of colorful throw pillows with paisley patterns were scattered across the back. Her kitchen cabinets were bright white with a colorful, modern backsplash of tiles. A ponytail palm tree and fiddle leaf fig flanked either side of a sliding door that flooded the space with light. Lime green pothos vined across the upper cabinets.

"I love all the color," I admitted. "It feels so good in here."

"You know, after I got divorced, I craved color. It became a metaphor for the life I wanted to live. Away from the grey and beige life I was stuck in, I yearned for a change. I embraced Rhyne's love of color, and this was our collaboration. It gave us a project to work on together to go from the sting of loss to a transformation of wholeness."

"Is Rhyne's dad in the picture?"

"Not anymore," Sarah said quietly. I wanted to ask more questions but didn't want to pry. If she wanted me to know, she would tell me. I took off my coat and shoes and yawned. I was depleted.

"I don't know how to thank you."

"Hush," she said. "I've been where you are, and someone reached out a hand to save me. Now, it's my turn to pay it forward."

"I hope I get the chance to do that someday, too," I said.

"You will. There's no shortage of parents needing support navigating this battlefield." She walked toward the kitchen, and I fell down onto the soft sofa, sinking into the cushions, grateful for a moment of solace given to us when we needed it most.

TWENTY-THREE

The next day, I went to the bank the second it opened and attempted to transfer four thousand dollars from our home equity line of credit to a new account at a different bank, ignoring the flurry of incoming calls and texts from John. We'd opened it for emergencies only, and in my book, this situation qualified.

Totally justified, the successful transfer sent a giddy tingle of power to my core and allowed me to breathe easier. Later that evening, I sent a text to John.

Me: I need to be able to take care of our daughter.

The incoming text bubble flashed, and I chewed on a fingernail, waiting for his response, wondering if his rage had cooled. Then it disappeared altogether, and even though I checked the screen constantly, no new messages came through. After twenty minutes, I put John on silent again. I tucked the phone back into my purse and spent the day trying not to look at it and trying not to think too far down the road we were on. Needing something to do to dispel the anxious energy, I found cleaning supplies under the sink and spent the next several hours scrubbing every surface, grateful to have something physical to focus on. Once the entire house gleamed, and I could see my reflection in the windows, I made a quick dart over to the grocery store, deciding to make some cookies for the kids and grab ingredients for dinner. I wanted to be useful, and the simple tasks were a welcome distraction from the thoughts stuck in my head.

In the late afternoon, the oven timer dinged and I pulled the cookies out, letting them cool on top of the stove. Ten minutes later, the door burst open as Rhyne strode in with Wren on his heels, rocking a dramatic smokey eye with glittery shadow. He was clad in skin-tight, red skinny jeans, six-inch heels that he wore better than most women, and a vintage concert t-shirt. Over that was a jacket he'd embellished with sequins. The back was painted with an elaborate tree design. I couldn't tear my eyes away from him. Rhyne oozed complete confidence; it was magnetizing.

"Mom." Wren's tone was a warning when she caught me staring too long at him, and it snapped me instantly back into reality.

"Sorry," I said to Rhyne with an embarrassed smile.

"Girl, I want you to stare!" Rhyne sang out, "You don't put in the work to look this fabulous without wanting an audience!" And then for my benefit, he sashayed down the hallway like it was a catwalk. At the end, he swung around and blew me a kiss over his shoulder before striding back to the kitchen. I laughed, unable to pull my gaze away. He *was* fabulous, like the word had been created for his benefit alone.

The front door opened again, and Sarah walked through it.

"Mama!" Rhyne sang out and teetered on his tiptoes over to Sarah for a hug.

"After school *cookies*?" she exclaimed with a smile. "Now you're just making me look bad."

"They're even warm. I just pulled them out of the oven," I said. "Oh, and we are having a pot roast for dinner."

"Dinner, too?" Sarah enthused. "You know you didn't have to do all that, but I'm so glad you did!"

"A mom that *cooks*!" Rhyne teased Sarah playfully, pushing on her shoulder while she laughed good-naturedly. "Can I get a refund? Because I think this one is broken."

The banter between them fascinated me. There was an ease and lightness to their interactions that had always been missing from ours.

"Hey!" Sarah pretended to act offended.

"Don't worry, darling, you have many, many other redeeming qualities." He wrapped an arm around her shoulders, pulling her in for a hug.

I glanced over at Wren, who seemed to be as fascinated with their interactions as I was. Her gaze shifted over to me, and I winked in an effort to connect that just confused her. When you aren't naturally a winker, it just becomes a bumbling exchange proving you are trying too hard.

I swallowed the awkwardness, poured glasses of milk, and dished up warm cookies on colorful plates I found in the cupboards. None of her plates matched, but somehow, the vivid colors pulled them all together. It was an eclectic bohemian style that felt effortless.

"After dinner, I'm reading everyone's tarot," Rhyne exclaimed. Wren's glance darted back to me. Tarot was considered borderline scandalous in our old home.

"Can't wait," I declared as the kids cleared out and went to Rhyne's room. "How was your day?' I asked Sarah.

"Pretty decent," she answered. "The city approved the parade route for Pride Fest. It's still almost a year away, but there's so much to do. You should come."

"I'll think about it," I mumbled, remembering the news from last year. This obnoxious Baptist church, known across the country for their hate, had staged a protest right outside the entrance, picketing with signs and shouting cliche slurs like, "God created Adam and Eve, Not Adam and Steve." Last year, a fight broke out on the last day, sending a stream of people to the hospital. There had been talk about canceling the event.

"Rhyne's already working on the fit."

"The fit?" I asked, confused.

"The out-*fit*," she explained with a grin.

"Oh." I laughed as I found a corkscrew and popped the cork on a bottle of cheap wine I splurged on as I picked up groceries after my successful trip to the bank.

"What are we celebrating?"

"My first act of independence? I set up my own bank account and funded it by drawing on our HELOC."

Her eyes widened and she leaned in, waggling her eyebrows. "You sneaky little minx," she exclaimed. "Look at you. That *is* something to celebrate." She hoisted her glass toward mine, and they chimed as they clinked together.

I took a sip. "It was definitely out of character for me. My hand was shaking as I filled out the paperwork." I confided. "I'm not sure where I stand financially or in my marriage, and I might have to get an apartment." I took another sip and confessed, "I haven't had a real job for fifteen years."

"Sure, you did." Sarah nodded. "You were the CEO of your family. Why do women do so much, yet take so little credit for their efforts?"

"That's a good question." I held up my hand. "Guilty as charged."

"Project management, you'd be good at that or maybe a home health aide?"

I nodded. "And you've been so generous, but I know we can't stay here forever."

"Hey, If you keep greeting me after a long day with a glass of wine, fresh-baked cookies, and a home-cooked dinner, we might be able to work something out." She smiled as she pulled off her heels and massaged her calves. She sniffed the air and glanced around at the sparkling room, "Wait… did you *clean*?"

My cheeks reddened in response, and the corners of my mouth took a downturn as I cringed. "I hope it wasn't overstepping," I apologized. "I needed something to keep me occupied."

That sent her howling into hysterics. After a full minute, she straightened up and said, "Overstepping? It's like you're my fairy godmother. I was supposed to be the one saving you, and you turned the tables on me."

Her praise made me smile. "Just trying to help out since you are doing so much for us."

"You can relax, you know. You don't have to scramble to prove your worth around here."

Her words stunned me. Was that what I was doing? "How did you get so smart?"

"Years and years of therapy," she confided and took a long sip of wine. "Have you ever been?"

"I haven't, although, I always thought confession was kind of the same thing."

"Whoa. The Catholic brainwashing runs deep in this one." Her throaty laugh made it easier to stomach the insult. "Confession and therapy couldn't be further apart from each other. It's helped me navigate all my feelings and support Rhyne the best way I can."

I pondered her words. "You seem so at ease with each other."

She laughed again. "It took a long time for us to get here."

"Really?"

"Of course, it did. I made so many mistakes."

"What kind of mistakes?"

"Thinking it was a phase. Ignoring what was happening. Checking out and not being available to them when they needed me. Refusing to use the pronouns. I thought I could control Rhyne and discipline them straight."

"What changed?"

"The day his school counselor called and told me they were suicidal and I needed to take them directly to the emergency room for an evaluation." She paused. "I am not proud of the job I did parenting them when they first came out. I got myself in counseling and learned I had this desire to control Rhyne and force them into a box that I thought would protect them. I used the word love, but nothing could be further from the truth. Real love doesn't demand a person to act a certain way to earn it. Real love accepts a person at their most basic level."

I was silent, thinking about the box I was trying to wrestle Wren into and the even smaller box John had built for her.

"We always think our children are an expression of us. That their behavior somehow reflects on us. None of that is true. Most of the time, we just need to get out of their way. Give them space to figure out who they are and believe them when they tell us."

A tear cascaded down my cheek. "I haven't done that at all," I admitted.

"That's not totally true," Sarah said and reached out to squeeze my arm. "You're here. You protected her from a toxic environment. The rest you can figure out as you go." She paused for a moment and then said, "Your only job is to love Wren."

"I do," I whispered. "She's my whole world."

"Careful," Sarah warned. "That is part of the problem, too. You have to let Wren embrace her individuality, and learn to embrace your own." She smiled. "As parents, we've been taught to live vicariously through our children. We put the weight of our happiness from our selfish expectations on their immature shoulders. Their shoulders weren't made to carry that burden. It's why they rebel. They want to walk down their own path, and instead, we want to force them down ours."

"I never looked at it that way."

"It took me a long time to see it, too. My official stance

now is, unless Rhyne is hurting themselves or someone else, I stay out of the way. If they stumble walking down the road, I don't rush in to save them anymore. I pause. I wait and pray for them to find the strength within themselves to find the solution. When they come to me for advice, I first ask: What do you think you should do here? It helps them develop coping strategies and strengthens their responses and inner strength."

"I would have never approached it like that," I mused at her way of looking at the world and the choices she made to parent her son. I had to admit, the proof was in the pudding. The person Rhyne had become was smart, funny, and engaging. Truly expressing who he... *they* were. It *was* refreshing.

"Try it," She encouraged. "Wren is having an identity crisis, but the bigger identity crisis is your own, Theresa. You are going to need to redefine who you are and what you need and want in your life. I get the sense you've never done that before."

"Man, you're good at this," I commiserated, swirling the wine in my glass before taking a sip and swallowing it along with my pride.

"It comes from years of experience." She laughed.

"I must be having my midlife crisis." I sighed, "I need to start looking for work, to build a life where I can stand on my own two feet that isn't dependent on anyone else, but where do I even start? I don't know what I'm qualified to do."

"I would urge you to consider the bigger picture. Who are *you* outside of Wren and John? What does *that* woman want?"

"I have no idea. I stopped listening to her a long time ago."

"She's still in there. You just have to turn down all the other noise so you can hear what she has to say." She reached out to squeeze my shoulder. "Alright, that's enough deep talk for now. I'm starved. Let's eat."

TWENTY-FOUR

I tossed and turned that night as Sarah's truths circled and circled my mind. At first, I was offended by her theory on parenting since it was in complete conflict with my own. But as I looked around her colorful house filled with art and love and witnessed the beautiful accepting relationship she had with Rhyne, I had to admit the evidence supported her theory. No matter how foreign it felt to me, or how much it clashed with my traditional values on parenting, I had to try.

Her home was a happy one filled with acceptance and love, and I had run from my own, escaping abusive words and controlling behaviors. The contrast between our homes, from oppressed to empowered, pained me to see. I now understood there were two destinations, and the map of my heart was intent on figuring out the navigation, but there was no clear path. There was no simple route to the life I wanted to give my daughter.

I snuck out into the kitchen, looking to make a cup of tea, only to see Wren already there, eating a bowl of cereal.

"Hey," I whispered as I leaned down to plant a kiss on the top of her head, feeling fresh stubble brush my lips. "What are you doing up?"

"I couldn't sleep," she admitted.

"Me neither. Anything in particular on your mind?" I knew I was opening Pandora's box, but she'd been so quiet since we left our home. I wanted to know where her head was at.

"I like it here," she admitted.

"I do, too," I agreed. "It was getting to be pretty destructive at home. I am sorry we didn't leave sooner. I was afraid."

"Of what?" she asked.

"So many things, honey." I sighed. "But none of it matters anymore." I reached out to squeeze her hand. "There are a lot of things that need to change right now, and the first one is me. I have to figure out how to let go and let you become who you were meant to be." I exhaled a heavy sigh. The room was silent except for the hum of the refrigerator compressor.

"I need to have faith in you, little one. You have a beautiful heart, you care about people, and you always fight for what's right. You have all the tools you need already inside you to create your own life. I keep getting in your way and intervening, thinking I know what's best for you."

I looked deep into her eyes and continued. "And I just figured out, when I am so engrossed in mothering you, it takes all my energy so I don't have to focus any of it on the parts of *my life* that aren't working. You've been my favorite distraction." I laughed at the bold confession.

Tears welled up at her lashes, and she swiped them away, looking down.

"But it's time to put the project back in your capable hands, sweetheart. From now on, I am going to work hard at letting you navigate. I'll be here for advice, but only when you ask for it."

"Are you sure you can do that?" Wren kidded me, laughing through her tears that were now freely flowing down her face.

I laughed back. "Might need to put some duct tape over my mouth from time to time, but I really am going to be taking a step back." I looked down, gathering my courage. "And I made another decision. I am enrolling you in driver's ed. I'm going to be looking for a job, and I will need you to be more independent."

"Okay." She nodded. "A job? What kind of job?"

"I don't know yet," I admitted. "Going to have to pull out the world's dustiest resume and get out there."

"Does this mean we aren't going home?"

"I don't know, honey," I said sadly. "I truly don't. I know your dad loves us, but we can't live like that anymore. It's not good for your well-being or mine." I tipped my head and studied her. "But there *is* one new rule. No more lies. No more hiding who you are and how you feel. Even if you think I don't want to hear it, I want the truth. Can we agree on that?"

"Yeah." She nodded, conviction strengthening her voice, then she stifled a yawn.

"Why don't you go back to bed and get some sleep? It's a school day tomorrow."

She nodded and disappeared down the dark hallway, leaving me at the kitchen island. I opened my tablet and registered Wren for driver's ed, wincing at the four-hundred-dollar fee, getting pinched from my first glimpse into the hard financial truth of being a single parent. Then I Googled apartments for rent near me. Scrolling, I gasped. Twelve hundred dollars for a two-bedroom townhouse with a washer and a dryer! Nine hundred if I could endure brown shag carpeting, window air conditioning, and didn't mind lugging my dirty laundry to a laundromat. I felt the walls closing in, making my chest heavy. I hadn't worried about money for decades. John took care of all the bills and gave me an allowance for spending money and extras for Wren. I had no idea what we paid for car insurance or utilities. John had taken care of it all, and I let him because it was easier. Now, it didn't feel easy at all.

I swallowed the lump in my throat as I tried to make a list of monthly expenses. Each one added to my anxiety. I was frugal but soon discovered my bare minimum expenses would be far higher than a minimum wage job could handle. I didn't have a degree or a career, and I was trapped, for the first time understanding why women stay in abusive situations longer than they should simply for survival. I ripped the offensive page from my notebook and crumpled it into a tight ball with my fist, letting it sit on the table next to an empty glass.

I pulled a purple pen from the container and a note-book that was nearby. At the top of the page, I wrote: "Jobs I'd enjoy." I sat there silent for a full minute, considering my options. I'd never had to go out into the world and get a job as an adult. I doodled absentmindedly, afraid to actually commit to writing an answer on the paper. Somehow, I understood if I did that, the die was cast. Instead, I made small loopy daises and colored in the centers until words began to form. Baking, gardening, mother's helper, cake decorator, flower delivery. They all sounded like enjoyable jobs, but none were actual careers.

I turned the page and wrote the word: "GOALS" in huge capital letters at the top. My mind was blank, and then I began to panic.

"Come on," I said to myself as I struggled to put thoughts together. When had I become so empty, so entwined with John and Wren's lives that I couldn't even remember who I was or what I wanted? I scribbled on the paper as I came to grips with where I currently stood. One by one, I had let go of my own dreams to help someone else in the pursuit of theirs. Now, I was a lost soul floundering in a murky sea of doubt. Why did I buy into the fallacy that women are supposed to give little pieces of themselves away in the name of love, to self-sacrifice until there was nothing left? Was that my decision, or was it thrust upon me? What did I want now that Wren was older? What would I do with my days when she was an adult and pursuing her own path?

They were questions I had never considered before. Panic crept in again, and then anger at the panic. When did I become this weakened version of myself? I hated that I allowed myself to erode as the other facets of my role as a mother consumed all my daily resources.

What did *I want?*

I walked back through my life before John. It was another lifetime I'd almost forgotten. I'd shed it like a snake slithering out of his old worthless skin, leaving behind a flimsy shell. Being a mother was the only real goal of my life, straight out of the 1950s and I was ashamed of it for the first time. If Gloria Steinem was around, she would be shaking one decrepit finger in my face, age spots dotting her translucent, feminist skin like freckles.

I loved making a house feel like home, and feeding people made me feel necessary and useful. I traced this feeling all the way back to my childhood, looking for clues to my future. I kept coming back to food, home, and family, those three values I held so close to my heart and wrapped my life around. They were the truest expressions of me. The most authentic version of the woman I was born to be.

Born this way.

Wren's shirt in the burn barrel flashed in my mind. I finally understood. She was becoming her truest, most authentic self and unknowingly having a hand in giving me the courage to become mine. My heart tugged at the epiphany. I'd always categorized our relationship as teacher and student, but my thinking had been flawed. It was actually student and student the entire time, and the fresh revelation shook me. I marveled at this new truth, adding it to the crown of them I had gained in a short period of time. They sparkled individually, infinitely valuable and hard-earned. I closed my eyes and said a prayer of gratitude before continuing to delve into the scary future.

Feeding people gave me a sense of satisfaction. I was a self-taught cook, watching hours of *30 Minutes Meals with Rachel Ray* and secretly coveting her bright orange, cast iron Dutch oven and her colorful utensils. I loved the Zen quality cooking had, almost feeling like meditation as I finely diced carrots and onions and celery for a base of the soups I seemed to endlessly make.

Soup. Maybe that is it.

In the early nineties, I was enthralled with the *Soup Nazi* on *Seinfeld*. "No soup for you!" I made soup when Wren was sick. I made stew for frequent church potlucks. Soup was forever a staple in my home, an easy way to use up leftover ingredients and transform them into something comforting and delicious. I doodled a soup bowl as I thought about it. I was happiest in my kitchen, with a stockpot bubbling on the stove and air scented by the thyme and rosemary I tied together into a bundle with cooking twine to flavor it. Soup was a food hug, nourishing to the body and the soul.

I'd watched one too many episodes of *Hell's Kitchen* to know that working in a restaurant as a sous chef was not for me. The pressure and drama those poor kids had to endure would burn me out. It would take away the calm feeling that washed over me as I stirred onions in the pot while patiently waiting for them to caramelize and release their sweetness.

I wrote: "Own a restaurant" on my list of goals, feeling a zing of accomplishment as I penned the letters with purpose. It was a big idea and hard to wrap my head around.

Starting a small business? Now? At my age?

I Googled "Restaurant failure rate" and felt nauseous when it retrieved the answer. "Around sixty percent of new restaurants fail within the first year. Nearly eighty percent shutter before their fifth anniversary." Then I picked up my pen and crossed it off the list, deliberately cutting through the paper in frustration. Too risky.

How could I cut costs? Overhead is what was the killer. Employees, food waste, it seemed like a mountain that was impossible to climb. I doodled a spoon and then bubble letters, S O U P, tracing and retracing the letters. I filled them in with cross hatches as I turned the idea over in my mind. A flash of inspiration hit, and I added an E and an R. Then another flash. Souper Duper. A catchy cutesy name that was memorable. Soup was something that could easily be reheated. Most even tasted better on day two or three, giving the ingredients a chance to meld together and the spices to infuse into the broth more deeply. A delivery-only business—that would fit into my life. I would be able to set my own hours. Cook and deliver during the school day and be home for Wren after school. Brainstorming which soups to offer and what the packaging would look like, a shift began to happen. What was once a grandiose idea began to transform into a real plan that could be carried out. I felt a rush of adrenaline, empowered and electric, as I wrote list after list, dividing Souper Duper into action items that would make the dream a reality.

Two hours later, my mind finally empty, I stood and stretched, entwining my fingers behind me to pull my shoulders back with a crack. Spread out on the countertop was my business plan, and seeing it there in black and white was a thrill. I gathered them together and straightened the pages, tapping them on the counter. Then I turned off the kitchen light and went back to the bedroom to go to sleep. Dreaming of dumplings and noodles, a smile spread on my face.

TWENTY-FIVE

The next morning, I expected my late-night Souper Duper epiphany to dissolve into nothingness by the bright light of day. Exhausted, I stumbled to the coffee pot and saw Sarah paging through the loose sheets of paper.

"Not trying to be nosy, but I like what I see here." She glanced up at me, already dressed for work in jeans and a sweater that morphed through all the colors of the rainbow as it walked down her torso. "Souper Duper?" she asked with a huge grin as she locked her warm eyes on mine. "What a name. It's perfect."

"Really?" I asked, a bigger grin spreading across mine, the thrill of the idea waking me up again. "It's a gamble," I explained. "I know we can't live here forever, and I Googled apartments last night."

Sarah's head tipped to the side, and her brow furrowed. "You know you can stay here as long as you like."

"You've been so generous, but I don't want to impose."

"Don't be silly. Rhyne loves having Wren around. They are like two creative peas in a pod."

I nodded in agreement. Instant besties, Wren followed Rhyne everywhere, practically taking notes on how to be fabulous. Going to public school, Rhyne expertly applied his daily makeup, a regimen that required at least an hour and a half of preparation each morning. He crawled through digital copies of Vogue and GQ, researching new looks. Using an ancient Singer sewing machine, he embellished the thrift store finds he brought home into an edgy fashion-forward look, looking more like he was headed to the Oscars instead of school. Wren was stuck wearing her St. Auggie's uniform but found creative ways to embellish her backpack and accessories.

"I'm taking my baby gay hunting this weekend," he'd declared after school yesterday.

"Baby gay?" I asked, confused. "Hunting?"

"This one just came out and won't shut up about it." Rhyne's cheeky response made Wren's cheeks pink up. "Thrifting," Rhyne explained as he waved a manicured hand in front of Wren, who was in her uniform for school. "This whole look is just sad." I loved that Wren had Rhyne in her life. It gave her permission to be bolder.

Sarah continued snapping my thoughts back to her, "And if you really want to make Souper Duper a go, it will be tough enough to start a new business, you don't need rent and utilities hanging over your head."

"I couldn't ask you to do that."

"I know." She smiled. "That's why I'm telling you to stay. Insisting on it, really." She held up the sheath of papers and handed them back to me. "I think you have something here, and I'd love to help you get it off the ground."

"Partners?" I asked.

"Yes!" Sarah enthused. "But a financial partner only." She continued, "I gotta keep the day job. I love it, and trust me, I'm useless in the kitchen."

"But I've never done anything like this before," I admitted as the fear churned in my gut. "It's pretty risky."

"Of course, it is! That's what makes it worth pursuing." Her excitement was rubbing off on me.

"But eighty percent of restaurants fail in the first five years." I threw out the statistic I'd learned last night.

"Then be one of the twenty percent that don't," she countered, simple as pie. "Stop trying to talk me out of it," she warned. "Did you ever hear that quote by Marilyn Monroe?"

"Which one?"

"We should all start to live before we get too old. Fear is stupid. So are regrets."

"What an icon," I exclaimed.

"One of my other favorites is, 'I believe that everything happens for a reason. People change so you can learn to let go, things go wrong so you appreciate them when they're right, you believe lies so you eventually learn to trust no one but yourself, and sometimes good things fall apart so better things can fall together.'"

"Wow," I said. "I had no idea she was so profound. The media always portrayed her as a blonde bimbo, leaning hard on her sex symbol status instead of giving her credit for having original thoughts."

"Only those who have had their heart crushed can articulate the depths of true struggle and pain." She busied herself putting her empty coffee cup in the dishwasher. "I've got to get to work, but you need to keep going with this. We can brainstorm on the way to group tonight," she offered as I nodded. "But you have to promise me one thing." She stopped, her expression serious, and waited for me to answer.

"What?"

"No fear, no regrets. Promise?"

"I promise." I crossed my heart with my index finger. After she left, the house was completely quiet and still. I washed the dishes in the sink, then made a quick run to the grocery store, gathering ingredients for my ham chowder recipe. Souper Duper was now more than just a fleeting idea in my head. Every minute that passed by, it was becoming more and more real.

———

The next eight hours passed in a blink.

"What is that?" Rhyne asked, sniffing the air when he burst through the door after school. "It smells so good and I'm starved."

"It's the bacon from the ham chowder," I answered. "Want to try it?"

"Well, yeah!" he said. "You're lucky your mom is such great cook."

Wren smiled and nodded. "Her ham chowder is the best."

Hearing her compliment made me gushy and excited. I ladled two big bowls of soup for them and warmed up some crusty French bread while it cooled enough to eat.

"God, this is so good," Rhyne said after his first taste.

"The angels are singin', honey!"

I laughed. "Really? But is it restaurant quality?" I asked shyly, knowing I'd hear the unvarnished truth. Teenagers were opinionated and unafraid to show it.

"No," he answered quickly.

"Oh." I sighed, and my shoulders drooped as I took a seat at the table, unable to eat mine as the bitter sting of disappointment smacked my tongue.

"It's *better* than restaurant quality." He continued to scoop huge spoonsful of it into his mouth, and when the bowl was empty, he mopped up the bottom of the bowl with the heel of the bread and leaned back in his chair. "I'm stuffed."

"Really?" I asked for validation again.

"Yeah, Mom. It's good," Wren answered me.

"So… I had a little idea."

Wren's curiosity piqued as she studied me.

"I was thinking about starting a small business called Souper Duper."

"That's not a *little* idea!" Rhyne enthused, making me smile. This apple hadn't fallen far from Sarah's tree. He picked up his bowl and began to lick it. "Seriously, if they all taste like this, you can build an empire."

I laughed. "An empire might be a bit of a stretch, but I'd take a viable self-sustaining business."

"Dream bigger," Rhyne said. "Let's talk branding."

"What?" I asked him, confused by this sudden shift.

"Logos, packaging. You know, the whole customer experience."

My head started to spin with all this new information. "But I just want to make soup."

"Trust me," Rhyne leaned forward, "we're learning

about this in my AP Marketing Class. The name? Perfection." He grasped his long fingers together and made a chef's kiss. "Now you need a logo, a website, you know, a complete social presence." He stood and began to pace. Wren looked at me with a proud grin. "I can do the logo and create the online menu."

"You can?" I was surprised.

"Yep, I'll whip something up right now. Do you have a color palette or a mood board?" he asked.

"A what?" I asked bewildered.

"Wren, we've got work to do." Rhyne snapped his fingers and she popped up. "Chop, chop, girl!" They strode toward me. "I'd like to be your marketing director."

"I can't pay you," I admitted.

"Not in actual dollars, but you could let me get experience for my portfolio. Our final project is launching a fake product. Doing all the research and the market analysis. Finding the right pricing and business model, and then finding your ideal customer persona. Email campaigns, social media content posts, and then there is the keyword analysis and getting the domain." Mumbling to himself, he opened his phone and began to feverishly type with his fabulous thumbs. The long fingernails were now bright green and, somehow, not an obstacle.

"www.souperduper.com is available. Buy it now." Then he turned to Wren. "Get up, girl. We have work to do!" They disappeared into his room, and I pulled up the domain company, set up an account, whipped out my new debit card, and paid for my domain. I hit the complete button with authority. Seconds later, it was official. An email sat in my inbox, declaring me the owner of www.-souperduper.com.

TWENTY-SIX

We left Rhyne and Wren at home and carpooled to support group. Sitting in the seat next to Sarah, I watched the streets whip by, then picked at the stain on the cuff of my sweater I hadn't noticed when I was packing up leftovers into Tupperware.

"Your son is something else," I said with a soft chuckle.

"What do you mean?" Sarah asked.

"He… um… they," I corrected myself; it was a constant struggle to say the right pronoun and I was failing at it. "They declared *themselves* the marketing director for Souper Duper. They were talking about logos and keyword analysis. Social media campaigns. I have to admit, it's making my brain hurt."

She laughed. "That's Rhyne. When they take on a project, it's all in. If it makes you feel any better, they are currently getting an A in that class."

"Don't get me wrong, I welcome the help," I admitted. "But I'm having major fish out of water syndrome over here. I just want to make the soup. Selling the soup? That's a whole different animal."

"Rhyne is probably plotting out a plan for total world domination as we speak." Sarah laughed.

"That kid can do anything. He's extraordinary. *They* are. You have to know that."

She softly smiled as she turned to me. "I do. I am just trying to stay out of the way." She pulled into an empty parking spot and we walked down the stairs into the hospital basement. I turned on the lights and set out a plate of the cookies I made while Sarah coaxed the ancient coffee pot to brew. One by one, people I recognized began to filter in. Mary and Craig waved at me, and I noticed a major shift in them. Their faces seemed smoother and softer; a transformation was happening and I was thrilled to see it.

I saw a face I didn't recognize hesitate by the door. She was skittish, and I picked up my pace, knowing in a few seconds she would likely dart back up the steps to perceived safety.

"Hi there," I said, offering my hand. "I'm Theresa. Are you looking for Fearless Parenting?"

"Um… yeah," she answered, making one more furtive glance to the stairwell before deciding to shake my hand. "I'm Becky, but I'm not sure this is the place for me."

"I wasn't either," I admitted with a disarming smile. "But there are good people here. Come sit by me and give them a chance. Just one, okay?"

She nodded and followed me to the ring of chairs as the rest of the group began to get settled. Standing there awkwardly, surveying the group gathered around her, I was relieved when Becky finally took her seat next to me, clutching her purse in her lap. She sat on the edge of her chair, unable to even unzip her jacket, in case she decided to bolt and make a quick getaway.

Sarah stood and called the meeting to order. "I want to welcome you to Fearless Parenting, a support group for parents of at-risk LBGTQ+ youth. I see some new faces and some old friends. I am happy you are here, whether it's your first visit or your fiftieth. Who wants to share first?"

I found my feet as the rest of the group's attention swung to me. "I'm Theresa, here to support my daughter, Wren. Life has been kind of a rollercoaster since Wren came out. I didn't realize it would bring up as many feelings of shame and loss as it has. I was totally unprepared." I stopped for a second, gathering the courage to admit what happened. "I'm currently couch-surfing with Sarah and Rhyne, and I am grateful for a place to catch our breath. My husband, John, and I have landed on opposing sides, and I'm not sure if our marriage can survive this."

I looked down at my wedding ring and wondered if it would be something I would tuck into a drawer someday. For the first time in my marriage, my mind wandered to the possibility of divorce and it startled me.

"I need to rebuild my life, create an identity separate from Wren, and learn to stand on my own two feet. That means being financially independent for the first time in my adult life. I know that sounds ridiculous and archaic." I paused for a moment looking down at my feet. "I am ashamed at the dependence I had on my husband and the level of control I gave him over our lives." I cleared my throat, then continued. "I didn't think I contributed enough to have a say, to voice a real opinion, so I let him make all the major decisions for our family. But a week or so ago, he crossed a line, and I had to leave to protect Wren. It's the scariest thing I've ever done in my entire life." The admission came with a buoyancy I didn't expect and I pulled my shoulders back and stood taller.

Sarah nodded at me, encouraging me to continue.

"And now that I am regaining control of my own life, I am paralyzed by the fear of making the wrong decision, of somehow hurting my daughter even more. I want to grow into the kind of woman Wren can respect, and I'm having to figure out who that is. It's almost like we'd all been sleepwalking through our lives and Wren woke us up."

I glanced around the circle of faces, some of them nodding up and down and not a single one making me feel dirty or ashamed. "I wasn't sure if this group was for me, but coming here for the last several weeks has given me a healthy perspective. I appreciate all of you for being brave enough to share the pieces of your lives that hurt. I'm learning that, when I share with you, coming from a truthful and vulnerable place, it takes some of the shame away." I turned toward our leader. "And I want to thank Sarah. You've given me a safe space, a new family, and possibly even a new business." The circle buzzed with excitement that made me feel validated, and warmth flooded my heart.

A rush of giddy newfound purpose welled in me. "I'm taking steps toward opening a soup delivery business. There's a lot to consider, and it's really early in the process, but I'm excited."

"If the soup is anything like your cookies, then I'll be your first customer," Mary said with a smile, waving a half-eaten cookie at me.

"We'd love to be your taste testers," Craig volunteered and patted his rounded belly affectionately.

"I might need to take you guys up on that," I answered with a grin. "Anyway, I am grateful for all of you and this new path I am on. Thank you."

I sat back down, feeling a wave of gratitude wash over me. I'd always lived on the edge of groups and never had a sense of belonging, taking on the perpetual wallflower persona, waiting to be asked to dance. I offered Becky an encouraging smile and was surprised to see her find her feet.

On wobbly legs with her hands shaking, she began, "I'm Becky and I don't know why I'm here." She stumbled on her words. The room was so silent you could hear a pin drop. "He's gone," she whispered. "I'm not a parent anymore." Stunned, we waited for an explanation.

"My son, Elijah, took his life after being bullied at school." She vomited the words rapidly, then a choked sob escaped her throat. "It's been seventy-four days and..." She glanced down at her watch for a long moment, calculating, and then continued, "thirteen hours without him. I don't know how to go on. I don't know how to do this, to live this life when I'm not a mother anymore." Now unleashed, fresh tears coursed down her cheeks and sobs wracked her thin frame. Her pain was evident in every line etched on her face and the dark circles under her eyes. She was consumed by it. My heart tugged and forced me to my feet, pulling her in for a hug. She clung to me, a port in her storm, both of us shaking. Then all around me, I heard squeaks and metallic screeches as the rest of the group got to their feet. Warmth enveloped me as they wrapped their arms around us. In my arms, Becky sobbed huge, heaving sobs that dampened my cheek, and we clung to her there as minutes ticked by on the clock. Eventually, her sobs quieted, and we pulled back and found our seats again as she let out a huge breath.

Sarah stood. "Becky, I know I speak for everyone in this room when I tell you how deeply sorry we are for your profound loss. Please consider coming back here so we can offer you support and help you grieve." She looked around the whole group. "I have never been prouder to be part of a group of people than I am at this moment." Choked up, she couldn't continue.

Eventually, Mary found her feet and Craig stood next to her, his arm around her shoulders. "We have some big news to share. Channel 11 wants to do a story on Tristan and interview us about our philanthropic work with his college fund."

"Wow. That's incredible." I marveled at their physical changes. The tightness of his jaw and Mary's dark circles had disappeared. They were beaming. "You both are glowing. I see a huge shift in you both."

My declaration brought tears to Mary's eyes, and she swiped them away as Craig answered for her. "She's having a hard time accepting joy and goodness in her life. Hell, we both are. It feels like a betrayal to be happy here on earth without our boy."

"Oh, Mary," Sarah empathized. "From what you've told me, Tristan was the absolute joy of your life. He wouldn't want you to suffer until the end of yours. It's okay to let yourself feel happiness again and to feel good about this new path you have been forced on. I have a feeling he has a hand in it."

"Us too," Mary agreed. "I feel him near us when we

talk about the foundation. I know he would approve and be so proud."

"Of course, he would. What a legacy you are creating in his name."

"That's what we focus on," Craig answered, "when things get rough and it's hard to carry on. This opportunity is a chance for more people to hear his name, to understand the path of his short life. It keeps him alive for us."

"That is something people don't understand about grief," Sarah explained.

"I agree!" Becky chimed in. "After the funeral, I noticed that all my friends stopped saying Elijah's name because they are afraid of my reaction. It's like he ceased to exist for them, but the truth is it makes this pain even more excruciating. I want to shake them and say, 'Please! Please say his name. Elijah was here. His life mattered. Please don't forget about him. Please tell me stories about my son. My heart has already been destroyed, and nothing you can say or do can make this suffering worse.'" Her voice cracked and she was silent.

"The world is definitely darker without the bright lights of Tristan and Elijah," Sarah offered, then the group fell silent, the only sound Becky's sniffling next to me. I passed a box of tissues over to her. Twenty more minutes passed as the rest of the circle shared, but my thoughts were stuck on Becky, Mary, and Craig. They were part of a group I never wanted to join: parents who have lost a child. It was unnatural to bury your child, for them to leave the earth before you did, and was my greatest fear.

I heard Sarah say, "See you next week." And then the group began to filter out of the room, but Becky stayed glued to her chair.

"Are you okay?" I asked her, then corrected myself. "Gosh, I'm so sorry, of course, you're not okay."

She forced a tiny smile of acknowledgment. "Do you ever get stuck in the land of what if?" she asked wistfully, her eyes glossy with fresh tears. "What if I'd paid more attention? What if I'd gone to the principal even though he begged me not to? What if I'd gotten a lock box for my Xanax instead of leaving it in the medicine cabinet?"

I pulled up a chair next to her. "You can't blame yourself."

"There's no one else *to* blame." She whimpered.

"This might be hard to hear, but if it hadn't been the Xanax, he would have probably found another way. Teenagers are masterful at hiding important information from their parents." I reached out to squeeze her hand and she clung to it.

"He was all I had, and now he's gone. I keep seeing him lying on his bed, his lips blue." She looked up at me. "At the funeral home, it took eight hours for me to gather the courage to leave, knowing I would never see his face again. I sat there, brushing his hair from his eyes. I just couldn't say goodbye." She shivered and then swiped at the tears on her cheeks. "I couldn't afford a casket, so he was cremated. They gave him back to me in a cardboard container, no bigger than a shoebox. That was all that was left of my sweet son. It crushed me to see his entire existence reduced to fit into such a tiny box."

I shuddered. Her pain was palpable. Sarah pulled up a chair and sat down next to us and I was relieved.

"Becky, you have found the right place." The woman nodded. "I'm sorry for your loss, but I am glad you found the courage to seek out this group. Nothing can bring your beautiful boy back, but hopefully, we can provide the support you need so you can move forward."

"But I don't want to move forward," she cried. "Not without him. I keep thinking this is a nightmare, and someday I will wake up and he'll be at the breakfast table eating cereal. Sometimes, I swear I can almost hear him calling my name, but then the truth comes flooding back in and I realize I have to get up and live another day without him."

"How are you taking care of yourself?" Sarah asked. "Are you in therapy?"

"No." She looked around. "I thought I would try a support group first."

"That was a great first step, but I believe in therapy and I know it will help you find peace in some of these questions you're asking. It will help you deal with the guilt." Sarah reached into her purse and handed Becky a card. "Give her a call."

"And one more thing," I added. "Keep coming back here."

TWENTY-SEVEN

The next night, I wowed them with my Italian Wedding Soup, a rich broth simmered with tiny meatballs I rolled by hand. Stuffed to the gills again, we gathered in the living room while Wren and Rhyne shut the blinds and attached the computer to the projector they'd arranged for Sarah to bring home from work.

Rhyne was all business today. Rocking horn-rimmed tortoiseshell glasses, he wore a pair of rust-colored corduroy slacks, and an ivory-colored shirt topped with a navy-blue sweater vest. His hair was tamed down, slicked back, and held in place with copious amounts of gel. Wren was in a navy three-piece men's suit, tailored by Rhyne, she'd found in a second-hand store and tan leather dress shoes. A dark, smoky eye enhanced her brown ones, and a glossy nude lip, arched eyebrows, and growing-out buzz cut gave her an androgynous model look. They were both fresh-faced and runway ready.

"Wow, you guys really committed."

"Dress for the career you want," Rhyne declared.

"When you go to war, honey, you have to dress for battle." His wrist shot back and forth in a fierce Z snap for emphasis.

The kids were so serious I had to pinch my lips together to stop the laughter. I locked eyes with Sarah, who was busy choking back her own giggles.

He cued up a PowerPoint presentation where white light flooded the screen and played music over the Bluetooth speaker. A solid twenty seconds of music swelled, getting more intense as each second unspooled.

"More than Soup. It's Souper Duper." Wren clicked to the first slide. The logo was a circle in lime green with a purple bowl. It popped off the screen.

Wren clicked to the next slide as Rhyne continued. "Eco-Friendly, the bowls will be completely biodegradable. Packaged with lime green napkins in an eggplant kraft paper bag. Everything about our packaging is made to compost easily."

"What about the spoons?" I asked.

"Even the spoons!" Rhyne declared, and Wren flipped to another slide that showed all the elements of the biodegradable packaging. With a red laser pointer flashing on the screen, he continued, "They are made from natural Corn PLA Resin. Cornstarch is heated and processed to form a resin, and from there, they can be molded into virtually any shape."

"That's a thing?" I questioned, shocked at the lengths their research had gone to already. "But what about the cost?" I asked.

"We are building an *elite* brand," Rhyne answered. "It only costs ten percent more to go first-class, Theresa. It's the difference between a forty-cent bowl of grocery store ramen and the twelve-dollar cup of seafood bisque at Alessandro's."

"Oh," I declared. They had a point. I nodded my head in agreement. "I like it."

Wren clicked to the next slide. "Your best channels for social media are Insta and Facebook. Lots of old people live on Facebook and would eat up your soup. Facebook is positively geriatric."

"Hey!" I protested. "Are you calling us old?" I glanced over at Sarah, whose eyes were twinkling.

Ignoring my outburst, Rhyne pressed on. "You should do some behind-the-scenes videos when you make the soup, maybe a series at the farmer's market or the grocery store when you shop for ingredients. You could also create some short videos teaching people how to pick out perfect produce."

"I don't know," I hesitated. "Would I have to appear on camera? It's not really my strong suit."

"You'll be great, Mom," Wren said, surprising me. "We make Tik-Toks all the time. Rhyne and I can teach you some tricks."

"Are you up for a make-over?" Rhyne asked as his eyes drifted up and down my usual frumpy mom uniform of yoga pants and old t-shirts. "Your brand is you." He winced. "And I mean this in the most loving way…" he pressed his hand to his heart and then held up one palm and made a quick circle in front of me. "That look is just sad, honey, okay?" His voice twerked higher with the insult.

I chuckled at the honesty, and next to me, Sarah dissolved into a pile of giggles.

"Brutal, isn't it?" she asked. "They always go for the jugular."

"Whoa. You are making my head spin." I declared leaning back into the sofa. "Let me absorb all of this."

Wren flicked to the last slide that showed a framework of the website, complete with an ordering page. It was fresh and modern, mostly white with punches of lime green and purple. The entire look was fun and cohesive. "I've been designing websites on WordPress since I was eight," Rhyne continued.

"They have," Sarah chimed in. "They're actually one of the designers on the team for Pride Fest."

"Wow." I was in awe. Sarah stood and pulled Rhyne in for a hug. "It looks so professional. You guys killed it!"

Wren walked over to the lights and flicked them back on. I was still on the couch, struck speechless and unable to move. The presentation left me dumbfounded, and I struggled to articulate my thoughts into words.

"I'm blown away. I love the logo. You put so much thought into every aspect of this. The packaging, the advertising, all of it. I can't thank you both enough."

"So, we can get started on the website?" Rhyne asked. "This project will be forty-five percent of my final grade in AP Marketing. I am also going to need you to submit a review of the process and how it was to work with me."

"Absolutely," I responded. Rhyne and Wren were so proud of themselves. "I can't wait to write you your first glowing review."

"Wren did most of the PowerPoint presentation," Rhyne admitted. "We worked on the big ideas together."

"The logo was Rhyne's baby," Wren acknowledged.

"Come here, you two, bring it in." I wrapped my arms

around them. "Beautiful. So proud of you both." Rhyne glanced over his shoulder.

"Mom, quick, take a photo so we can push it out to socials on the new Souper Duper page."

"What? I have a page?"

"We took some liberties," Rhyne answered. "Since you bought the domain, I scooped up the Facebook business page and the Insta handle."

"Wow! You thought of everything," I admitted. "Can I take you to the Creamery for some hand-rolled ice cream to celebrate?" The kids worked so hard; I had to reward them.

He stroked his cheek, acting like he had to think the proposition over. "I'll allow it." Rhyne cracked with a smile.

A few minutes later, Rhyne and Wren chattered from the back seat as I drove everyone to the Creamery. Wren was animated and laughing more than I'd seen her laugh in the entire last year. I stole glances at them in the rearview mirror. I loved seeing her walls down and her cheekbones popping when she smiled. Sarah caught my eye, giving me a wink in the seat next to me.

It was amazing how, in such a short time, Sarah and Rhyne became like family to us, and how quickly John had drifted away.

TWENTY-EIGHT

The next month was a blur. I was consumed with the tasks of getting a sales tax ID number set up, printing stickers, and ordering biodegradable spoons and bowls. I learned when we cranked up the Rhyne and Wren marketing machine, it was like putting a steam roller into action. There was no stopping them. Every day after school, they slaved away in their bedroom, and at night, I could hear murmuring through the walls and muffled laughter until the late hours finally made me drift off. Even though the kids were biologically a boy and a girl, I was able to easily reconcile in my mind it was just a fierce and fast friendship. I didn't even question what John would think about them sharing a bedroom. As far as I was concerned, he lost his veto power when he froze us out.

I felt totally justified in making the decision on my own when Wren asked to be enrolled in public school with Rhyne. I just filled out the paperwork and enrolled her, simple as that. We both breathed easier when her last day at St. Auggie's was finally over. Other people might see the decision as an extreme move, but from where I stood, it was a protective act that would make vast improvements in Wren's self-esteem.

And in a rite of passage, I found myself choosing to use Wren's preferred pronouns. Hearing Becky's story killed the will I had to fight Wren on who they were becoming. The idea of rebelling against such a small request from Wren now seemed ignorant and dangerous. If this one concession would make Wren feel comfortable in their own skin, I would do it. There was no way I would be bringing home my child in a cardboard box over something so trivial.

I enrolled Wren in therapy, and even though I never got more than two-word answers when I asked them how it went, I could see a small but significant shift happening. Wren was flourishing in this home built in living color. They were thriving and becoming a more confident version of themselves. It was like watching them be re-born, casting off the old version and fully stepping into the new. One of my favorite parts of the day was when the kids walked into the kitchen before school. They both went to great lengths to express themselves with clothing, makeup, and accessories. Every day, I took a photo. Each morning was like walking into an impromptu fashion exhibit at the Met.

Once a week, I went to the bank to withdraw five hundred dollars for us to live on. To my surprise, John left the account open. Every time I went to the bank, I was certain it was going to be emptied or closed, but it never was.

Weekly support group meetings and fine-tuning recipes made my days begin early and end late. I was starting to fall into a rhythm of a daily life that didn't include John. It astonished me how easy it was to continue living a life outside the one I had been living for so long. The old one was small and cloaked in routine, but this new one was bigger, in full color, and ripe with possibilities.

Early summer brought farmer's markets and festivals, all kinds of events where I could find a hungry crowd. After getting an A on their final presentation for AP Marketing, Rhyne had already set up my simple website with our summer event schedule and flavor round-up. Wren let their hair grow out a little and then one day surprised me at breakfast when they came down rocking a punk mohawk, the sides of their head shaved smooth and bare. The strip of remaining hair was platinum blonde with hot pink fringes, thanks to Rhyne's salon skills. They experimented with their look every day, sometimes wearing prairie dresses and combat boots and sometimes wearing a white wife-beater, rainbow suspenders, and black skinny jeans with pumps.

"Wren! Hurry up! Driver's ed is in twenty minutes," I called out to them, and they finally joined us at the table wearing seven-inch-tall platform shoes.

"Really?" I said, annoyed. "You can't possibly drive in those."

"Yes, I can."

Wren tittered out to the car when I dropped them off, and I knew I should have waited, because no more than eight minutes later, I received a phone call from Wren that they were dismissed by the driving instructor. Instead of running right up there, I let them sit and wait. It was a brand-new parenting style for me, and the more I embraced it, the easier it became.

One Sunday morning, Sarah invited us to her church.

On the scale of St. Auggie's Catholic Mass to Jerry's Extremist Conversion Camp Nightmare, it hit about in the middle. I was apprehensive, still bitter with the way things were handled when I lost my cantor position at St. Auggie's.

Rhyne wore a military jacket they found thrifting and a long plaid kilt, With their hair pitch black and swiped across one eye. "You're wearing that to church?' I heard Wren ask them, and I strained my ears to hear their response.

"I could go naked if I wanted; that's how accepting our church is."

Rhyne made quick work of styling Wren in pink platforms with stonewashed baby-blue skinny jeans and a fitted jacket.

"Come on," Sarah urged at breakfast, "just this one time, then I'll never ask you to go again."

"Okay," I answered. She'd done so much for us, it seemed like a small request.

I fidgeted as we walked up the steps of the unassuming brick building from the early nineties that housed the Unity Church. Inside, rows of chairs were set up with a stage on the righthand side. As we walked in, a full praise band, including drums and three guitars, was belting out powerful vocals whose lyrics were projected above them for the crowd to join in. It was the energy that got me. From the chairs, the congregation harmonized and danced between the rows. There was a bold undercurrent of joy I wasn't accustomed to in church that surged and made the whole building come alive. Intrigued, I followed behind Sarah, who led us to a place in the middle and seated us behind a family of four. Two women were huddled together. With an arm wrapped around each other's waists and a child on either side, they rocked back and forth as a single unit to the beat. I looked away and caught Wren watching me. Glancing behind her shoulder, one of the women gave me a wide, open smile, then the song ended and they settled down in front of us. The couple held hands, an intimate gesture I thought would make me feel uncomfortable, but the longer I sat with it, the easier it was to accept.

A pastor draped in a black choir robe with a long sash made of triangles in rainbow colors walked to the podium. Her hair was cropped close to her head, and she was very plain, wearing no makeup or jewelry. "God is love, and all who live in love, live in God, and God lives in them." She waved her hands in the air. "It's beautiful, isn't it? And so simple in theory. But when it's distilled into the actions of humans on earth, it can get twisted." She smiled out into the congregation. "I love you," she said into the micro-phone and then paused for emphasis. "Three little words, not longer than four letters each, and yet when spoken together have tremendous power that can start wars or can uplift and inspire. I believe you would be hard-pressed to find three more powerful words in the english language. When used for good, they bring us closer into communion with one another. They inspire peace and generosity. When they are seen in a bad light, they can incite violence, cause people to act in inhumane ways." She fell silent. I glanced over at Wren, who was listening, hanging on her every word.

"It's so hard, yet so easy, right?" she asked gently. The pastor continued her sermon, and my mind drifted to John.

The right to love had divided us, and now, I intimately understood the power of those three little words. If Wren had said, "I love Mason" or "I love Will," our lives would have likely remained unchanged. But the words "I love Sammie" had sent us spinning out, had destroyed our family unit, and set us on this new path. I glanced over to Wren, who was sitting close to Rhyne, engaged instead of zoning out like I often saw them do at St. Auggie's. I realized something as I caught their eye and gave them a small smile. It didn't matter to me how God got into my daughter's heart; I just wanted to make sure He did.

———

Since we'd left, once each day I would scroll through texts from John. At first, his anger colored every exchange, and then he tried freezing me out. When we left, I never thought we'd be apart for months. I always figured that, after a few days, we would find a way to work it out. But the days stacked up, one after the next, the way they do. Then one day you look back and it's been too long. One day you realize too much time has passed to pick up right from where you left off. Our prolonged estrangement brought with it an awkwardness. I didn't know how to reach out to him. I didn't know what to say to the man I had married. I didn't know how to scale the walls of the massive fortress that had been built between us and to be honest, I felt he was the one who needed to do the scaling.

For months, I had been waiting for a text that never came. Four months after we left our home, I finally got it.

· · ·

John: *T, Come home. I'm sorry.*

I stared down at his message on the phone in my hand. I typed out four different responses and then deleted them all. It finally occurred to just ask him for what I wanted and not dance around the topic or try to explain anything away. Keep it simple. I tapped out a response and hit send before I lost my nerve.

Me: *Thank you for your apology, but the only apology I am looking for is changed behavior. Are you willing to change?*

The incoming text bubbles had me waiting impatiently for his answer. I waited and waited. After a full five minutes, his dead silence told me everything I needed to hear. He wanted us to come home, but only on his terms, and I finally understood that wasn't the kind of marriage I wanted anymore. The truth set me free, but not before it gutted me.

TWENTY-NINE

Aweek later, the kitchen was a flurry of activity. Huge ·stainless steel stock pots were simmering on the stove. I was wearing an apron, stained orange from the marinara sauce I'd made for the lasagna soup. All four burners were lit up, the blue flames licking the bottom of the pots. Chicken noodle, chili, and chicken tortilla were bubbling away. A stack of biodegradable bowls and spoons sat on the countertop.

Humming, I stirred the pots; it was the easiest part of my day. I turned the burners off to let the soup cool before we packed it up and readied it for delivery.

Sales were flying in on Facebook, and most afternoons after school were spent delivering soup throughout the neighborhoods in Eden Prairie. Wren was a logistics genius, mapping out the orders closest together for efficient delivery, a skill I knew came directly from their father. He would have loved to see this side of Wren.

When I was tired, a little nudge of homesickness would spring up out of nowhere. The texts had stopped coming, and I'd developed a stubborn streak. There was no way I was going to make the first call. He was the one who needed to make the effort, and at the end of each day, right before I drifted off to sleep, he would pop into my consciousness, flitting around my exhausted brain. I knew I couldn't ignore him forever, but working toward my own dream every day made it easier to delay.

I was building a solid nest egg for our future since staying with Sarah helped me tuck money away at an astonishing rate and reinvest it in the business. Each dollar I saved reinforced my new way of standing secure on my own feet. I didn't know what the future held for me and John, but I now knew without a doubt Wren and I would be okay with or without his support.

On Saturday, the kids lured me out of the house with promises of sugar. They'd been acting odd for the better part of a week, and I was hoping to find out what they were scheming about as Sarah drove us to our destination.

"What are we doing here?" I asked when Sarah parked the car at a quaint downtown parkade. Small mom-and-pop shops ringed the cobblestone street. During the entire twenty-minute ride, Rhyne and Wren conspired in the back, whispering with their heads bowed toward each other. Their brightly colored mohawks fanned away from their scalps in a showy display that gave them the illusion of gothic human birds. A box sat on the seat between them. "What's in the box?" I asked. Sarah kept silent, clearly enjoying my nervous nelly reaction.

She zipped her fingers across her lips and then turned a fake key at her cheek before tossing it away.

"What have you guys been conspiring about? You're all in cahoots. I can tell."

"It's nothing bad, Mom. Just relax," Wren finally voiced from the back, knowing I wouldn't stop asking questions unless I was given some information.

I unbuckled my seatbelt and stayed in the seat, searching for clues, when Wren opened the door and pulled me by the hand and down the sidewalk where they stopped in front of a beauty salon.

"Ta-da!" Rhyne and Sarah chorused. "It's makeover day!"

"I didn't think you were serious."

"As a heart attack, honey!" Rhyne sashayed into the shop, a bell jingling as they walked through it and checked me in at the counter.

Over the next hour, I was washed, cut, colored, and straightened under the watchful tutelage and full direction of Rhyne. I tried to steal glimpses of myself in the mirror so often, Rhyne strode over and whispered into the stylist's ear.

She took a step back and Rhyne swiveled me completely away so I couldn't so much see a single hair on my entire head.

"That's not fair," I whined. "Can't I have a little peek?"

"No. We want you to have your fairytale moment at the big reveal." Their freshly manicured hands spread out like fireworks. Big reveals were huge in Rhyne's world. "Have I ever let you down?" they asked, and I had to grudgingly agree.

"No."

"Then trust me."

"Fine." I gave in. Working with Rhyne over the last few months gave me the opportunity to see what a creative genius they were. Rhyne was a makeover magician, and I was putty in their skilled hands.

After two hours in the stylist's chair for hair, Rhyne opened their tackle box of cosmetics. Plucking an eyebrow pencil out, they leaned me back in the chair and drew out the shape of my eyebrows. It was a painstaking process that seemed to last an eternity. When they were finally satisfied, they waved in the esthetician, who applied warm wax. I closed my eyes, enjoying the comforting warm sensation of the wax on my skin. She pressed it down and then, without warning, ripped the wax off, tearing what felt like an entire head's worth of hairs out by the root in a single rip. After the first pull, I howled in the chair and covered my other eyebrow with my hand, bucking my body upright and out of reach while they dissolved into a fit of giggles.

"You have to warn a girl before you rip off half the hairs on her face," I cried. The esthetician cracked a smile and smoothed a cool, calming lotion under my brow where it stung.

Fool me once.

I playfully strained to get away from him. Rhyne laughed, pulled my hand away, and then gently pushed me back into the chair. "Beauty is pain, Theresa."

"Then I don't want to be beautiful," I reasoned as I bucked up. "I'll settle for plain or unassuming, or how about cute with a good personality?"

"First rule in life: Never settle."

Rhyne waved the rest of my excuses away as if they were an annoying gnat and gently pushed me back down to complete the rest of their planned torture.

Sarah snickered in the chair next to me while Wren

made short video clips and took photos I was sure would soon grace my social media accounts. They gushed about being authentic and letting people see the woman behind the business.

Initially, my insecurities about appearing on camera had been a hurdle to overcome. During the recording of my first few behind-the-scenes videos, when Wren would push the red record button, my entire vocabulary would vanish. Then my face would flush red, and every sense would heighten with the fight or flight response, reducing me to a bumbling idiot in mere seconds. The first videos were painful to record, took at least twenty takes to get one useable video, and were hard to watch without cringing.

Tasked with being my social media manager, in a stunning role reversal, Wren had to give me the first pep talk of her life. "Can I talk to my mom in private for a minute?" they asked sweetly. I was sweating profusely and grabbed a potholder, fanning it under my arm pits.

An exasperated Rhyne nodded in agreement and left with Sarah.

"You have to relax, Mom."

"I can't. I'm stuck in my head and the words won't come. This is so far outside my comfort zone. I don't know if I can do it."

"You can do anything," they started to explain. "Look at where you are." I was confused; we were where we always were—in Sarah's kitchen. "You've been outside your comfort zone for months. We're in a different house, a new school, and you have a new business. You've been doing things I bet you thought you'd never do."

"Hmm," I mumbled, listening to them. "You might have a point."

"I'm so proud of you," Wren said, and it choked me up. I was melting into the pile of goo mothers do when their child notices a significant positive change in them.

"Really?"

"Yes!" Wren practically shouted at me. "I know the sacrifices you made for me. Putting me first. Standing up for me in front of Daddy."

"That's the first time I've heard you mention your dad since we left. Do you miss him?"

They squared their shoulders, and I knew they would never admit it. The hurt overshadowed all else and prevented the revelation. "Not really."

"Do you want to see him?" I asked. "I don't want you to think you can't, you know."

"I know, but has he even made an effort to apologize?"

"Kind of," I answered. "Talk is cheap. It's actions I want to see, and I'm not sure he's ready to do that for us yet."

"Will he ever?' They asked the question I'd been asking myself since we landed at Sarah's.

I pulled Wren in for a hug. "He's your dad, and he loves you. Of course, he'll come around." I said the words, but I wasn't so sure. He was a man of convictions that ran deep, and I knew he'd never been pressed to go against those to this degree before, even if it meant choosing between his family and his faith. I was trying to give him the benefit of the doubt, but the longer he took to apologize and right the wrongs he'd made, the more my wary heart hardened. I didn't want to poison Wren's heart toward him. I wanted her to make up her own mind and draw her own conclusions about her father, not piggyback her decisions on mine out of loyalty.

Her pep talk worked, and over the last several weeks, I lost the deer-in-the-headlights, vacant look in front of the camera. The fear of putting my full self on display publicly lessened. Instead of fading into the background, I stepped forward into the light.

It was Wren's coaching, taking Rhyne's directions, and refusing to give up until we had solid videos for social that made all the difference. They amazed me, putting so much effort into this enterprise, and I wanted to help pull my own weight. I was proud of what we were building together.

I should have seen this makeover coming weeks ago. Each time they suggested it, I pulled away, offering one excuse or another. They had conspired against me, luring me out of the house with promises of chocolate shakes and crispy loaded tots. I felt a little like a dog being told he's going on a ride only to be taken to the vet for shots. My eyes drifted up to Rhyne's, who was intently swiping the perfect shade of blush across my cheeks, then to Sarah behind them, who gave me a radiant smile of encouragement, then finally over to Wren, who was slowly circling me and Rhyne with their phone on a gimbal, for a smooth flawless video, and my heart burst. Being the center of their attention felt… strange.

When the stylist spun me around, I didn't even recognize my own reflection.

I gasped and searched for any remnant of my former self that remained. My skin glowed, bright and smooth. My pores had disappeared. Convinced my eyes were playing a trick on me, I reached my hand up and stroked it gently across my cheek, turning my face back and forth in the mirror. It was me.

Sarah crept closer, a huge smile on her face. "Look at you! Just incredible."

Rhyne let out a sorority girl squeal and then clapped their hands. "I'm a genius? Right, Mama?" they gushed, fanning their hands dramatically in front of their immaculate face. "I promised myself I wasn't going to cry." They pressed their lips together. I laughed and rolled my eyes at them both. Their fawning over me made me uncomfortable.

"You're beautiful, Mom," Wren said with a smile that melted me.

I grinned, enamored with my reflection, still unable to believe it was me.

"There's one more surprise," Rhyne said, finally addressing the mystery box. He placed it on my lap, and I opened it. Inside were four embroidered shirts with Souper Duper's logo emblazoned across the front. The colors popped from the pristine white t-shirt and the purple cardigan resting inside.

"Oh, my goodness. I don't know what to say." I was overwhelmed.

"Stop that! There's no crying allowed!" Rhyne chastised me with a smile. "If one gets by the goalie, remember to dab, not rub." They pulled a tissue from the box on the table and demonstrated their flawless dabbing technique. "Look up and dab. Up and dab."

My eyes met Wren's and welled up again. "Look away!" Rhyne cajoled. "Do not make eye contact with that woman," Rhyne shouted at Wren. "I did not just spend the last hour applying a flawless fresh face for you both to ruin it."

THIRTY

I'd packed three dozen cookies into trays and was busying myself getting set up for the support group when I heard a voice talking to Sarah that stopped me cold. My stomach fluttered in recognition as I strained to hear the words.

"Is this Fearless Parenting, the support group for parents of LGBTQ+ at-risk youth?" he asked. The commanding tone was instantly recognizable.

"Yes, it is," Sarah responded with her usual warmth as my hands began to shake. "Is this your first visit?" I turned the crockpot to warm, filled with bacon cheeseburger soup, and wiped my sweaty palms on my pants. I then took a deep breath, bracing for confrontation. It was the moment I'd both wondered and worried about for months thrust upon me in the place where I turned to for safety and acceptance. To have him there felt like an ambush I was unprepared for, and I struggled to calm my hammering heart. I was not the woman who left our home five months ago. I had rebuilt myself from the inside out with the help of Sarah and Rhyne.

"I actually came last week, but couldn't bring myself to come inside. I guess this time it got a little easier." I heard a stiff chuckle that I knew was his.

"Well, I'm glad you made the decision today to join us," Sarah said as I heard her heels tapping on the linoleum as she walked closer. "Let me introduce you to some of our members." I fiddled with the platter, turning it slightly and then readjusting it. My nerves were shot. Feeling a flush of heat, knowing he was standing behind me, I turned slowly around.

"Theresa…" Sarah started in, seeing the glint of recognition wash across his face. "Do you…?"

"There's no need," I cut in. "This is my husband, John."

Sarah stiffened, her eyes widening.

"It's okay. I've got this," I said to her. She nodded, then walked away, giving us some space. John looked smaller somehow, the gray in a new beard beginning a full-on assault across his face in the time we'd been apart.

He bounced from side to side, clearly as uncomfortable as I was. It was a hollow victory.

"That's new." I motioned to his beard, brushing down my cheeks with my thumb and forefinger.

"Yeah," he said softly, looking down at his shoes. "I kind up gave up on some of my rituals when you…" He stopped himself short. He cleared his throat and cocked his head as he studied me. "Your hair, it's different. I like it." He was clearly trying, but I was determined not to make it easy on him.

I brushed a few locks away from my face. "Yeah, the kids gave me a makeover."

"The kids?" he asked, confused.

I changed the subject. "I'm surprised to see you here," I said, wanting to get down to the nitty-gritty as fast as possible. The room was beginning to fill up, and I didn't want to cause a scene.

"I've been thinking about a lot of things," he started as I studied his posture, looking for signs of deception and finding none. "How's Wren?"

"*They…*" I emphasized the word, not bending and tiptoeing around the truth anymore. I had come too far to revert back to conforming to fit his wants.

He smiled a guilty smile. "How are *they*?" he asked again to my surprise. I felt one of my eyebrows arch up as I considered his response.

"About as well as can be expected under the circumstances," I finally answered. "Look, I don't want to cause a scene here. I've been attending this group for a while now and consider these people my friends." I finished fussing with the cups and faced him, closed off with my arms folded.

"I don't want that either," he agreed. "I can leave if you want me to."

"No. You're here, you might as well stay." I walked away from him and sat down in the circle of chairs, purposefully picking one in between two occupied chairs so John couldn't sit by me. He sat down in a chair opposite. Sitting ram rod straight in the chair, his hands folded in his lap, he waited.

At ease, Soldier.

Sarah glanced at me, then to John, then to me again. I

gave her a slight nod that everything was okay. "Welcome, everyone, to Fearless Parenting. I am happy to see some new faces." The next hour passed as I struggled to keep my focus. When asked to share at the meeting, John gave a smile and waved it away.

"We don't allow lurkers in this group, John," I cautioned boldly, and Sarah's eyes widened.

He cleared his throat and stood stiffly, his khaki pants wrinkled and hitched at his thighs. His shoulders sprawled back as he stood to his full height, and he began to speak.

"I'm here to figure some things out," he began. "My daughter… is…" he stammered, unable to say the words.

"Gay?" I offered.

He cleared his throat again. "Yes. I think she is gay."

"No," I corrected. "*They* are gay."

"I'm sorry." He admitted, "That is right, *they* are gay."

I folded my arms across my chest, defensive.

"I've made some mistakes." I couldn't bring myself to look in his eyes. "I was raised differently," he muttered in explanation. "I really just want my family back. I want another chance to prove to my wife and my child that I love them."

I struggled not to roll my eyes and shook my head in barely contained disgust.

"I said and did some things that I am not proud of." He reached up and rubbed his forehead "I've had some time to think about how I handled it, and I want to make amends."

"What's changed?" I asked.

"The conditions," he answered, "I guess. Being the head of the household, I thought it meant raising my child with the same values my parents instilled in me, and being in the military didn't help much in regards to becoming more accepting and tolerant." He looked down at the floor. "But none of that matters anymore. If I am a failure as a father but held strong on those values, I'm still a failure at my most important job."

His voice softened, and I felt my resolve following suit. "Theresa, I am sorry. I know I hurt you, and I know I've hurt Wren in ways no parent should ever hurt their child. All I am asking for is a chance to make it right."

Putting the pieces together, Mary gasped. I turned to face the group. "I'm sure this has been awkward for you all to watch. I'm truly sorry and hope you can forgive us."

"Sweetheart," Mary began, her eyes boring into mine. "Can I speak?"

"Of course," I said gently.

She turned to John. Craig wrapped his arm around his wife. "Why don't you let me talk to him, man to man?"

"Anything you need to say, you can say here, Craig. I think that was always part of the problem. Man to man. Stiff upper lip. Toxic masculinity. Please speak your mind, but I would prefer you do so in front of the entire group," I said, feeling powerful advocating for myself. Sarah glanced at me with a nod, shoring up my confidence.

"You're right," Craig said to me. "I meant no disrespect, Theresa. Old habits are hard to break."

"No offense taken. Please continue," I said.

"I've walked down the same road you're on, John, and I can tell you the darkest place it might lead if you continue to walk down it. When our Tristan came out, I threw the bible at him, forced him to go to confession, thought I could change him, get him to conform to my way of thinking. All it did was create this huge wall between us. It didn't change the way he felt. It just made him feel isolated and alone." He paused.

"You're Craig Meyer. Tristan is the boy who was found at…" John's voice trailed off as he put the pieces together.

"Yes, sir," Craig confirmed. "And I can tell you from experience your child needs you to love them, to protect them, to shelter them, and look out for them. That is what a real father does."

John closed his eyes and nodded. Craig's story hit him like a sledgehammer between the eyes. It was one thing to read about it in the newspaper. There, it was condensed to an act of hateful atrocity carried out by a stranger *to a stranger*. Putting a face to the tragedy made it hit home in a way I knew nothing else ever would.

"You have a gift right now. Every day your child is alive is a chance to prove to them that, no matter how ugly the outside world gets, no matter how vile and destructive and nasty it can be, they always have their father. They always have a home, a place they can retreat to for safety, where they are cherished and loved." Craig's voice broke, and then he choked out, his voice gravelly with emotion as he waved a strong finger at him for emphasis, "Don't you dare waste it."

I watched John's Adam's apple rise and fall. He was affected deeply. He leaned forward resting his forearms on his thighs as he wrung his hands together, clearly distressed. I felt vindicated, but then Craig waved one finger at me. "And don't think you're getting off so easily, missy."

Confused, I waited for him to continue. "Don't let your stubbornness drive away a father who wants to be in their child's life. Kids need a mom *and a dad* whenever possible, whenever it is healthy," he cautioned. "Theresa, people make mistakes. But he's here and he's learning. I am a pretty good judge of character, and I can see this is a man who has a deep love for his family. His actions might not have always shown that, but I've always been one to believe in second chances. Now, that's all I'm gonna say. Let's eat!"

To his credit, John stayed. He got in line behind Craig, and I watched him navigate the group while I hung back with Sarah.

"Are you okay?" she asked in a low voice out of earshot.

"I never saw that coming," I answered. "Honestly, I never thought I'd live to see the day John's shadow would darken the door of an LGBTQ+ support group."

"Maybe he's had enough time to think and is ready to make some changes," she offered.

"I love how you always see the best in people," I praised, "but sometimes it's really annoying."

She laughed. "What are you going to do?"

"It's time we talked. I don't know where it will lead us, but it's time we faced what is happening with our family and our marriage head-on."

"No matter what has happened, Wren's coming out has changed you both. I would say you changed for the better. The jury is still out on John. All you can do is be open-minded and see what he has to say. Don't compromise, you've come too far to go back now."

THIRTY-ONE

After the meeting, we walked to his car, and as we approached, he picked up his pace and eagerly opened the passenger side door for me. An act he'd done when we were dating that had fallen to the wayside over the last several years.

"Thank you," I offered and slid into the leather seat, folding my hands in my lap.

He drove us over to Millie's, a pie shop deeply downtown we stumbled across one night in search of dessert. The silence between us was thick, and I wondered when he would breach the divide. Feeling the burden was his responsibility; I waited him out.

He parked the car, and after opening the door for me again, we walked quietly down the stairs and into the pie shop.

"Sit anywhere you like," a voice called from the back, and I followed John to a booth as far away from the door as possible.

The room was dim, most of the light coming from flameless luminaries placed in the center of each round table. In the soft yellow-tinged light, after the waiter brought us glasses of ice water and left menus, his gaze drifted to mine and softened.

"You look really beautiful, T."

The compliment was disarming. I wanted to be angry with him, but I felt it dissolving and melting away my defenses the longer his eyes were glued to mine. He wasn't one for flowery language, and it tempered my anger. I reached up to tuck a few hairs behind my ear and quickly grabbed the glass of ice water and took a sip, grateful to have something to do. His gaze seared into me, tripping me up, making me feel shaky and unsettled.

"Did you mean what you said today in group?" I finally asked.

"Yeah." He nodded as our waitress sidled up to the table with two empty coffee cups and a pot of coffee.

"Yes, please," John said, and she set one down and filled it to the brim. Turning to me, I nodded, and she did the same.

"Can we order now?"

"Of course."

"I'd like the strawberry, and also a pecan." He motioned toward me.

"French Silk?" I asked.

"Yep." The waitress scribbled something down on a pad, tucked the pencil behind her ear, and then walked away.

"I thought we could share like we used to. Remember that?"

"I do," I answered. "Life was easier then."

He nodded in agreement. "I know I don't deserve it, but I want another chance."

"You're right, you don't. I'm…" I struggled for the right word to explain the ocean of feelings churning inside me. "Gob smacked, really. I don't know how I feel. How could you stay away for so long? I could never turn my back on you or my daughter and not have any contact for months, and I don't understand how you could cast us off like that. We had a life."

He swallowed hard. "I understand why you would say that." The humility in his voice was new and forced the rusty steel of my heart to give a little.

The waitress appeared at our table and set the three pie plates in front of us. I watched John thank her, studying him for visible changes. His thick hair was trimmed close with more gray at the temples. His polo had been ironed, and his arms were muscled and tanned. On the outside, he was the same man, but there was a quietude that wasn't there before.

"After you left, I was just so goddamn stuck. The anger, I didn't know what to do with it, so I just wallowed in it, telling myself I was making the righteous choice, that eventually you'd come to your senses and come crawling back. All I had to do was wait you out."

"The credit cards, John? That was unforgivable."

He visibly winced at the reminder and exhaled deeply before continuing. "That was dirty," he admitted. "I am not proud of that moment."

"It was! I had been a loving wife and faithful partner to you for seventeen years."

He nodded in agreement, his head hanging low in shame. "I know. You didn't deserve it." He took a sip of his coffee and slid the pecan pie over to me with a sweet smile. "First bite is always yours."

The gesture made a little grin tug on my lips. There was something deeply satisfying about pressing a fork through the tip of a piece of pie and slicing a perfect triangle. I took a bite, enjoying the sweet and salty decadence.

"I went to therapy," he declared. I recoiled like I'd been slapped and choked on a single pecan that sent me into a coughing fit. My reaction made him laugh a deep belly laugh. "You never were very good at hiding your emotions."

"That's true." I waited for him to explain.

"I know I always said therapy was useless and a joke, but when you get to be my age and your world implodes, it drives you to re-think a few things."

"What did you learn?" I asked, warming my fingers around the coffee mug, fascinated by this seemingly evolved creature sitting in front of me, looking and smelling like my husband.

"A lot of things," he said quietly. "Mostly that I parented using fear and control because I was afraid of what would happen to her."

"Them," I interrupted.

"Them," he repeated. "Please help remind me," he asked and then continued. "I also learned a lot of the beliefs I had about honor, discipline, and duty worked well in combat but not so well at home."

"That's the truth."

"It's hard to explain, but working with my therapist has

helped me open up and relax and learn to allow things to happen instead of forcing them together. There was a lot of old junk in my head from the way I was raised and the deployments and being away for so long. It took time to start to unravel my way of thinking. Now, I'm far from finished, but I do feel different. Something inside me is lighter. I waited because I wanted to work on myself. That day at the burn barrel…" He stopped abruptly and pressed his hands to his face. "I am so ashamed of what I did to Wren. I know it hurt them. I just didn't know what else to do. The fear was screaming inside my head, and I started this chain of events I couldn't stop. The rage was all I could see, and I let it get away from me."

I sighed. "You definitely did some damage."

"I know." Then his tone deepened. "All I am asking is for a chance to prove to you and Wren that I can be the type of father they need."

I bit my lip as I turned his words over and over in my mind. His voice was sincere and his gaze steady.

"I'm not the same woman I used to be," I said boldly, leaning forward. "I started a business."

"What?"

"I'm a small business owner."

"That's fantastic."

"What?" Now, it was my turn to be dumbfounded.

"I always thought you were sacrificing too much for our family, but the selfish part of me let you."

"Wow." I was startled by his revelation. I'd never looked at it that way. "I wanted to. I have no regrets about the life we lived."

"I wish I could say that." He shot me a sad smile and

spooned a bite of strawberry pie into his mouth. A dot of whipped cream clung to his new beard, making me smile. "What?" he asked, unaware.

I pulled the napkin off my lap and dabbed the cream off. He pulled my hand into his, unwilling to let go. It was warm and strong and felt like home.

"Tell me more about this business."

"It's a soup delivery business, Souper Duper."

"No way!" he interjected. "The guys at work can't shut up about that place."

"Really?" I asked, swelling with pride.

"Yeah, you're an amazing cook. God, I miss your cooking." He patted his belly, which seemed a little softer than I remembered. "Living on burgers and fries lately."

"Rhyne and Wren are running the show. They helped me build a website and a social media presence and do most of the deliveries."

"Wren's driving?"

"Yep," I answered, "and they're going to public school."

His eyes widened, but he didn't react. "That was probably a good decision," he finally admitted. "I wish I'd been part of it."

I nodded.

"It was the right thing to do. I've always trusted your judgment."

"Almost always," I corrected.

"Touché," he said. "You're not letting me get away with anything anymore, are you?"

"Nope."

"I think that's good." He squeezed my hand. "I want

you to come home. I want to keep going to therapy and learning how to be a better man, a better father, and a better husband." He looked down at my hand, caressing the top of it with his own as his voice lowered, and he continued tenderly. "Enough about what I want, what do you want?"

"I want to raise my daughter in a home where they feel safe and loved. I want to grow my business and learn to stand on my own two feet, and I want to work on rebuilding the foundation of a marriage that fits us both. I don't want to be dominated or have my future decided for me anymore. I want to help make the decisions. I want a true partner, someone who can help me navigate all of this and who always has my back."

"I want that, too," he whispered. "I can do that. I want to."

The rest of my defenses dissolved away. He wasn't perfect, but none of us are.

"Okay." I nodded.

"You'll come home?" he asked.

"Eventually. When Wren is ready."

"Deal." Then he dipped his index finger in the whipped cream and tapped my nose playfully.

"Who are you and what did you do with my husband?" I wiped the cream off with the napkin.

"I like that."

"What?"

"Hearing you call me your husband." He tugged my hand toward him and kissed me, a sweet soft kiss that tasted like strawberries and hope. It was so endearing and earnest my eyes filled, and I blinked the tears away, turning away from him.

"Come here," he whispered and pulled down to grab my chair, tugging me close to him. "I'm sorry, sweetheart." I rested my head on his shoulder and snuggled into his warmth. I had a feeling I was going to love this new version of my husband very much.

THIRTY-TWO

"Daddy?" Wren's voice was wistful, then sharp. "What are you doing here?" Thankfully, Sarah and Rhyne were the world's best buffers.

"I missed you," he admitted. "I ran into your mother at her support group, and we had a cup of coffee."

"What?" Rhyne and Wren chorused together. They were shocked.

"Hey, buddy," Sarah chimed in, knowing we needed some space to sort things out. "Let's go grab a frosty at Wendy's."

"Can I get fries?"

"Of course." With an encouraging smile, she cleared her house for us to talk. I tugged at the St. Christopher's medal on my chain again, begging for patience. My daughter and my husband were cut from the same cloth. I loved that about them, but they could also both be bullheaded and stubborn.

"You, my father, John Allen Churchill, Master

Sergeant United States Army, went to an LGBTQ+ Support Group?"

"He did," I interjected. "It was a chance meeting, honey. He was as shocked as I was."

"What were you doing there?"

"I was looking for information. Learning how I could better support my daughter."

In disbelief, they shook their head, exasperated.

"You have every right to respond that way," John admitted. "First, I need to apologize for my behavior the last time we were together." His words were as awkward as his posture. He shifted uncomfortably on the balls of his feet.

Wren wouldn't let him get off that easy.

"The last time we spent time together? You're referring to an incident of abusive behavior like we were having Sunday dinner." Utter disgust and outrage coated every word.

He blinked several times, and I felt a flush of panic. I knew what always came next with him—yelling and an unwillingness to back down. He surprised me when his voice was calm and almost softened enough that you had to lean in to hear him. "I owe you an apology."

"Damn right you do."

"Wren," I cautioned, trying to diffuse the tension.

"No," Wren shot back at me. "You don't get to intervene and play peacekeeper. He has something to say, let him say it."

John smiled, which only confused Wren more. "I have always loved your gumption, kid. Okay." He readjusted. "You want a direct approach. I like that. Let's cut through the bullshit." He looked at them. "I'm sorry I let my emotions get the best of me. I should have been strong enough to disengage. It should have never escalated to the level it did."

"Talk is cheap, Dad. I want to see changed behavior." They glanced over at me and I smiled, thrilled to see some of the lessons I wanted to instill *did* sink in. Seeing Wren set boundaries with someone who wounded them made my heart swell with pride.

"All I am asking for is a chance to prove it to you," he asked.

"Does that mean we're moving back home?" Wren demanded.

"We've decided to leave it up to you," I intervened. "The easiest way for him to prove it to you will be on a day-to-day basis. If you're willing to try, we can move back again."

"Don't think you can come in here and pick right up where we left off," Wren challenged him, and I held my breath, waiting for him to take the bait. He never did, dumbfounding us both.

"I wouldn't dare," he said behind a suppressed smile. "I know I did damage. It is on me to repair it, and I will."

"What about Souper Duper and Rhyne?" Wren asked.

"He knows all about that, too, and you and Rhyne will be friends for life," I answered.

"They wear makeup, Dad." Wren tested him again, narrowing her eyes. "Yep, that's right, they are one of those theybies."

"*They* have an interesting look," John offered, shutting Wren down instantly. "Not my cup of tea, but I'm a changed man. My new theory is live and let live."

"Why don't you get your things packed up, and we'll

wait for Sarah and Rhyne to come back so we can say goodbye." Wren strode away, and I was able to take my first full breath. "That went better than I thought it would."

"While I don't love being on the other side of their ball busting, we both have to take some pride for the fire in that one. They don't back down an inch."

"Yep," I agreed. "The apple didn't fall far from the tree."

"You think I'm the tree in that scenario?" he asked. "If I remember correctly, just a few hours ago, you were the one busting my balls."

I laughed. "You're right."

"You should be proud of the child you raised. They are going to do great things someday."

"They already are."

———

Twenty minutes later, I was packed and Sarah and Rhyne came home and realized what was happening when their eyes landed on the two suitcases by the door. Rhyne clung to Wren, waxing dramatically, showing me for the first time how close they had gotten in such a short period of time.

Rhyne dropped to the floor and clung to Wren's skinny leg. "Don't go. Please don't go." They dramatically groveled at Wren's feet and fake sobbed.

"Get over here, you big baby," Sarah said.

"Rhyne, come meet Wren's father, John," I said.

Rhyne's perfectly manicured eyebrow arched as they got to their feet and stood eye to eye, thanks to Rhyne's platforms.

"Rhyne's my marketing director," I explained as John took in their entire look head to toe without a flinch. "They are an incredible human, with such raw natural talent. Come give me a hug goodbye?" I asked. "I'm going to miss seeing your wardrobe choices every day at breakfast."

"I'll text you a photo," they offered and I smiled.

"Yes. You better and just because we don't live here doesn't get you off the hook for deliveries," I cautioned.

"Slave driver, this one," Rhyne said with a wink.

"Can you guys take the luggage to the car? I want to talk to Sarah."

The teens jabbered together, a constant stream of disses and gossip, and John picked up the suitcases and led them outside.

"Are you sure?" Sarah asked.

"I think so," I answered. "Thank you. I'll always be grateful for you and Rhyne during this dark time in our lives. I don't think Wren or I would have..." My voice broke. "You cushioned our fall and have brought me so much clarity and understanding in the short time we've known each other. I've never met anyone like you. You're extraordinary."

Sarah teared up and waved off the compliments. "Extraordinary women raise extraordinary kids. You know one because you are one." She hugged me.

"You've modeled to me every day the kind of parent I want to strive to be for Wren."

"I'm so proud of you," Sarah shared, and it choked me up again. "And it looks like you might get a second chance, but make him prove it to you."

"Oh, I intend to, and if I don't, Wren will make sure he does."

Walking out of her home was like leaving a warm cocoon, a safe place filled with color and people we loved. For a moment, terror griped me and I wondered if we were moving too fast. Then I remembered that it was my foot on the pedal, not John's.

THIRTY-THREE

"You're not going to like this new church." Wren almost rejoiced, pushing their dad's buttons, testing him to find weak spots in his new persona. We were eating breakfast before the 10:30 service began. John was at the stove stirring scrambled eggs and adding his secret weapon —slivers of crispy bacon and freshly grated cheese. He didn't take the bait.

"No more 'stand up, sit down, kneel.'" Wren sang out the commands. "And what's even better is there is no more Father McDonnell!"

"Even I am not going to miss that old blowhard," John admitted as he brought the pan to the table and scooped sunny yellow eggs onto our plates. After dropping the hot pan into the sink, he pulled the biscuits out of the oven with purple oven mitts up to his elbows and quickly filled a bowl with warm biscuits.

He sat down at the table and glanced over to Wren as he handed the biscuits to them first. I saw their shoulders soften as they grabbed two biscuits and passed the bowl to me.

Twenty minutes later, we were in the car, headed to church. The worship band was already on stage and was belting out a song that sounded like it belonged more on the top forty than part of a church service. At the door, John hesitated. The wave of sound hit him like a blast to the face. I reached down and gently pulled his hand toward mine and made my way down the aisle, finding an open spot in the fourth row. He stood stiffly next to me, getting acclimated to the room as his eyes darted around in the near darkness. I knew he was locating and making mental notes of the closest exit, a leftover habit from his long years in the Army. Undeterred, I clapped to the music, letting it wash over me. Closing my eyes, I unabashedly felt the energy surging. When I opened my eyes, John gave me a thin smile. He was like a fish out of water and having a hard time reconciling this rock concert vibe with the high-pitched hymnal songs we sang at St. Auggie's. I felt the urge to make this easier on him well up in my gut, but then I tamped it down and gave myself an inner pep talk.

This is a good test. If you want a different result, you need to do things differently. He's a big boy. He can handle it.

He shifted from foot to foot as the worship band segued into their last song, and the music softened and became almost like a lullaby. Delicate strokes from the man at the keyboard brought the tempo down as the congregation swayed from side to side.

The young girl on the microphone, almost swooning, crooned, "Thank you, Father. We bring our hearts to you, like little children, washed clean from our sins because of your sacrifice."

Finally, the congregation took their seats and the house lights illuminated the space as I felt John's shoulder relax next to me. Two readings went quickly, and then the pastor cloaked in a brightly colored tunic stepped in front of the bright stage lights.

"Go forth and multiply," she started in, "and when you take note of the almost eight billion people that currently exist on this earth, I'd say we've followed that direction quite perfectly. Wouldn't you?" There was a collective chuckle from the packed audience.

She paused for a moment then continued. "He also directs us to love them—everyone. That, my friends, is where I think we're coming up short. What does love mean?" Her face softened. "Think of the love between a mother and a child. That soul-stirring kind of love, that purpose-driven woven in the womb kind of love." I nodded in deep understanding. Glancing over at Wren who was seated next to me, listening, I reached out to squeeze their leg and they laid their head on my shoulder. It was a sweet gesture from Wren's childhood that brought the pastor's words home even harder for me.

"Love doesn't have room for shame. It doesn't say, 'I will love you when you act like I want you to act and when you do what I want you to do.'" The pastor paused letting her words sink in.

Next to me, I felt John sit up straighter and lean toward her, listening more intently. "When love has conditions, it is control, not love. We welcome with open arms all who come to Unity Church. We strive to make this a place where you leave shame and intolerance at the door. Where you can be free to be the person God created you to be, free from the expectations of society. With open acceptance, we meet you where you are, in your brokenness and despair. We hope to give you the tools you need to heal yourself. To see, sometimes for the first time, you are truly and absolutely loved by God the Father. There is nothing more you need to do, be, or have to step into this welcoming love. You are enough already as you are and as you will continue to be. It is your birthright."

I felt a prickle of tears at the corner of my eyes and lifted a hand to brush them away as John reached out for my other hand to squeeze it, a gesture that cramped my heart before it burst and fat hot tears began to course down my face. I glanced over at Wren, whose brown eyes were dampened and glossy, then felt John's arm behind my shoulders pulling me in closer to him.

"God does not make mistakes. He planted the seeds of you into the depths of your mother's womb, and waited, nurturing her until they took root. There is nothing that needs to be repaired, nothing that is faulty or broken. You are a beautiful child of God, created in his likeness yet as unique as every snowflake that gently falls from the sky. You may doubt a million little things about yourself, but never, not for one single moment should you doubt the Father's love for you." I felt a stirring deep in me which was normal and familiar, but what surprised me were Wren and John's reactions. Wren bolted upright in the chair like they'd been shocked, and then I felt them break. Wren's cheeks were wet with tears, black eyeliner washing gray tracks down their face. I wrapped my arm around their thin shoulders, pulling them to me and planting a kiss on their forehead.

Her words were a balm to my soul. It felt like the sermon was handpicked for my little broken family. We felt the power of them slowly tugging us back together by the heartstrings. The heaviness that had burdened us for months lifted and shifted, floating away, and my soul was buoyant. Sitting in the modern sanctuary with my family, I felt God's love wrapped around us, knitting us back together.

In a daze, we floated to the car. John was silent and pensive as he drove us home, and I wondered if he felt the same weightlessness and peace filling him. Silently, we followed him into our house, and Wren's arms were crossed at their chest in a protective stance. I understood their need to protect themselves from feeling exposed and vulnerable, and I pulled Wren closer to me.

John broke the silence first. "Can we talk?" he asked, looking into Wren's hardened eyes. They nodded, and we sat on the sofa in the living room.

"I don't know where to begin," he admitted, and I was puzzled as he wasn't often at a loss for words. He pulled up a kitchen chair and placed it directly in front of us, so close I could smell his aftershave. I closed my eyes and breathed it in, praying this time would be different.

"I've made some terrible mistakes," he finally uttered as Wren's eyes widened. They still weren't used to him willingly accepting blame.

"I know this will be hard for you to believe, Wren, but it's the truth." He looked down at his hands. "For the longest time, I prayed that God would heal you or fix this brokenness in you. I was afraid of the world and what it would do to you, and so I panicked, thinking I could force you to change. That it was my responsibility to put you on the right path and keep you safe and protected. I was afraid for you. I was ashamed of what the rest of the world would say, the judgment we would get from others, and it clouded my own. From the very first second I knew you existed, I promised to love and protect you, and I have fallen far short on both. I am deeply sorry."

Tears coursed down both of our cheeks, the last of their mascara rolling down the side of Wren's face. Their forehead crinkled, and I saw a glimmer of hope flicker in their eyes.

"I can see now how flawed my thinking was. I need to be your protector and your biggest fan. You need to gather strength from the steadfast love that is found in our home so that when you go out into the world and have to fight battles for basic acceptance, you have vast resources to pull from. Without a doubt, I want you to know that your father loves you, the real you, the authentic you that you feel compelled to be. I don't want you to hide any slivers of yourself from me any longer. I accept you as you are, completely and fully from this moment forward."

His voice cracked, and I heard a sob rise from Wren. Stunned, we squeezed closer together. "I spent many hours watching you sleep when you were a tiny baby. It had taken us so long to make you that, when you finally arrived, I never let you out of my sight. I rejoiced when your chubby baby thighs kicked and your arms waved at the sound my voice. It tore me in half to leave you and your mother and go halfway across the world to fight the battles I was asked to fight, knowing I would miss out on so many marvelous and wonderful things."

He reached out for their hand and held it in-between his own.

"You're the one I read stories to and taught how to track deer in the forest and what berries to eat in the wilderness. Today, when the pastor said God doesn't make junk, I want you to know that I see that now. You are the best parts of both me and your mother, fused together in the most astonishing way."

He wiped a tear from his eye and then looked deeply into her eyes. "When I take my last breath on earth, I want to be able to look back on a long lifetime of memories of our family together, where you have felt the permission to fully become the person you were meant to be. Despite the turn our lives took the last few months, I want that time to be reduced to an ugly blip on the radar of our long lives together. A glitch that gives contrast to the better way I promise to love you from today forward."

He pulled them from my arms to stand, grasping both of their hands in his own. "I am asking for your forgiveness, sweetheart. I am asking for your guidance as we learn to live this authentic life together. If you see me slip, I hope you can find it in your heart to gently guide me back. I am not a perfect father, and I have hurt you and your mother. I see that now. I love you, Wren, and now I can say that nothing will ever diminish that love. Nothing." He pulled Wren into his arms, and they both sobbed. I stood and wrapped my arms around them both. This warmth was a welcome change from the deep freeze we'd experienced.

"I love you, too, Daddy," they breathed out, and I knew they meant it.

THIRTY-FOUR

L ater that night, I found myself falling into my old routine. Changing into pajamas, I pulled a book from the nightstand and crawled into bed. John sat at the edge of the bed and removed his shoes, then put on his flannel pants and an old t-shirt.

"I made something," he said shyly, and in his hand, he revealed a tiny pride flag made with a wooden dowel and felt.

"For the dollhouse?" I asked as tears welled in my eyes.

"Yeah," he admitted. "I can't wait to give it to Wren."

"They will love it," I said as I took it from his hand and gave it a little wave. "Go put it on the dollhouse and see if they notice it."

"That's a great idea!" He disappeared into the living room, returning a few minutes later with a sweet smile.

"Thank you," I said.

"For what?" He was preoccupied with getting ready for bed.

"For today."

He nodded and sat next to me on the bed. Gently, he brushed a few of my stray hairs away, tucking them behind my ear. "I don't want you to thank me. I don't deserve it. It's what I should have been doing from the beginning."

I nodded quietly, agreeing with him. "I know that must have been hard for you."

"That was nothing. How hard was it for Wren?" he asked. "Just a kid trying to grow up, trying to discover who they are, and I stunted it with my own fear and ignorance."

I brought one of my hands to his cheek, and he nuzzled closer. "I've never seen this side of you before," I mused.

He laughed. "I guess, after seventeen years of marriage, I still have a few surprises up my sleeve."

"I guess." My voice was soft.

"I'm sorry, T," he whispered and pulled me closer to him as we lay on the bed. I heard the comforting thump of his heart in his chest and pressed my palm against it. Closing my eyes, I relished the sound of it, the strength of it beating, and acknowledged the new growth of his heart in the face of diversity. In it, I found my safe place again.

"I know." I let the calm wash over me and lull me closer to sleep.

———

It took a week for Wren to find the flag.

We heard a little surprised squeal while we were eating breakfast. They ran over to the house and plucked the tiny flag from the front porch.

"Which one of you is responsible for this?" Wren came

closer, waving it at us, trying to suss out the answer. I looked away and sipped on my coffee as John's eyes twinkled.

"I don't have any idea what you're talking about," he proclaimed.

"It wasn't me," I admitted, knowing the act would melt any remaining ice around our daughter's heart.

"Daddy?" Their voice cracked on the last syllable. That's all it took, one tiny rainbow flag on the front of a homemade dollhouse.

The next two weeks passed, and I watched Wren rebuild their relationship with John with college visits and cutthroat Monopoly battles that waged late into the night. I was wary yet hopeful, knowing our family's heartstrings, tenuously stitched together, were still raw and tender from the events of the last few months.

On a Saturday in late September, I was bustling around the kitchen, getting ready for our final farmer's market of the season. Wren boldly walked into the room, rooting around the cabinets for snacks to take in our cooler. At first glance, I did a double-take. Pre-occupied with getting the rest of the soup packaged, I stole glances at their profile. The window light carved out their high cheek-bones and delicate nose where a newly adorned nose ring glinted in the light. I braced for impact, but John looked up at them, took it in, and then clamped his mouth shut. I wasn't so agreeable. I strode right up to Wren, tipping their chin back into the light, examining the jewelry, exasperated.

"What is that?"

"It's a nose ring." Their nonchalant answer was irritating.

"Body modification?" I asked, "Why do you always have to push the envelope?"

"Chillax, Mom. It's just a magnet." They reached up and opened it, and I let out a sigh of relief, smacking my hand over my hammering heart. "But when I'm eighteen, I'm doing all the things. I'm talking tattoos, an industrial, maybe some cheek piercings."

"Don't do that," I begged. "I made 'dis." I waved my hand in front of them. "You're perfect without all those adornments."

"When I'm eighteen, I'll be an adult and it won't be up to you," Wren pushed. "My body, my choice."

John laughed at their audacity. "Kid, you're one of a kind."

"At least, make sure you put those tattoos where you can hide them. You don't know what kind of work you'll end up doing. Make sure you can cover them up with a long sleeve shirt," I advised.

"Your mother is right," John said.

"You guys are a buzzkill," Wren assessed then shrugged their shoulders. "But at least you're consistent."

We loaded up and caravanned over to the market to set up. I had bowls in the cooler for reheating and was going to serve ready-to-eat options along with puff pastry breadsticks and homemade garlicky croutons.

"What do you think about a food truck?" John asked after the booth was set up and just minutes before the biggest group of visitors would come through.

"That seems a little excessive," I said as I kneaded the tight muscles in my back with my hands. "And expensive."

"I don't think it is at all," he stated. "Think how much

easier it would be to cook the food in one place and keep it warm, and then all we'd have to do is drive it to the venue."

"You might have a point," I conceded. Then I cocked my head at him, wondering.

"Say it. I know there's something on your mind."

I smiled. "You know me." I took a step closer, wanting to bridge the gap between us. "It's just… it feels like you're overcompensating a little bit."

The tips of his ears pinked up, and he wore an embarrassed grin. "Maybe. But I believe in you."

My eyes welled up with tears.

"It's time to build something new," he continued. "Let's at least look into it." He edged closer and wrapped his arm around my waist. "You know, we've spent a lifetime already being pulled apart and coming back together." He pulled me in for a hug. "I don't want to do that anymore. It stops here."

I pulled back to look him in the eyes. "I like that. It stops here."

Wren whisked by the booth, rolling their eyes at us. "Gross."

The next hour passed quickly as hundreds of quarts of soup found new homes in the hands of strangers. Wren was front and center, charming the crowd, holding a tray of white paper sample cups, and offering them to passersby. Wren disappeared into the thick of the crowd, and I got distracted serving bowls to hungry people in line.

"Isn't that Sammie?" John remarked, and my head shot up to where he pointed only a few feet away. Sammie was smiling at Wren in the sunshine, basking in the glow of a harmless teenage crush. Almost in slow motion, I watched

Wren rock back and forth on their platforms, daring to inch closer… closer… closer. Even from a distance, I felt it. The undeniable pull, their natural nature bending one toward the other. Distilled to its essence, it was a tender moment of mutual adoration. Their smiles were sweet and genuine, eyes dancing. My heart understood their body language immediately. *You are my favorite person.*

Then Wren jerked back, and I heard them gasp and drop the tray. It clanged when it hit the ground like a bell, and tiny soup samples shot all over the asphalt.

"Get away from my daughter!" Mike shouted.

Every head in the vicinity whipped to see the spectacle. Standing only feet apart, Jennifer and Mike were staring Wren down as Sammie burst into tears and ran away.

John immediately crossed over to Wren in two steps, using his arm to guide them behind him, shielding our daughter from their hate. "Look at me," he said quietly as he grasped both their shaking arms in his and looked into Wren's face. "Go to your mother. I'll handle this." Wren shuffled back to me, and I wrapped my arms around them. With an audience, John held his ground, like he always had, staring down the smaller man. Jennifer and Mike eventually moved along, Jennifer tugging at Mike's arm as the crowd closed behind them. Wren was inconsolable and begged to spend the rest of the afternoon in the car, waiting for us to finish. I handed them my keys and, with a tight smile, served soup until we'd sold out.

THIRTY-FIVE

Sarah was swamped with work in the week leading up to Pride Fest. Souper Duper was going to be one of the food vendors, and I was making a special Love is Love Rainbow Chicken Tortilla Soup, with red and orange peppers, yellow and purple onions, and green celery, served with blue corn tortilla strips. It was a limited edition run along with some of my other best sellers—cheesy broccoli and ham and bean.

Rhyne and Wren made us pride shirts to wear in flamboyant colors, with huge white letters screaming free mom hugs and free dad hugs on the back. Surprisingly, John took it in stride when Wren handed his over to him. They still felt the need to test him.

"So, I'm supposed to hug random people?" he asked. "Isn't that weird?"

"Only if you make it weird," Wren responded, watching for signs of flinching.

"So, we hug a few strangers, what's the harm?" I

asked, and when Wren left, I pulled him aside. "I appreciate your willingness to show Wren how committed you are to talking the talk and walking the walk."

"It's getting easier every time." John then admitted, "But I'm not going to lie, this will be a challenge."

"I think effort is what Wren is looking for. They are forgiving as long as we attempt to acknowledge and use the pronouns and participate in events that are important to them."

"By hugging strangers?"

I laughed. "Yes, even by hugging strangers."

"Did you know in the fifties, gay clubs were raided and people were arrested for being in them? I just watched this documentary last week where two eighty-four-year-old women had been living together for sixty-two years. When they first started dating, they'd hear horror stories from their friends who were arrested during club morality raids. They never officially came out, and no one knew they were gay."

"Come on," he said. "That's hard to believe. Sixty-two years?"

"They lied to their families that they were only friends and splitting the high cost of living in Chicago. To keep up appearances, they would often date men from time to time. When gay marriage was finally passed into law in Illinois, they decided to come out and tell their families and get married."

He thought about it for a long minute.

"Can you imagine perpetuating a lie like that for six decades? When the only thing you're doing wrong is loving someone who loves you back? Having to hide one of the truest parts of yourself to make other people more comfortable?" I asked.

"That's why it's such a monumental decision in anyone's life. It can completely change the trajectory of who they are and who they become. It can be met with hatred, disgust, and isolation. Even now, when we say things have changed drastically from where they were in the fifties, while that is true, there is still so much further we need to go."

"I understand that now," he answered.

"So, I guess what I'm saying is yes, the simple act of offering a dad hug can help heal a tiny sliver of a heart that was destroyed by someone they loved. You never know how much someone is hurting, and I would venture to guess that the LGBTQ+ community has collectively been hurt more than most."

"Okay," he relented, nodding. "I'll do it for Wren. Where are they anyway?" After school, Rhyne and Wren disappeared into their bedroom to work on the "fit" for Pride Fest. It was a deadly serious undertaking that required seventeen trips to the vintage store, about as many Amazon deliveries, and several sketches that were vehemently discussed and then discarded. Crumpled balls of paper that sometimes missed making it into the trash can were littered all over Wren's floor.

"I'm not an athlete, honey! Okay?" Rhyne would sing out and punctuate it with a few dramatic snaps. This time, their lips were a bright fuchsia, and they rocked a black hat reminiscent of *Boy George.*

The night before Pride Fest, Rhyne and Wren descended the stairs into the kitchen, in full feathered showgirl finery, where John and I were slicing and dicing carrots and celery. Massive feather plumes fanned dramatically behind them, both of them wearing ruffled white booty shorts, a tank top, and white patent leather knee-high go-go boots. I don't think either John or I was prepared for the spectacle. Wren cued up dance music at the bottom of the staircase.

"Whoa," was all I could say as Rhyne sashayed across the kitchen floor, then cut to a pose with their hands on their hips and stomped away. "Careful," I warned, fanning the air behind them with a towel to keep the wispy feathers from floating down into the food. "You two need to *slay away* from the carrots," I joked, shooing them out of the kitchen.

The fashion show wasn't quite over. Rhyne executed a second dramatic whipsaw about-face and then fell to the ground, deep into what looked like a painful knee injuring split. Wren let out a loud whoop.

"Ow!" I ran over to them, still laying on the ground with a grin, and offered a hand. "Are you okay, buddy?"

"Mom, get out of the way!" Wren directed, and I stepped back in time to see Rhyne pop right back up and stomp back out to the living room, leaving me utterly confused as to what I'd just witnessed.

"I have no idea what in the hell just happened," John said, shaking his head after the show.

"It's called a drag queen death drop," Wren advised as Rhyne stomped back over, still in character, all proud smiles after their performance.

"I'm at the age when, if I go down like that, there's no way I'm popping back up." I groaned, "My knees just can't take it."

Wren pulled up a video on their phone on YouTube called *Falls and Drag Queen Death Drops*. It was a hysterical compilation of about fifty slips and falls on ice that would cut to the same move we just saw Rhyne execute. Four minutes of precise razor-sharp editing had us all laughing so hard our stomachs hurt.

"What in the world?' John was still in shock and huddled closer to watch it a second time.

"Sweet Jesus," I said. "I'd be covered in bruises."

"Thigh-high boots will cover most of those," Rhyne offered, tapping their temple. "Modern problems require modern solutions."

"You guys are too much," John said.

"Just enough," Rhyne corrected with a smirk, and then the kids disappeared back into Wren's room.

"I have to say, this house has a lot more life now," John mused. "That Rhyne's a character."

"Agreed." I stirred the pots of vegetables and measured out quarts of chicken stock. "How are you doing with all this change? I know their energy is a lot to handle and something you're not used to. You can always escape out to the garage, you know."

He thought about it for a second, and I saw a shadow pass his face as he remembered the times he would sequester himself out there, especially after deployments when he was struggling to reintegrate back into our lives.

"Honestly?"

"Yep. That's what we do now."

"I *don't* understand it, but I gotta say I'm enjoying it. You never know what's tumbling around inside the brains of those two knuckleheads. They seem to bring out the best in each other."

To confirm what he was saying, we heard squeals of laughter from Wren's bedroom.

"They just get each other and have from the moment they met. Wren is lucky to have a friend like Rhyne."

THIRTY-SIX

P ride Fest was blessed with a picture-perfect, blue-sky day and Indian Summer weather that was a balmy seventy-four degrees. The booth John researched and purchased for our stand was packed into the trunk of his SUV. He'd already contacted a custom food truck builder out of Chattanooga and was pouring over spreadsheets of financials and schematics of the truck design. We'd gone to the bank and secured a loan together, a far cry from the visit to the bank I'd made alone right after Sarah took us in. I still hung on to the account; the difference was he knew about it and supported my decision to keep it separate. I also had my own credit card now. I was never going to be in the dark about finances again. Just knowing it was tucked away in my purse gave me the peace of mind I needed to feel secure.

After making endless trips to the cars to fill them with our coolers packed with pre-packaged take-home soup bowls, the four-burner warming station, and huge stainless-steel kettles filled with ready-to-serve soup, I was becoming an expert at the game of *Tetris* required to get packed for an event.

"Whew!" I leaned back to stretch my lower back muscles. "I'm exhausted. It's going to be a long day. I've already got eight thousand steps in today."

"Just think, next year, we'll have the food truck, T."

I nodded and wiped away a trickle of sweat with the back of my hand. "That day can't come soon enough."

I'd never worked a live event this size before, and I was anxious about it. I'd made endless checklists and remembered to stop by the bank for a huge stash of cash I tucked into a locked metal box with a little key that dangled from my wrist. Thankfully, we had plenty of help to unload. Sarah met us there early, having to be on-site already for last-minute preparations and to help get volunteers organized. At the entrance, a massive rainbow balloon arch flanked temporary fencing, creating a makeshift tunnel to guide the flow of foot traffic. It wasn't the garish type you'd see at middle school dances. It was art. An actual sculpture with balloons of different sizes combined in clusters that morphed from one end of the rainbow spectrum to the other, draped in long, elegant swags down to the ground.

"Is that everything?" Sarah asked with a big smile.

"I think so," I answered. "Thanks for your help. I know you have a million things going on today."

"Always ready to help a friend." She grinned. "Besides, I've been here for hours, fretting about little things. Now that the volunteers are in position, it should be smooth sailing from here on out."

Rhyne sauntered up to Sarah and casually draped an arm around her. "Mommies?" They playfully dangled the question at us, a glimmer of mischief flickered in their eyes.

"It feels like you two are buttering us up for something," Sarah declared.

Feigning shock, Rhyne walked away dejectedly to where Wren was standing. They plucked the keys off the table and jingled them together. Then both hammed it up, resting their chins on their clasped hands while they batted their eyelashes at us.

"What is it?" Sarah asked.

"Moms, you *know* we love you, and this is a busy day for you both, but Wren and I need to be free to mingle with our people," Rhyne reasoned, pleading for their early work release. "It's time for our Cinderella at the ball moment, and we need to go home and get ready."

Sarah laughed. "Saw that coming a mile away. Theresa, are you okay with that?" I knew she was consumed with all the last-minute details being the event emcee and coordinator entailed. At her hip, a phone rang, and she turned away and took the call, leaving the decision up to me.

"Alright," I caved. Between myself and John, I was hoping we had enough help to work the booth. "But you two stick together. From what I hear, Sarah is expecting a record crowd. I want you to check in every two hours here at the booth. Got it?"

They groaned.

"It's non-negotiable. Don't make me run up on stage and page you from the microphone in between acts."

"You wouldn't dare." Rhyne was aghast at the idea.

"Oh, she would," Wren answered for me and turned back to Rhyne. "We should accept her terms. It's the best deal we're gonna get."

Rhyne let out a squeal, and they clapped their hands together before running to the car to head home before I changed my mind. Knowing it would take them hours for makeup alone, John and I organized the booth and the table, setting out mason jars filled with spoons and napkins. We finished just in time as the first visitors began to file in.

———

I don't know what I expected a Pride event to look like. I was thinking that maybe we'd see a few rainbows and a smattering of elegantly dressed fashion-forward guests, but when the crowd started to pour in through the arches, it was all the color that captivated me. It was the saucy t-shirts shouting "Wild Feminist" and "Wish You Were Queer" in rainbow colors and "Come as You Are" in simple black and white. There were men in rompers and scarves, wearing heels with chiseled calves and faces full of makeup with dramatic lashes. The crowd surged with energy and a festive attitude of freedom on the one day a year a collection of outcasts could come together and celebrate life. A lot could be learned here. Acceptance in its truest form, all were welcomed with open arms.

Music pulsed from speakers close to our booth. The opening act was belting out covers from 1980s bands. I recognized a little George Michael and some Bee Gees. At the booth, hungry festival goers kept us busy at a steady clip. We shoved handfuls of cash into the lockbox, and I was already envisioning our purple truck with the logo and lime green awning set up for Pride Fest next year.

Big, puffy clouds began to collect in the sky, giving us a break from the sun and making it even more picture-perfect. I couldn't remember a more spectacular late September day. When I wasn't serving food, I was people watching. Pride Fest was a smorgasbord for the eyes, awash in bright colors and decked out to the hilt. Peaceful crowds gathered together, rocking to the music and dancing. A t-shirt cannon blasted t-shirts out to the crowd in between musical acts Sarah was charged with introducing on stage. Her throaty voice resonated far and wide throughout the venue with the jokes Rhyne and Wren wrote for her.

A festive parade kicked off the day, and elaborate theatrical floats featuring musical acts and drag queens drifted by, throwing out fistfuls of colorful condoms. John was as curious as I was, but he struggled to figure out where to put his eyes. We saw for the first time, men holding hands and kissing each other on the mouth. He got an eyeful of slow dancing women paired with women, men paired with men, swaying to the music like any couple in love would. I caught his eye and smiled, knowing this was not anywhere near his comfort zone, but he was trying. He was doing the real work to leave his fears at the door and accept what was in front of him without the need to pass judgment.

"Can I get one of those?' the next man in line said to John. He was delicate, a gorgeous twink, barely five-foot-tall, all legs and elbows with perfectly coiffed hair styled in a sky-high platinum pompadour. Streaks of rainbow glitter covered his eyebrows and traced down his face. His chest was bare, and he was wearing what could be considered quite possibly the tiniest shorts ever created, held in place by a pair of rainbow suspenders. His skin was like chiseled ivory, almost translucent.

"I'm sorry, what flavor can I get you?"

"Oh." He looked down sheepishly. "I meant your shirt. It says free dad hugs."

John instantly reddened. A flash of fear in his eyes made him freeze, but he recovered quickly. "Oh yeah, it does. I've been working so hard, I forgot all about it." He walked from behind the booth and opened his arms slowly like a statue, and I pressed my lips together and looked away. The man teetered into his arms, wearing five-inch stilettos. Even in the heels, he was tiny, only reaching the top of John's neck. The hug was awkward, but John fought his way through it.

"What about me?" I asked, turning around and hiking a thumb to my shirt. "Fancy a mom hug?" He smiled and flew into my arms. I squeezed him tight, then he pulled away.

"My dad disowned me when I came out at sixteen." His confession sucked the breath out of my lungs, and John's jaw tensed.

"It was great to get a Dad hug, but they are as awkward as I remembered," he murmured with a teasing smile that made John's cheeks pink. "I'm Simon. I feel, since we've gotten so close today, we should probably know each other's first name at least." He held out one delicate hand to me, his nails long and painted fire engine red.

"Fair enough, I'm John." John shook Simon's delicate

hand, tipped back at the wrist, that disappeared into John's larger one.

"I'm sorry that happened to you."

Simon shot us a winning smile, his teeth white and perfect with skin so healthy it glowed. His voice was higher pitched and soft. "Don't you worry about me one little second. Everything turned out as it should. If I'd stayed there, I'd still be miserable in Ohio, working some dead-end job. I would have never made it here." He spread his arms wide behind us. "This is as close to happy as I deserve. I get to live the life I want to live. I don't have to hide who I am anymore. I am surrounded by people who love and accept me."

"Maybe someday your dad will change," I offered, ever hopeful. John had come around, so maybe Simon's father would, too.

"It's too late for us. He got sick last year, and I had it all in my head that we were going to have this big come to Jesus moment, where he'd be looking over all the decisions he'd made in his life and all the regrets he had and would finally love me the way I am."

I felt my throat choke when John asked, "Did you get it?"

Simon's head shook sadly. "I didn't. And then he was gone. That man hated me right up until his last dying breath."

"That's terrible," I commiserated.

"Oh, honey, I made peace with it. You know, lots of therapy and lots of self-forgiveness and exploration."

"He's the one who missed out," John said.

Simon choked up this time, nodding. "He did. He

missed out on seeing the person I'd become because he was too busy hoping I'd transform into something else."

"One more for the road?" John asked, opening his arms wide, and Simon squealed and wrapped them around John. I snapped a photo.

"I have to tell our daughter your story."

"Please, it's the only thing that gives us our power back." He gave a little wave, and then we watched him dissolve into the crowd as John wrapped his arm around my waist.

"Sometimes, I feel like God sends me people to teach me things at the exact right moment I need them," he mused.

"I think that's how He works."

———

Two hours later, the streets were filled, and the headliner act, a twelve-piece big band, took the stage. After the concert would be our last rush of the night, and my feet were screaming. I sat down heavily on the empty coolers and yawned. A few minutes later, I felt John's warm hands on my back. His strong thumbs dug into my shoulder blades, massaging out the tension that felt permanently lodged there after eight hours on our feet.

"Don't ever stop that," I begged, finally taking a moment to relax. "I think we might have hit a Souper Duper sales record today." The lockbox was stuffed full of cash, and I'd swiped so many credit cards on the reader, I'd developed a small blister on my hand.

"I was hoping you'd say that," John said behind me.

On stage, a diva behind the mic sported a bouffant

bright green wig and all the sparkles, but her voice was a deep powerhouse. She bellowed into the microphone, "We're the weather girls, and have we got news for you!" And the crowd went wild. On stage, umbrellas in a rainbow of colors opened and closed in tune to the music as the first few notes on the keyboard tapped out on *It's Raining Men*. It started in a low range, gathering speed as background singers chimed in, energizing the crowd whose arms were in the air. Twirling and dancing, the crowd was enjoying being alive. It was an energetic wave of rainbow color that surged. I knew, somewhere in the thick of it, Wren and Rhyne were bobbing and bopping up and down to the music. The energy was invigorating, pulsing, and it compelled you to dance.

Then the band morphed into the Abba hit, *Dancing Queen*. The trilling sound of the keys on the piano being swiped by an Elton John-meets-Liberace look-alike made the crowd shift into swaying and twirling, singing the words out in unison in a massive chorus. The wave of sound from the raw power of all those voices together made my chest thrum. In the crowd, hands raised, there wasn't a single wallflower in the bunch. Today was a day about self-expression, where people were free to be who they were. No more hiding. Unabashedly enjoying the concert. Carefree.

Even in my exhausted state, I couldn't help myself and got lost in it, too. My shoulders shimmied, and then I stood, unable to sit still any longer. The desire to be part of this colorful chorus took over. I found the words of the lyrics somewhere in my mind and joined in full tilt with the crowd, singing with them. Singing at full volume and enjoying every second. I felt alive.

Dancing in a circle, John twirled me around awkwardly and pulled me back to him. I loved seeing this softer side of him now. Little pieces of my soldier I thought he'd left in Kuwait and Bosnia were still there, and every now and then, one would surprise me with its appearance. We swayed to the music, and he twirled me again.

Then one manicured hand stroked the piano keys, and a person with the biggest afro I'd ever seen channeled Gloria Gaynor and started singing, *I Will Survive.* The crowd joined in, the wave of sound becoming so powerful it was electrifying. Their unofficial anthem being voiced was a kind of religious experience.

"They sure know how to throw a party," John said with a smile as he pulled me in for a sweet kiss. That's when I heard the first pop, rapidly followed by another. Confused, I felt John stiffen in my arms. He knew. He knew exactly what it was.

"Get down," he demanded, shielding me with his body. "Run to the car and do not leave it until we get there. You understand? Call the police."

Stunned, I wanted to argue, but another quick succession of shots was fired, like black cats on the 4th of July. Then the screaming began, and pure pandemonium broke out.

"Wren! Rhyne!" I tried to pull away and hammered him with my fists. "I can't... I won't leave without them. I'm coming with you."

Having only a split second to decide, he said, "Okay, but you listen to me. Whatever orders I give, you follow. No questions."

I nodded and we ran headfirst into the terrified crowd

that was rushing to the exit in the opposite direction. Desperate to fight the tide of humans scrambling for cover, I clung to John's hand. More shots rang out. John pulled me in close to him. "Run in a zig-zag pattern. It's hard to hit a moving target, and don't you dare stop." He guided me further into the crowd as we screamed their names. I searched every face as they ran by in a panic, afraid to look at the bodies on the ground. They were being stumbled over as people raced to find the exit, their costumes and heels impeding the process, tripping them up and sending them reeling.

"Wren!"

"Rhyne!"

On the ground, tattered and dirty feathers lay. Another round of shots rang out, and two more bodies dropped to the ground as John scanned the area.

"There!" He pointed to a window in a hotel across from the venue. "The shooter is up there. Keep running." He shouted our daughter's name, yanking me further into the crowd.

"Wren!" Screaming, my throat was hoarse, my stomach in knots and nauseous. I hunkered down to catch my breath as my eyes scanned the faces of the frantic rush of the masses that raced past me to safety.

Around us, it was like a war zone. Bullets kept coming, and I knew fireworks would never hold the same beauty for me again. The never-ending shrieking, the ringing in my ears, and the color of blood red now overshadowed the rest of the rainbow. Bodies crumpled to the ground as chaos continued. It was a concert of blood-curdling screams and heart-wrenching sobs. A cacophony of utter terror that ripped out my heart.

Another wave of humanity crashed into us as we forced a path against the tide. More shots rang out, and a man ran by me before dropping to the ground, a fresh bloom of red sweeping across the pristine white of his shorts. Then finally, blessedly, sirens, trilling through the darkness, piercing through the screams. Blue and red lights flashed as they raced toward the scene. Ambulances, fire trucks, and squad cars, all with sirens on and lights flashing.

"Wren!" We screamed their name together, willing for them to respond. "Rhyne!"

"Mom?" I heard a voice, and my heart leaped to my throat.

"There!" I shouted to John. "Wren's okay. They're okay." Rhyne and Wren raced toward us. They bowled us over in relief, clinging to us while trembling in fear.

"We have to find cover and protection. NOW!" John shouted at us. Yanking Rhyne by the hand, he led us to an alley, scanning and scanning for threats as I assessed the kids who were clearly in shock.

I held Wren out in front of me, eyes searching for wounds, inspecting their skin inch by inch. "Are you hurt?"

"No."

"You have to stay here," John shouted at us. "We don't know if they've gotten the gunman yet." I strained to listen, pulling the St. Christopher's medal out and praying for the madness to stop. I was grateful my family unit was still intact.

"My mom," Rhyne cried. Their eyes scanned the carnage in a panic.

"We'll find her," I promised, and for a brief second, I

wondered if that was a lie. "We have to look for Sarah," I said to John.

"I'll go. I need you to stay here. Take care of the kids until we know it's safe." One more shot and then an awful silence that filled with a wailing I will never forget. I hugged the kids tight to me, all of us sobbing. The sounds of agony surrounded us, ragged breaths being drawn, and my heart broke knowing some people were drawing their last. Human carnage was everywhere. Ten long minutes elapsed where I struggled to catch my breath, a heavy weight stuck on my chest. The children were okay, but where were John and Sarah?

Finally, from a megaphone, a calm and steady voice offered words of reassurance. "The suspect has been apprehended. You are safe. Please exit the venue slowly, and if you or a loved one requires medical attention, we have a triage center set up at the entrance."

John ran back, this time with a beleaguered Sarah, her eyes wild. Rhyne ran at her and tackled her, sobbing. They clung to each other in relief.

"I have to help the first responders," John said, "but we have to get the kids out of here." We followed him, dodging bodies on the ground, seeing others limp to the ambulance triage station. Halfway to the car, John stopped and gasped, recognizing a face we'd met hours earlier. It was Simon. He was a still form, unmoving on the ground.

"T, I can't leave him here." John kneeled next to him. Simon was shot in the torso, and John pulled his shirt off and pressed it down into the wound to stop the bleeding.

I nodded watching him press his fingers to Simon's throat.

"He has a pulse, but he needs help now."

"Simon?" He shook him. "Open your eyes for me, Simon. Someone special is here to meet you. It's my daughter." He was pale and still, the red in his chest blossoming bright against the stark white of his skin. "Stay with me, Simon."

John reached down and scooped him up easily, running to the nearest ambulance. "He needs a doctor." The crew pulled out a stretcher, and John laid him down on it.

"What hospital are you taking him to?" John asked.

"County," the attendant answered and tucked him into the cab of the ambulance. Another of the crew slammed the door shut and sped away.

"Take the kids home, T," John said. "I'll catch a ride with Sarah."

Sarah was grief-stricken and dazed. "Are you okay?" I asked and immediately hated the word choice." She shook her head no and began to cry.

"Are you whole?" John reworded, and she nodded.

"We have to help," she finally decided after a long sigh, digging deep. "Take the kids. We'll text when we know more."

"What about the booth?"

"Leave it. Grab the cash box and head home. We'll worry about the rest later." I nodded, following his directions.

"Let's go, guys." I pulled them closer to me and led them to the car, while the chaos around me filled with cries for help, and an influx of firefighters and medical professionals worked on the most critical cases. I settled the kids in the car as it began to rain, washing away my tears and leaving me shivering. I took one last look before I got in the car to drive the kids home. The balloon arch was destroyed, shredded into pieces that bobbed up in tufts while other parts collapsed under the sharp spike of heels that ran through it. I knew we were the lucky ones. The ones left behind, scarred by events that would haunt our memories forever. Sheets were draped over at least ten others who weren't as lucky.

THIRTY-SEVEN

ours later, we met John at County. He was sitting in a chair in the waiting room, picking apart a Styrofoam cup. His face was filthy, and he wore a t-shirt I didn't recognize that was covered in blood and dirt. His face was haggard, sporting a full-on five o'clock shadow, and sitting next to him was a dazed Sarah. She rested her head on the wall behind her, eyes closed. Seeing their mother, Rhyne ran to her seat and sat next to her. Rhyne was barely recognizable after a shower and swimming in John's sweatpants and a t-shirt. It was the first time I'd seen Rhyne without a trace of makeup. Their face was pale and gray, and their usual jovial expression empty and blank.

"Hey, you," I whispered to John, trying to stay quiet in case Sarah was asleep. John got to his feet and pulled Wren closer to him for a hug. He clung to their trembling figure as a deep sob clawed its way up Wren's chest and heaved out into the crowded waiting room that was filled with other survivors and terrified family members. I wrapped my arms around them both and squeezed my eyes shut. Every room in the ER was filled to capacity with the lesser urgent cases filling the chairs around us.

I heard the *whoosh* of the automatic sliding door open and a shrieking wail. Turning, I registered the deeper voice speaking to the nurse behind the desk, who was fielding phone calls and distraught visitors with care.

"Our daughter was brought here," Mike demanded as he relayed the information to the nurse. "Samantha Reilly." His hands were balled into fists, his face red and tight. Jennifer's eyes were wild, scanning the room. Compassion surged in my chest as I remembered feeling the same desperation when we were running through the crowd just hours before, desperate to set our gaze on Wren and Rhyne.

Hearing her name, Wren stiffened and pulled away. Seeing Sammie's parents rattled them, and their eyes darted over to me, panicked. "Mom?" Their voice cracked. "Dad?" I felt their legs give out and John swept Wren into his arms as a chair was offered from a woman with a buzz cut wearing a sling and waiting to be seen. He gingerly placed Wren in it, and I bent down to their level, holding their shaking hands in mine.

"I'll be right back, kiddo," he said, then turned on his heel, heading to the nurses' station to get information. The nurse said something I couldn't make out, but the new information made Jennifer collapse and fall into John's arms. Beside me, Wren began to sob. "No, Mom. She wasn't there. There has to be some kind of mistake."

I didn't know what to say. Wren's mind was grasping at straws, and I didn't have the heart to reason with them. If Sammie's parents were here, without a doubt, she was in this hospital.

"I begged her to sneak out for Pride Fest, but she was afraid. I was so angry at her." Wren began to wring their hands. "I told her if she wasn't willing to take the risk to be with me, then maybe we needed to not see each other anymore."

"Honey, you cannot blame yourself."

"But she would have never been there if I didn't say those things. It was so selfish. I just wanted to be with my girlfriend at Pride Fest. I didn't know it would end up like this. Oh, God," they wailed. "I think I'm going to be sick," Wren warned, and I popped up and pulled a blue biohazard bag from the dispenser on the wall in the nick of time, seconds before Wren retched into it. I rubbed their back in clockwise circles, making soothing sounds, but they would not be comforted. I wrapped my arm around them, but Wren shook it off. Their eyes were glued on their father, who was speaking to Mike after settling them into chairs across the room.

A few minutes later, he walked toward us, and I tried to decode his expression. He was stone-faced and, with an exhausted sigh, sat down heavily in the chair next to us.

"She's in surgery," he offered Wren, who hiccupped into their hand. "Two gunshots to the chest. She snuck out of the house to attend Pride Fest. Jennifer and Mike had no idea until an officer showed up on their doorstep."

"That's terrible." I sighed, wishing I could go to Jennifer and offer support. I watched her pace, wearing a path up and down the hallway, mumbling to herself. Her arms were wrapped around her waist. A stunned Mike sat statue-still, glaring at us from across the room. His hatred was palpable even from a distance.

Sarah's eyes opened, and seeing Rhyne, she clung to

them as fresh sobs wracked her body. "I can't believe it. Do we know how many yet?"

"The first reports are saying ten."

"Ten." Sara pressed her face into her hands in despair. "Gone. Ten lovely, beautiful souls wiped out forever."

"That number would probably be higher if you and John hadn't been on hand to help." I tried to bring her comfort, but she shook it off.

"This world is so filled with hate," she mumbled, and I considered what to say. I couldn't disagree.

I turned to John. "You both look exhausted. There is nothing more we can do here. You should head home and take a shower."

"I'm not leaving," Wren demanded next to me, and I didn't have the heart to argue.

"We can stay," I offered. "Let me walk your dad out, and we'll wait for Sammie to get out of surgery." Satisfied, Wren nodded and settled into the chair, biting their thumbnail.

I stood and walked with John to the door. He made it to the car before he crumbled, pulling me into his arms, and I felt his body quake. I'd only seen my husband cry on three occasions in our entire marriage.

"What is it?" I asked gently.

"Simon," John choked out. "He didn't make it."

"Oh, honey." I pulled him back into my arms. "I'm so sorry."

"I didn't even know he existed twenty-four hours ago. How does a person come into your life in such a short time and have such an impact?"

I exhaled, searching for words to comfort, but they

didn't come. There were none to offer. It was unexplainable, a heinous act of destruction and hate.

"He didn't deserve to die." John's lips trembled as he struggled to regain his composure. "None of them did. It could have been Wren and Rhyne under those sheets." He shivered. "God, if something happens to Sammie…" He stopped himself. He didn't need to fill in the blanks, because I already had a million times in my head since I heard the news. I knew the devastation it would wage on Wren. I was terrified of having to cross that bridge, pleading with God and whatever saints who would listen to avoid it.

"I know," I offered. It was all I could say.

"You need to get back in there with Wren," John finally said, wiping his eyes with the back of his hand and pinching the bridge of his nose. "I'll be back after a shower. Call me if anything happens."

I nodded and started back to the hospital, glancing up at the darkened sky filling with twinkling stars now that the rain had passed. Stopped dead in my tracks, I marveled as a single shooting star zinged across the dark navy of the night sky. Simon. I just knew it was Simon.

THIRTY-EIGHT

A few hours later, John was back by our side. The waiting room had thinned out, and one of the rooms was dedicated to informing next of kin. One by one, hopeful faces were pulled into it, only to have their world destroyed in mere minutes.

On the television that hovered close to the ceiling, we huddled with a small crowd for an update after reading the ticker. "Twelve slain by sniper at Pride Fest."

"Twelve?" Sarah cried out, inconsolable. I wrapped my arm around her shaking body. "So many."

The anchor, a woman with a deeply sympathetic voice and a razor-sharp bob began, "A festival about love and acceptance was the scene of the deadliest act of gun violence in Eden Prairie history. Last night was a devastating blow to our local LGBTQ+ community. A sniper from the fourteenth floor of The Plaza opened fire, killing twelve and wounding dozens more before turning a gun on himself."

A photo of a bespectacled bald man wearing military

fatigues popped on the screen. "The gunman has been identified. Shawn Michael Douglas had been a guest at The Plaza during the last week. More details will be coming as events develop. Victims' names have not been released as officials work to notify the next of kin. If you have a loved one who is missing and are thought to have attended Pride Fest, officials are asking you to call 599-213-9827. We will bring more details to you when they are available. Our thoughts and prayers go out to the families affected by this tragedy."

I pulled my coin purse out and offered it to Wren. "Why don't you go grab some snacks?" Grateful to have something to do, Wren walked away. From my chair, I studied Jennifer. Her hair hung limply and her hands were clasped under her chin, her lips forming fervent words I was certain were prayers. Next to her, Mike sat stiffly, staring directly in front of him. Every time a doctor padded out in scrubs, he'd pop up filled with hope, only to be forced to sit back down seconds later.

"Let's go talk to them," I decided, "while Wren is out of earshot."

"Are you sure?" John was wary.

"They were our closest friends," I said. "If it was me over there waiting on an update about Wren, I'd welcome any support."

"Okay," he agreed, standing, and reached out for my hand. I grasped it and slowly walked over, studying Mike's expression as we got closer for signs of anger, grateful it had been replaced by exhaustion and fear.

"No updates yet?" John asked the obvious question, already knowing the answer. Mike just shook his head no and rubbed his weary eyes with his palms.

"Is there anything we can do for you? Grab you a coffee or something to eat?" I asked gently.

"I can't eat anything right now," Jennifer mumbled. "Not until we know Sammie's going to be alright."

Mike let out a long sigh. "I guess it's better to be gay and alive than dead and straight." The statement was cold, and next to him, Jennifer recoiled like she'd been physically slapped.

"How can you say that when our daughter is in the ER right now fighting for her life?"

John sat in the seat next to him, and I saw Wren walking back down the hall, arms full of chips and sodas. Their eyes widened as they got closer, seeing us sitting together.

"Any news?" Wren asked, their voice twisting up in a hopeful tone that, in the midst of all the wreckage, made tears tingle at my lashes.

"Not yet, honey."

"Can we pray for her?" Wren asked. "I lit a candle in the chapel for her and the twelve victims."

Jennifer reached her hand out to Wren, a tentative gesture that I knew took incredible inner strength. Wren pulled her to her feet, and Mike softened enough to stand. We formed a circle, holding hands as Wren began.

"Dear Father, we ask you to bless the doctors and nurses that are working on Sammie right now and guide their swift hands. Heal her and restore her. Don't let her become another casualty in this war of hate. We all love Sammie and need her to return to our lives." I reached out a hand to squeeze Wren's shoulder, and their voice cracked. "I can't live without her here. She's my best friend and my first love. I'll make whatever promise I need to make if you'll let her survive," Wren bargained. "Even if it means never seeing her again. I'll stay away. Whatever it takes. I just want her to be okay."

I felt the *whoosh* of air, and a surgeon pulled a surgical hat off her head and stretched her back while cracking her knuckles.

"Samantha Reilly?" she asked, and we huddled over to where she was. Jennifer grasped Mike's hand, her shoulders tight.

"She made it through surgery, but she's still in critical condition. We were able to remove two bullets from her chest. They missed her aorta by half an inch. She's very lucky. The next few hours will be touch and go, but she's young and strong, and we have every hope she is going to make a full recovery. She's being moved to the ICU soon. You can see her in a few hours."

Wren collapsed on the floor in a relieved heap, sobbing. I bent down to pull them back to their, feet tears obscuring my vision.

"Thank you, doctor." Mike's voice wavered as he shook the doctor's hand, who strode back to the automatic door and disappeared down the hall. "Thank God!" he declared as he clung to his wife. His eyes squeezed shut as tears leaked from their corners and they rocked side to side.

The hope returned to Jennifer's eyes. "That's amazing news!" I beamed up at her, letting go of the tension from the last few times we'd seen each other.

Jennifer nodded and swept me up into a hug, and I hugged her back. It's easy to find forgiveness in your heart when faced with the reality of losing a child, and I never was one to hold on to anger.

ONE YEAR LATER

"You ready to take this thing out for its inaugural spin?" John asked while I was preoccupied running through the checklist.

"Ladles, dish soap, napkins." I paged through the list, scanning for missed checkmarks.

The food truck was a dream that had now become a reality and was parked in our driveway.

"This thing cost more than our first house," I mused, and John agreed. It had been hard to stomach the initial quote. $172,000! It felt indulgent and selfish, knowing that money could fund a myriad of other things, vacations, an addition to the house, or our retirement. It was a gamble. There were three sleepless nights as we tossed and turned, deliberating over the pros and cons in our minds. I found endless ways to talk myself out of it. John found endless ways to justify the expense.

He argued, "You spent almost twenty years of your life giving me the freedom to chase my dream, and you never once complained. You raised our kid practically on your own. It's high time I get the chance to return the favor."

His earnest words melted my heart and the rest of the ice that shielded it. It was the act that solidified his commitment to our family. It was the final gesture that restored our trust fully, and I dared to let myself dream again. To see the happy future he'd promised me when he got down on one knee in our twenties, when decades spooled out before us and we had no clue how life would test us. God, we had been through it together and had come out the other side, not unscathed, but beautifully broken and skillfully restored. Our marriage had become our most prized possession now that we had the newly discovered knowledge of its frailty and its strength.

I claimed my seat next to him, and he turned the key. "She purrs like a kitten," he declared.

"She should for $172,000!" I exclaimed. "How do we know she's a she? Maybe she's non-binary!"

He laughed. "Still worth it." He leaned over to kiss me before shifting it into drive. "If we fill our calendar with festivals, we'll make the initial investment back in two years, and then this baby is a profit machine." His faith in me restored my own, and I felt myself step into a new place of contentment and love with my life. A steadfast enduring love that had been tested and had overcome the greatest of obstacles.

"Wren is so nervous," I mentioned. Sarah asked Wren to speak at Pride Fest. They were observing the first anniversary of the shooting, the deadliest act of terror in Minnesota history. At first, there was talk of canceling the event altogether, but it was Sarah who led the impassioned plea to the city leaders. Her rousing speech in front of the

City of Eden Prairie's city council meeting had been televised and was the most well-attended city council meeting in a solid year. Arm in arm with Rhyne, Wren, and an army of allies and members of the LGBTQ+ community, she stood and spoke with conviction for those who lost their lives. She demanded the chance to memorialize the twelve brilliant lives cut short, to pay their respects, and to gather as a community to grieve the act and celebrate their survival. In a vote of six to five, they were granted a permit for the event.

John navigated our food truck into its booth space, parallel parking the beast and relying on mirrors to navigate. He'd insisted on a spot he'd carefully chosen for its unobstructed view closest to the edge of the event to ensure a rapid exit if the need ever arose again. Combat parking. It was in his blood and one of the ways he took care of us.

Once in place, I opened the window and John set up the purple and lime green awning, cranking it with a hand crank that was clipped to the inside of the door.

"Open for business," he declared, setting out a handwritten folding sign that listed our flavors and hours. He glanced at his watch with a smile. "All of thirty seconds to set up. I think we're going to love this thing."

"Let's go find Wren," I said, and he nodded, locking the door behind us. A small line started to gather at the curb that John addressed.

"I'm so sorry, but our daughter is giving the welcoming address. We'll be open for business at noon. Please come back and see us then."

We walked toward the main stage, and at the entrance, twelve massive white butterflies standing over seven feet tall flanked either side of the aisle. In front of each one was a stone-carved tag. We passed two before John stopped in front of a stone marker labeled "Simon Sturgis." John looked down, and I felt him pull away like he often did when his Army memories fought to resurface. My mind drifted to Simon, who just one year ago was a vibrant lesson in pure love for us both. I squeezed John's arm, and he jumped and swiped at his eyes. Pulling me closer, he whispered, "I hope his soul is free. I hope he's dancing on a cloud somewhere, content and feeling nothing but love."

We navigated to the front looking for Wren, who wasn't answering texts. "They're probably running through their speech with Rhyne," John offered in explanation. "The welcome address is in ten minutes." People began to shuffle in, a quiet respectful crowd clad head-to-toe in white. All the vibrant colors from the prior year had been sacrificed to honor the loved ones lost. Security was heightened, and the police presence was strong, though they remained back and allowed the crowd to congregate. Tears were shed as participants filed in, awestruck by the sheer size and beauty of the butterflies, reconnecting with old friends and mourning those who had been lost. The party atmosphere was replaced with a more pensive, somber tone.

Ten minutes later, we stood shoulder to shoulder with scores of men and women. Families pushing strollers with children. We clung to each other as Sarah took to the stage to a wave of applause.

"Welcome to a very special Pride Fest." She paused. "We want to open this year's ceremony with a moment of silence. I will read and we will get the chance to acknowledge those precious lives we lost and those who were wounded just one year ago. I want to commend you for pushing past your fear and coming together for our community to heal. Whether you are a member of the community or an ally, you are welcome here. Thank you for being present."

A gong was rolled out, and a man dressed in a white flowing robe and a stunning pair of white feathered angel wings stood next to it with a mallet, waiting for Sarah to continue. "I will now read each name."

The man swept his arm through the air and struck it, and a somber wave of sound rippled through the crowd.

"Mal Cardone."

After a long pause, he rang the gong again.

"Brendan Williams."

Another reverberating tone from the gong.

"Simon Sturgis." I squeezed John's hand and he looked at his feet, pressing his lips together.

Sarah continued, her voice strong and unwavering as she called out the rest of the names of the fallen. A solid minute of silence was so well-observed that you could hear a pin drop, and in the distance, a baby wailed.

"We are survivors!" Sarah declared. "We will not back down in fear. We will not let a bully destroy our lives with their selfish demands."

The crowd began to applaud, and Sarah waited for silence once again.

"I will now read the names of our survivors, who we ask to join us on stage with their allies."

"Thomas Conor." Soft music began to build as Sarah read the names.

"Samantha Reilly." An obviously nervous Mike and

stiff Jennifer flanked Sammie as she walked across the stage. Twenty-two more names were said, and the music ended as thunderous applause began and only strengthened for a full minute.

After it had calmed down, Wren walked out onto the stage. Wearing white coveralls and high-top Converse shoes, their hair was twisted into a mohawk of white-tipped spikes, with white candy bracelets covering their left arm. Seeing them take the stage, my heart began to flutter and swell.

"Now, it is time to hear from the next generation. To pass the torch to those who will continue our fight for acceptance and equality. I'd like to introduce someone who has become like a second child to me: Wren Churchill."

Applause thundered again, this time with whoops of joy and excitement.

In their shaking hand, Wren held a piece of paper. They spoke into the microphone with a strong, clear voice.

"We remember." They stopped and glanced up, their eyes connecting with John, who beamed up at them with absolute pride. "Today, we remember the eyes that forever closed, the smiles that vanished, the dreams that died. The arms that won't hug, the legs that cannot dance, the joy that won't be celebrated."

Tears sprung to the corners of my eyes. "We pick up the shattered remains of our angels, piece by piece, carrying slivers of them forever in our hearts. Grateful for the sacrifice of our twelve brothers and sisters, we look forward to the day we are reunited with them. Not a single life was taken in vain. Not a single one of these souls will be forgotten. Their names have been carved into the chambers of our hearts forever." I swiped at the tears falling down my face as I heard the collective sniffles around me. Couples clung to each other, all forever changed by an unfathomable loss.

"We honor them by living our truth more deeply. By having the courage to step into the people we were born to be, lighting the way for those who will come behind us. Offering an arm back to help the next person find their own courage within. While we have suffered a devastating loss, we will not allow it to chase us back into the closet from fear. We will stand here together, united by our right to love the one our heart is called to love. Nothing about us needs to change. It is the world that does, and we will be out there in it, inspiring that change from the inside."

The crowd erupted in applause, and John stuck his fingers in his mouth and whistled a long, sharp sound that disappeared into the ocean of love, crashing onto the stage where the survivors stood with their families. Wave after wave ebbed and flowed, and we stood shoulder to shoulder, clapping our hands until they were pink and stinging.

Two minutes later, the first musical act took the stage, and the sadness began to lift. John and I picked our way back to the food truck and began to serve the line that formed. Twenty minutes later, we got our first break and heard a timid knock on the back door. Unlocking it, I swung it wide, seeing Rhyne and Wren outside waiting.

"Oh, honey. I don't think I've ever been more proud of you," I gushed, hugging Wren tight.

"Incredible," John said, "and at such a young age." He pulled them in for their own hug.

I glanced out the window where a fresh line was forming.

"You guys are busy, and we gotta run anyway. Coco Caliente is taking the stage in five minutes," Rhyne said.

"Oh, yeah," Wren interjected. "My girlfriend is saving us seats in the front row." Wren blew us a kiss and scooted out of the back of the food truck.

Using the word girlfriend liberally was one of Wren's new favorite habits. 'My girlfriend would like a slice of pizza.' 'I don't know, I'll have to ask my girlfriend.' 'I need to go call my girlfriend.' It reminded me of when a couple gets engaged, and they constantly refer to their partner as their fiancé ad nauseam.

After Sammie's surgery, I invited both Mike and Jennifer to our support group. The shooting created an influx of new members and pushed John and me into leadership roles. The first couple of meetings were uncomfortable, but Becky, Craig, and Mary shared their stories with them. Their testimonies coupled with almost losing their daughter transformed their hearts and they chose to love her. That's all it took. Life has a funny way of forcing you to learn its toughest lessons. No one gets a free pass.

I watched them dart away.

"Who's Coco Caliente?" John asked.

I gasped in fake shock. "Only Rhyne's favorite drag queen in the entire universe. How could you not know that? Weren't you paying attention when they forced you to watch all those episodes of *RuPaul's Drag Race*? It's like you're not even trying." I winked.

He *was* trying. It was new territory we were thrust into, and not by choice, but we were finding our sea legs as proper allies. We asked questions, adding definitions to our vocabulary for nonbinary, omnigender, and cisgender. It was a whole new world we were struggling to understand

and accept, and we learned that the community was patient. So patient to constantly correct us when we slipped and misgendered them. Endlessly forgiving when we asked questions. They *wanted* to be understood. To be allowed the same God-given rights as any other person on the planet. They corrected us with grace delivered with a heavy dose of humor.

When Wren came out, I thought I'd lost my child forever. I thought the life I'd fought to give them was destroyed. Turns out, Wren was fully capable of stepping into the life *they* designed. A life built on authenticity and being comfortable in their skin, no matter what it looked like outwardly, no matter who they chose to love. There would be no more hiding, no more cover-ups, no more pushing down their truth so I could live mine. It was never about me in the first place. The only thing I was required to do was love Wren, and when I finally understood, it set my daughter free to become the person they were meant to be, and that is all that any mother ever wants.

———

If you loved this book, please leave a review where you purchased it and on Goodreads as well as send a copy of it to me at books@tealbutterflypress.com

I'm an indie author with the dream of writing stories full time, but the high cost of health care for a single mother in America keeps it out of my reach. I've been working almost three years toward the fulfillment of this dream by putting in 40 hours a week at my regular job and another 40 hours a week writing and marketing my books. After three years of struggling to find success, I am at a pivotal point in my journey. The 80 hour work weeks are taking a toll on my physical and mental health and I am letting you (and the universe) decide my fate. I need to make the decision whether or not to continue.

To Encourage this Insanity, You Can Help in Three Ways.

1. Check out my other books for quirky down-to-earth characters who will win your heart. https://tealbutterflypress.com/

2. Write a review of the book on Amazon, BN, Kobo or Apple Books, and also post the same review on Bookbub and Goodreads.

3. Share my books on social media.

Thank you for reading this book. I hope to earn the opportunity to tell you other stories.

This book will always hold a special place in my heart. I am the proud mama bear of a queer teenager. Although the character of Theresa is very different from me, I have shared some of the same thoughts and feelings with her that are written in these pages. I was raised Catholic, graduated from Catholic schools, and was time and time again indoctrinated with bible teachings that homosexuality was an abomination and against God. As I got older, I broke away from the Catholic church and began to question my beliefs, and when the stories of rampant sexual abuse surfaced, I was done with organized religion.

As a parent, you want your child to love and be loved, but when society has rules about who that person can be, it opens up a whole host of fears in your heart. I was always accepting, but in the most secret chamber of my heart that I am not proud to admit exists, I hoped my children would be spared this reality. I feared it would make their lives harder, make them targets for hate in an already hateful world.

It's been a journey to understanding and re-learning who this person is that I thought I knew intimately as their mother. I struggled and continue to struggle with the pronouns, but my child gives me grace. It is more about the effort I am making to see them and acknowledge them in their most authentic form, which with teenagers can fluctuate daily. I am working to give them space to wonder, to question, and to discover themselves. To be completely honest, it hasn't always been a journey I have understood, but it has taught me some valuable lessons about myself as it did Theresa.

I'm learning it isn't about me. It's about giving my child the space to step into their truth. It is giving them the freedom of expression and the acceptance to love in the way that calls to their heart. In my estimation, that is the true measuring stick of success as a mother. If my child is happy and content living a life that makes them feel fulfilled, then I consider it a job well done.

When an LGBTQ+ child has one parent as an ally, the suicide rate goes from 41% down to 6%. I first heard this statistic while researching for this book, and it was a pivotal moment in my own life. When you think about it like that, using the pronouns and loving the child you were given wholeheartedly becomes easier. It is truly a life-or-death situation.

I was terrified when I stumbled upon the Wikipedia page on hate crimes against the LGBTQ+ community. The scene in the book was a real moment ripped from my real life. I vividly remember being physically sick, reading painful accounts of hate that seemed to scroll on forever.

The catalog of hate crimes carried out against one of the most marginalized groups in existence was hard to stomach, and I sobbed for loss after loss recorded in those pages. These victims were someone's *children.* As a mother, it crushes my soul to see those precious lives destroyed for nothing.

I hope the ultimate takeaway of the book is a peaceful one. I hope it resonates with mothers and fathers and turns more parents into allies because that is what these kids need more than anything.

A special thank you to Brooke, who read this book in its early stages and gave me much food for thought. Your insight has been valuable in my writing process and has made my books better in every measurable way. I appreciate you. I also need to thank my incredible editor, Kendra. She polishes my books until they shine. I don't know how to use a comma properly, but she always makes me look like I do. It's been almost three years now, and I am grateful for you.

I will leave you with this: Love one another. Three little words. That's all we need to do, yet we can fail at it so miserably. Love one another anyway.

Blair Bryan

Support Bursting Through

Bursting Through is a member supported, grassroots storytelling movement building the worlds largest library of stories celebrating the Queer/Straight relationship.

Stories are the most powerful change agent that exists and have the ability to change attitudes, hearts, and minds.

Bursting Through stories collectively highlight our shared humanity, discuss our differences with emotional maturity and amplify our connection.

To join the movement and tell your story go to https://burstingthrough.gay/

Support LGBTQ+ Family Connections Center

LGBTQ Young Adults Experience Homelessness at More than Twice the Rate of Peers.

LGBTQ+ and Two-Spirit youth find it difficult to find

housing and often are asked to leave shelters after revealing their sexual or gender identity. As a result of harassment and negative experiences in shelters, LGBTQ+ and Two-Spirit youth are especially vulnerable to living on the streets, physical and sexual exploitation, and experience high rates of conduct disorder, post-traumatic stress, and suicidal behavior.

This is why LGBTQ+ and Two-Spirit targeted services are so very important to statistically change the numbers. Family rejection doesn't change quickly, and for some, it never does. LGBTQ and Two-Spirit youth account for 40% of the total unaccompanied homeless youth population, even though they make up 10 percent of the overall youth population.

We provide LGBTQ+ and Two-Spirit youth and adults access to food, medical services, mental health services, housing stability, career counseling, and much more.

https://lgbtqfamilyconnectionscenter.net/

The best way to buy my books is direct at tealbutterflypress.com There you can save 20-25% and find autographed paperbacks. They are available at most booksellers too.

I write under two pen names, Ninya for Non-Fiction and Blair Bryan for Contemporary Fiction.

Non-Fiction

Scotland with a Stranger: A Memoir

Treehouses with a Teenager: A Memoir

First You Then Him

Fiction By Blair Bryan

Back to Before

Better than Before

The Sweetest Day

The Funologist

When Wren Came Out

AnaStasia Lived Two Lives

Steamy Sexy Series Velvet Guild

Velvet Guild Collection 1

Velvet Guild Collection 2

Velvet Guild Collection 3

Velvet Guild Collection 4

Velvet Guild Collection 5

ABOUT THE AUTHOR

I've always been a risk-taker, so at 44 I decided to write and publish my own books. It has been a roller coaster ride with a punishing learning curve, but if it were easy, everyone would do it. I write under the pen names of Ninya and Blair Bryan.

I love to travel and a trip to Scotland with a complete stranger was the inspiration for my memoir. I also seem to attract crazy experiences and people into my life like a magnet that gives me a never-ending supply of interesting storylines.

If you love a good dirty joke, a cup of coffee so strong you can chew it, and have killed more cats with your curiosity than you can count, I might be your soulmate.

Visit me online www.tealbutterflypress.com

Join my facebook reader group: https://www.facebook.com/groups/ninyons

www.ingramcontent.com/pod-product-compliance
Lightning Source LLC
Chambersburg PA
CBHW061058190726
48286CB00006B/1798